Releasing the Wolf

Aimie Jennison

A Note For The Reader

This book has been written using UK English and is set in Australia. I apologise if there are words or phrases you do not understand. Please feel free to contact me for further explanation, or to discuss the meaning of a particular phrase or word, via my author page on Facebook, website or email.

Dedication

To the best friend.

Remember you mean the world to someone.

This is for you.

Prologue

Jesse

Seventeen years ago

Placing the handset down, I stare at it in disbelief. Did I really just hear that conversation right? *"Meet me in the back paddock, near the cemetery fence," My Alpha said in a gruff voice.* There is one order that the whole pack follow: pack are to stay away from the Alpha family's cattle farm. The paddock is part of the farm. Giving the phone one last curious glance I turn on my heel and leave the office to meet my Alpha.

I make my way through the woods and away from my home. I can't help but think about how it almost wasn't my home. It was the Alpha Couple's home until one day - almost seven years ago now - Anthony Rossi found another Alpha in his home. Not only had he managed to enter the pack house he'd also been found standing over Rossi's baby daughter's cot. Needless to say the Alpha didn't live long enough to leave. Rossi was so angry he didn't feel that his family was safe under that roof any longer. So the next morning he offered to swap his mansion - the pack house - for my cattle farm. I immediately agreed, wanting nothing more than the Alpha family to be safe and happy. Once they'd moved out the whole pack had magically forgotten they even had a daughter. Being Beta, or the Alpha's second, I was the only one unaffected by the voodoo magic that had been used to remove her existence from everyone's memory.

I spot Rossi leaning his back against the fence watching his daughter running through the field giggling as her mother, Maria, chases her. "She's a little beauty, she's going to have all the boys chasing after her when she's older. You'll have your work cut out for you." I say as I approach. Expecting a growl to come out of his mouth at the idea, I'm surprised by his reaction.

A grimace crosses his face as he turns to look at me. "That's why I've brought you here. You may be the one scaring the boys away in the future, not me."

I can hear truth in his words and it chills me to the core. "Talk to me."

He sighs. "I've been invited to a hunt with Rick Maleny's pack."

"Say no. It's dangerous enough joining another pack to hunt, but a hunt two days from the full moon is suicidal." He shouldn't need me to tell him this, he knows it, but I can't stop the words from leaving my mouth.

"He knows about Rosa, he wants to talk," he says referring to his daughter.

I run a hand through my short hair. "I don't like it. You know as much as I do it'll be a trap."

Rossi paces away from the fence a couple of metres before turning back. "I know, but what choice do I have? He knows, I need to know what he's thinking," he says on his second time back.

"He'll talk shit about being allies. You can't trust a word he says." I catch sight of Rossi nodding agreement as I glance at the happy little girl in the field and my heart hurts. There is no way I'm letting Rick take her father away from her. He'll have to kill me first. "So, who are we taking? Giuseppe will be staying to protect Maria and Rosa, won't he?" I say referring to Rossi's Father as I try to come up with the best plan of attack.

"No." The authority in his voice pulls me back to attention and I find him standing before me. "Giuseppe will be coming with me. He's a good fighter and I know he'll handle anything thrown at us. Maria is insisting on joining me too, I don't like it but she won't take no for an answer, and she'd never forgive me if I used my Alpha authority on her for something like this."

Knowing I'm the only person left that knows Rosa exists, I realise where he's heading. "No. You need to take me with you. The three of you aren't strong enough alone."

"I'll take Mark, Caleb and Bart with me. Any more and he'll think we're there to attack him." Clearly he worked these details out before I arrived.

I can't be left behind. "Please, Ant," I beg. "Swap me out with Bart. Surely the magic can be broken and he can be told about Rosa."

Rossi pulls me into his chest and thumps me on the back before quickly releasing me. "I appreciate your loyalty, and need to protect Maria and I, but Rosa is my daughter, my world. I need you to protect her with everything you have." I nod my understanding, not necessarily my agreement. "If we've guessed Rick's intentions right and I don't return, you'll become Alpha. If you came with me there'd be no-one strong enough to hold the pack together. Rick would try taking over what ever is left of it."

As much as I hate his plan, he's right. We have to think of the wellbeing of the whole pack. This plan puts our Alpha Couple in danger, but it keeps everyone else safe. I sigh, feeing a little disgruntled at the hand we've been dealt. "Okay."

I watch as Rossi's shoulders drop in relief. "Promise

me you'll protect her no matter what."

"I, Jesse O'Keefe, give my word to protect Rosa Francesca Rossi until my dying day." The formal promise is made with a grim smile.

"Thank you. Madre knows what's happening and she'll feel safer if you're watching over the house while we're gone."

Madre. She isn't his mother in the biological sense, hell - he's a hell of a lot older than she is but she's been married to his father for the last sixty something years so she's grown into a mother figure for him. He even named his daughter after her.

"Of course. I'll be right outside if she needs me," I state with the sincerity I feel in my bones, hoping he feels it too. They're Pack. I want them safe as much as he does.

He nods and starts walking towards his wife and daughter. "We'll be leaving at four this afternoon in wolf form," he calls over his shoulder effectively dismissing me until four o'clock.

***

At a quarter to four I make my way back across the paddock to the farm with three wolves following behind me, Mark, Caleb and Bart. When we come to a stop at the edge of the paddock, the wolves settling down next me in the long grass. We all suddenly stand to attention as we watch another three wolves make their way down the porch steps. Maria pounces up to me and licks my hand. I stroke my hand over her head and down her flank.

"She's insisting I tell you to look after our baby." Rossi's voice says in my head. As an extremely old and strong Alpha he has the ability to talk to any pack member in their mind, even if they aren't in wolf form. His strength allows us as pack mates to talk to each other like this too but only with another pack member who is in wolf form. Not all Alphas or packs can do it, but the Rossi Pack is lucky.

I put my hand to my heart. "I'll protect her as if she was my own... always."

Rossi stops before me, cocking his head as he looks up at me. I drop my eyes thinking he must want my submission. Feeling a sudden nip at my hand and glance down to see he's drawn blood.

"As Alpha of the Rossi Pack, I leave the pack in your hands to control and protect as you see fit. May I not return, you shall be the new Alpha of the Rossi Pack." The formal statement rings in my head as Rossi communicates with me. I can feel the power of the blood oath running through the bond. For him to do something like this makes me realise exactly how dangerous even Rossi thinks this hunt is. This is his contingency plan. He doesn't think he's coming back. There's no need for me to give a formal response, his words are strong enough to ensure what he said happens. He's Alpha after all.

I feel the need to say something. "Make sure you

come back."

I hear his laugh in my mind, mocking my authoritative tone. *"You're not Alpha yet."* I drop my eyes in submission once again. *"You'll be a great Alpha."*

Shocked, I lift my eyes, watching as the wolves leave as one being – a *Pack* – and head north through the bush that lines the farm leading to Rick's territory. The sinking feeling in the pit of my stomach terrifies me. I know this may be the last time I ever see my Alpha pair and my four other pack members heading for the enemies territory.

***

Hours pass and with nothing to do but pace. So I pace. The trench forming on the edge of the field under my feet doesn't stop me from taking the repetitive steps. I was told to guard the house, and that's what I'll do until Rossi returns. It's all I can do.

Suddenly, there's tugging in the pack bonds followed by an excruciating pain. One by one, I lose the connection to Mark, Caleb and Bart. Their bonds snap as they die, and now they cease to exist. I throw my head back and howl into the night. Feeling a pain that matches my own, other pack members in the vicinity join in the song, and I know the whole pack will be howling wherever they may be.

"He doesn't know Rosa is still alive. He thinks the other Alpha I found by her cot killed her. Keep her hidden and safe." The words in my head pull me from the need to howl. Rossi has never spoken to me from such a distance.

I didn't even know he could. As the silence fills my head once again, a horrendous pain fills my chest as Rossi's bond within the pack is severed. The Alpha is dead. My wolf bursts out of me and I take a moment to pray that none of the other pack members were in a public place right now. No one would be strong enough to fight this change. It's just as powerful as the pull of the full moon – if not stronger. I release a howl and one by one pack members arrive in the paddock. My wolf knows what we must do, Rossi's earlier blood oath in the front of our minds.

We walk into the centre of the field and our pack mates form a circle around us. As the last wolf arrives they all drop into a bow - accepting me as Alpha. In any other pack there would be a number of fights for the title of Alpha but, as a pack, we have respect for each other and for Rossi's oath of which they will all feel through the bonds. It helps that I'm the strongest and most capable pack member for the job.

Chapter One

Frankie

I keep finding myself in the same place, stood staring at the four gravestones of my family - my grandmother's, whose name I share, Rosa Francesca Rossi; my mother's, Maria Sunshine Rossi; my father's, Antonio Giuseppe Rossi and my grandfather's, Giuseppe Lucas Rossi. Being here always takes me back to that day, the day my birthday turned into the worst day of my life.

On the eve of my seventh birthday, way past my bedtime, I was pacing around the living room waiting for Madre, Papà and Nonno to return from a trip to a friend's house. I'd cried for hours when they wouldn't let me and Nonna go too, someone needed to look after the cattle. They promised me they would be back in time for my birthday so when there was a knock at the door I ran to it as fast as my little legs would carry me. I ran right into the sideboard in the hall causing a photo frame to fall with a crash. I didn't stop to pick it up. I pulled the door open, disappointed to find a man I didn't know staring back at me.

Nonna walked up behind me and greeted him. "Jesse, is everything okay?"

He ducked his head. "Can I come in, Mrs Rossi? It's not something I'd like to discuss on the doorstep." Even my seven-year-old eyes could see the sadness fall across his face.

We entered the living room and the man looked at me. "Maybe little Rosa could go and play with her toys for a few minutes while we talk?"

I only allowed my father to call me Rosa. "My name is Frankie," I snapped.

Nonna looked at the man, the uncertainty clear on her face. "It's late. Go pick out a bedtime story and I'll be up to tuck you in when Jesse leaves, okay?"

I nodded and ran off to my room. After choosing a book I leant against the window and watched for Mamma, Papà and Nonno's arrival. I saw the man leave and ran down the stairs. I found Nonna sat on the sofa sobbing quietly with her head in her hands. I sat down beside her and hugged into her side as the grandfather clock in the corner struck twelve. "Don't be sad Nonna, it's my birthday." Her sobbing got louder with my words. It was the first time I'd ever seen her cry, unsure what to do I hugged into her side and let her cry.

It felt like a long time before she pulled her hands away from her face and kissed me on the temple. She took what I know now to be a grounding breath before speaking. "Oh sweetheart, I'm so sorry. Let's go get a bedtime snack and then we'll have a talk before opening your presents."

She still seemed so sad so I didn't question why she'd want me to open my presents before going to bed. I followed her into the kitchen and helped her mix up the cookie dough.

Once we'd eaten and made our way back into the living room, she sat me on her knee and hugged me into her chest as she explained that Mamma, Papà and Nonno had gone to heaven after coming across a nasty wolf in the bush, so they wouldn't be able to come and watch me open my birthday presents.

That was the first and last time I heard her relate to wolves in a negative way, she used to tell me bedtime stories about a man who turned into a wolf. Every story was different but it was always about the same man, 'Tony' she called him.

I lived on the same farm I was born on with Nonna

until she died peacefully in her sleep a month ago. I'd inherited the farm when my parents died since it was theirs, but Nonna had control of it until she died. She did a great job and I wasn't willing to step in while she was still here. Now she's gone I still can't step in. In fact, I had to move out because I couldn't bear to live in the silent house. Nonna paid some guys to do the heavy work and now they do the same for me.

A twig snapping behind me jolts me back to reality. I spin on my heels, coming face to face with a wolf as black as night. He's frozen in place, staring at me. I've always had mixed thoughts on wolves since the explanation of that '*nasty wolf*' being somehow involved in my parents' deaths. But this wolf *is far from nasty*'. This wolf is my friend.

He's visited me many times over the years. He turned up just after the funerals and whenever I was alone I knew it wouldn't be long before he'd join me. I haven't seen him much since I left the farm, though I guess it's not so easy for him to get into my fourth floor apartment. Whenever I'm here I can be certain he'll join me. Sometimes I come here just to see him and enjoy his comforting presence.

I hold my fist out for him to sniff. I can't remember who taught me to do that but I do it with every dog, or in this case wolf, I meet. He rubs his snout along my hand not really caring to sniff me, and I scratch behind his ears the way I know he likes it. His coat is as black as night but that's not what's extraordinary about him – it's his eyes. They're just like a flame, his pupil has a ring of that bright blue - almost indigo - just like in the centre of a flame and surrounding it is a ring of yellow.

"How's it going, Tony?" I ask, sitting down on the grass beside him, "Have you missed me as much as I've missed you?"

I called him Tony after the wolf man in my Nonna's stories. As a kid I hoped he would change into a man when no one was looking. Maybe he even had a family that he went home to. Following my lead, he flops down on the grass and lays his head in my lap. I lay back and he repositions his head onto my stomach. I run my fingers through the fur on his head. "I guess you did." I say answering my own question.

Chapter Two

Frankie

"Wake up sleepy head." I hear Joey shout as a cushion hits me on the head.

I groan, annoyed by the intrusion. "Remind me why I gave you that spare key again?" I ask, snuggling further under the covers in an attempt to evade any more flying cushions.

He laughs. "Because I'm your best friend and without these wake up calls - which you love so very much - you would never leave your pit."

I feel another pillow hit me through the security of the covers. "Okay, I'll make a deal with you. I'll go in the bathroom if you have fresh coffee waiting for me when I come out." I offer peeking out from under the covers.

He jerks his head in a sharp nod. "Deal."

I throw the covers back and get up before grabbing some clothes out of the chest of drawers, Following through on my end of the deal, I head for the shower. My studio apartment is tiny. It's made up of one room that's big enough for a two-seater sofa bed, TV cupboard and a chest of drawers - all of which makes up the lounge/bedroom area. And then there is the kitchen - *if you can call it that!* It's just a corner of my lounge that has a sink, a two seat dining table and a fridge against the corner of the wall; my food has to go in the cupboard under the sink. The only other room that is separate from the main room is the bathroom, which contains a shower, small sink and toilet. I have to return to the farm when I want to do my laundry, unless I manage to sweet talk Joey into taking it for me.

One day, some six years ago, Joey Metcalfe turned up on Nonna's doorstep asking for a job on the farm. There was always plenty of work to be done so she took him on immediately, not even taking time to consider it. I'd just turned eighteen and had started working on the farm myself to help pay my way through University to get my veterinary degree. I have no doubt that the fact that Joey was a year younger than me made Nonna think that he'd be good company for me. I wasn't big on friends and she was always nagging at me to make some. Come to think of it, that hasn't changed much as I've gotten older. I'm twenty-four and still only have one real friend but he's more than enough.

Walking out of the bathroom, I'm greeted with the smell of pancakes and coffee. I take a slurp from the big mug, and then pull Joey into a huge bear hug. "Thanks Jo. What would I do without you?"

"You'd starve for one thing." He nods towards the plate of pancakes on the table. "Eat up. We have a job to go hunting for."

Not being able to face the silent farm house means I've given up my job there too, and my funds are really starting to run low. So today my best friend, Joey, has taken the day off work to spend it job hunting with me. *Have I mentioned that he's a godsend?*

***

We must have been in every store, café and bar in my local suburb of Joondalup. A couple of places took my name and number but nothing ever comes of that. Most of them just shoved my resumé back at me and told me to apply online. It looks like I'm staying unemployed for the time being. Not that I can stay unemployed for long though because I can't afford to pay for my crappy apartment without a job. I might just have to face my grief and go back to the farm, no matter how quiet it is without Nonna.

We're exiting one of the shops in Lakeside Shopping Centre when Joey makes the best offer. "Let's call it a day. I'll treat you to a late lunch." He grins as he digs me in the ribs with his elbow.

We walk to the Sovereign Arms pub that's attached to the shopping centre, since it's a hot summer day we choose a seat inside making the most of the air conditioning. I take a seat with my back to the bar knowing Joey would want the one facing the room. He always chooses a seat where he can see everyone in the room. I've been kicked out of too many seats over the years to know not to take them in the first place now. Joey heads to the bar without bothering to ask me what I want. I have the same thing every time - vodka and coke in a tall glass, and Fish and Chips. I turn in my seat, watching the show as the two female barmaids rush their current orders just to try and get to serve Joey before the other. They do it every single time; it's hilarious to watch. The blonde barmaid hands over a beer with the biggest head I have ever seen, and her customer glares at her as she asks him for his money. A mortified look crosses her face as she glances down at the glass and notices her mistake. While she apologises profusely, the brunette with a pixie cut takes Joey's order, clearly happy to be winning today's battle. The blonde hands her customer a more presentable pint of beer and walks off glumly.

I let my eyes roam around the bar before turning

them back on Joey who's now making his way back towards me with our drinks in his hands. "One vodka and coke," he says placing it down on the table before me. He takes the seat I knew he would and has a mouthful of his beer.

"Thanks, I need it after today's wasted effort." I say, unable to keep the misery out of my voice.

"You know we all miss you at the farm. I know you're worried about it being quiet in the house, but what if someone moved in with you?" Joey asks, hope shining in his eyes.

"I... I can't, not yet." Just the thought of it makes my stomach churn and I quickly change the subject. "Are you going to give her a call?" I ask, nodding towards pixie cut.

He looks at me, furrowing his brows. "How did you know she gave me her number?" he asks, confused.

I laugh. "They always give you their number. Every. Time." I can't wipe the grin off my face. Him being there with me never stops them slipping him their number; we must look as platonic together as we are.

"You know I'm not," he says in reply to my earlier question.

I glance over at her chatting to one of the other girls behind the bar. "Why not? She's pretty and looks nice enough."

He shakes his head, no. "She's not my type."

In all the years I've known him he's never once

mentioned a girlfriend. "I've never seen you with a girl. What is your type?" A thought suddenly hits me and I can't hold back my gasp. "Oh my God, are you gay?"

He laughs. "Frankie, do you really think I'm gay?" When I give him nothing but a questioning look he shakes his head, disbelief written on his face with the slackening of his mouth and the widening of his eyes. "I'm not gay. I'm just not attracted to her, that's all."

"But—"

Joey cuts me off before I can question him anymore. "Just leave it, please," he begs.

I hold up my hands in defeat. "Okay, I give in. I'm going to put some decent music on."

Weaving my way through the crowded tables, I head for the jukebox. I choose three songs - Bon Jovi's *Livin' on a Prayer*; Adam Lambert's *Whataya Want From Me* and Adele's *Someone Like You*. It must have been running on a random loop until someone made a selection because *Livin' on a Prayer* comes on immediately.

As I dance my way back towards the table I notice Carter sitting at our table. Carter is a guy I met at University who's studying psychology. We've been on a couple of dates, but it's never progressed further than a kiss. I guess I'd call him my boyfriend if someone asked, although I'm sure his answer would be different. Carter's six-foot, lean athletic body always gets plenty of attention from the girls, which he loves. He's got short spiky white blonde hair and hazel eyes. In fact, he reminds me of Spike off the TV show *Buffy*. Now I think of it, I always did have a soft spot for Spike as a teenager.

Upon reaching the table, I notice Carter has taken my seat. My drink is now sitting on the table in front of the chair with its back to the door and room. I'm not comfortable with my back to the door but I don't want to cause a fuss, so ignoring my gut instincts I pull out the chair and sit down.

Carter leans across the table and kisses me deeply, causing me to blush and pull away. "Hey Babe, I saw you come in here with this loser," he motions to Joey with an upward nod, "and I thought you might want some decent company."

"*Carter!*" I say, astonished by his rudeness. "Don't be horrible. You can't call random strangers *losers*."

Joey doesn't appear affected at all by Carter's rudeness. "Its okay, Frankie," he says, staring him down from across the table. "We know each other, he's just being a dick, as usual."

I want to know how, but before I can ask a dark shadow falls over me. Someone's standing behind me and it's someone big. *Really big. I can feel it.*

I turn to face some nice abs showing through a tight grey t-shirt, which are matched with a pair of light faded jeans. I look up to an attractive yet intimidating man who looks to be about thirty. Some men ooze sex like Carter, but this guy oozes power. Mr Big and Powerful has a strong jawline with kissable full lips and a nose that fits his face perfectly. I catch a glimpse of blue from his eyes before he slips some sunglasses on. *Who puts sunglasses on indoors?* His dark blonde hair is short to his head in a military style cut.

"Joey. Carter." He nods at each of them before looking down at me. At least I think he's looking at me, with those sunglasses on he could be looking at the table for all I know.

"This is Rosa Rossi, my boss, I guess?" Joey says nervously. I glance at him stunned; I don't think I have ever seen carefree Joey nervous.

A large manly hand appears in front of me and I have no choice but to take it, feeling a jolt of energy that shoots straight to my heart as we touch. I quickly pull back, discreetly rubbing my hand on my jeans under the table.

"Nice to meet you, Rosa Rossi." His voice is casual, giving no hint that he'd felt the spark too. "I'm Jesse, Joey's other boss. Carter's too."

"Call me Frankie. Nonna was Rosa, so I go by my middle name. I'm more Joey's friend than I am his boss." I glance across the table to Joey, trying to get out from under Jesse's hidden gaze. "I've only been your boss for a month."

"Carter, I need to speak to you in private," Jesse informs him, clearly dismissing both Joey and I before he turns and leaves the pub.

Carter jumps up and follows Jesse out of the building, shouting "*bye!*" over his shoulder just before the door closes behind him.

The pager Joey had brought back from the bar with our drinks starts to vibrate, flash and beep on the table, signalling that our food is ready to be picked up from the bar.

"Finally! I'm starving." He picks up the pager before heading to the bar for the food.

Joey comes back with a plate in each hand and another balanced on the crook of his arm. I give the extra plate with a cheeseburger and chips he's holding a second glance. "You weren't kidding about being starving," I joke.

He laughs, placing it on the table next to his own plate. "It was Carter's order. I'm not a complete pig."

I lift up a piece of fish on my fork but, before I take a bite, I focus my attention to Joey. "Why did that big guy make you so nervous?"

He slowly chews on a mouthful of burger, deliberating. I can practically see the cogs in his brain turning over. I've never felt like Joey has secrets but seeing him with Jesse and Carter has left me thinking he may just have some.

I tuck into my own meal while I wait for his response.

"There's been some tension between Carter and Jesse. I didn't want them to start fighting while you were sat in between them," he tells me, sounding honest enough. He practically inhales the rest of the food on his plate before moving onto Carter's plate. "There's no point letting good food go to waste." I stare at him in disbelief, inciting a cheeky grin. *Has he got hollow legs or something?*

Chapter Three

Jesse

Striding out of the Sovereign Arms, there is no doubt in my mind that Carter will follow me – not if he knows what's good for him anyway. Wanting Carter to see my eyes, I remove my shades. As I come to a stop outside the boarded up store next door, I take a deep calming breath before turning to face him.

Carter nods stiffly. "Boss," he greets, not quite meeting my eyes.

"What the hell do you think you're doing, Carter?" His flinch tells me he hears the growl behind my words.

"You told me to watch her." He shrugs. "I am."

"*No!*" I snap. How fucking dare he twist my words like that. My whole body tenses in an effort not to pounce and cause a scene. "You're dating her, not watching her." Unable to contain my anger, a wave of energy flows out of me and hits Carter full force.

"I... I thought... that, that would be the best way to protect her," he stammers, wincing in pain as my energy burns against his skin.

"You and your bed post notches. I knew I should have put Nate onto this. *Dammit!*" I take a deep breath, trying to reign in my temper. "You will not sleep with her, Carter." I place all my Alpha power behind my words, making sure he understands the consequences if he defies my order.

"I understand," he agrees, looking down at his feet.

On the drive home I can't help but kick myself for giving him the job. I'd gone into this thinking Rosa wouldn't fall for his player attitude. Clearly I'd been mistaken. The only reason I hadn't given Nate the job was because I was worried that she'd fall for him. In fact, I knew she would fall for him. *All women do.* She is just his type too so I know the feeling would be mutual. This mess serves me right for being so selfish thinking I can keep her to myself. Who am I kidding? She didn't even know I existed until ten minutes ago.

Chapter Four

Frankie

We leave the pub just as the sun is setting. Both Joey and I often enjoy the short walk back to my apartment in silence. It's comfortable, and today is no exception. I can't help wondering about Joey's employer Jesse, Carter, and what causes the obvious bad vibe between the two of them. If things are that bad why wouldn't Jesse just fire him? Not that I want my boyfriend jobless or anything.

"What are you thinking so hard about?" Joey asks.

Unlocking the main door of the apartments without my key sticking takes all my concentration. "Nothing," I mumble. The lock clicks and I let out a little cheer. "*Yes!*"

I glance at Joey as I hold the door open. "What are we watching today? It's your choice this week." Once a week we have a marathon night of watching a TV show. Last week I chose *Game of Thrones*, season one, so this week it's Joey's choice.

His eyes glint as he flashes me a cheeky grin. "You'll have to wait and see."

I open my apartment door and walk straight to the kitchen, grabbing a bag of popcorn and placing it in the microwave. Even though Joey just ate two meals, I know he'll have no trouble eating some popcorn too. As I watch the popcorn spin around, I send up *'thanks'* to the angels or whoever it was that sent Joey down to me the day he knocked on Nonna's door. He really is a gift and I love him to bits. Joey is like the little brother I never had. The microwave beeps and I pour the popcorn into a large bowl. "Stick the disc in, Jo. I'll turn out the lights on the way."

I sit down on the sofa and cuddle up to Joey. He hits play and the opening theme song, *"Bad Things"*, comes on with its creepy videos. "Yay," I cheer excitedly as I clap my hands. I've needed a good *True Blood* fix for a while now.

We both sang along giggling to the song until the opening scene comes on the screen. "SHHH!" I say as I flap my hands in the air, emphasising my excitement.

"I was, you're the one shhh-ing," Joey says with a laugh. Pulling me into his side, he shoves his hand into the bowl of popcorn.

We're no more than five minutes into it when there's a knock on the door. Knowing I never get any visitors, Joey makes a move to get up, concern is clear in the frowning of his eyebrows.

I pat his leg. "It's alright, it'll probably be Betty from across the hall wanting some milk or something." I watch as he settles back, but the tension doesn't leave his body.

Getting up, I dash across the room to the door, pulling it open. "Did you forget to buy your milk again, Betty?" Instead of my forgetful old neighbour, I find myself faced with Carter sporting a cheeky grin. "You're disturbing a very important *True Blood* marathon, it better be worth it." I say in jest, trying to hide my surprise at seeing him.

"Only you can answer that." He leans forward kissing me quickly and thoroughly. I can taste alcohol on his tongue. "Am I worth it?"

I pull away and turn to look at Joey, asking with my eyes if I can invite Carter in. It's our night and I'll turn Carter away if he wants me to. Joey gives me a smile but I can see the disappointment in his eyes. "Hurry up you two, I can't hear a thing," he says, waving us both in.

I give Joey an appreciative smile and answer Carter's question. "I guess you are. You can only come if you'll be quiet and watch the show." I step back, giving him room to enter.

"Of course I will. I can smell popcorn; that'll keep me

quiet," he says walking straight over to my empty spot on the two seater sofa. Joey and Carter are both quite large men, so I grab my pillows and quilt - which are always folded up in the corner of the room waiting for me to use them when I change the sofa into a bed on a night - and use them to sit between their legs on the floor.

"Do you want to sit here, Frankie?" Joey offers. *Always the gentleman.*

I shake my head and pat his leg in thanks.

Joey gets up when the closing credits of the third episode start rolling on the screen. "I'm gonna head off, it's getting late."

I frown. We'd planned to make a full night of it and watch until we fall asleep. I'd guessed from the atmosphere in the pub earlier, it's not only Jesse and Carter that don't get along, and tonight's atmosphere hasn't been much better. I get up and walk him to the door making sure to step out into the hall and I give him a hug as always. I want to say sorry about Carter turning up and spoiling things, but he places his finger over my mouth before the word escapes. He inclines his head towards my door and he mouths the words *"don't worry"*.

"I'll call you tomorrow," he says out loud.

I know I'm sporting a puzzled look; I can feel my frown forming. Joey doesn't seem to feel the need to explain anything further and stays silent. "Okay..." I mutter. "Be careful," I add, giving him a quick friendly peck on the lips. I stay in the hall watching him go through the door to the stairs, and then turn to find Carter leaning against the door jamb, a strange look plastered on his face.

"I thought he'd never leave." Leaning forward, he reaches his hands around my waist and pulls me into his embrace. "Now I've got you to myself, what shall we do?" He kisses me as he manoeuvres me into the room, closing the door behind us with a swift kick.

I pull away to look at him. "What's got into you?"

His eyes roam up and down my body. "You, and your sexy body."

I look down at the flannelette pyjama's and fluffy slipper socks I'd changed into after the first episode finished, before bursting out in laughter. "I think you need your eyes testing." I bat at him playfully and walk over to the sofa. I give it a kick and a tug and it pops out into a bed, like magic. Well not really, I've just learnt the knack to it. Grabbing my quilt and pillows off the floor I throw them on top and climb up. I glance at Carter who's stood staring at me with a predatory look, and pat the bed next to me. "Are you joining me or do you want to stand there all night? Whichever you choose, can you turn the TV off since you're right next to it?"

He's suddenly next to me having already turned off the TV, my eyes flick to the TV. *Had he done that quicker then I thought was humanly possible?* I shake my head and berate myself. *Don't be silly.*

It doesn't take us long to strip each other of those pesky things called clothes. His kisses start to roam from my mouth down my jaw and neck. He licks at a nipple before nipping it between his teeth, making pain and pleasure mingle together. I can't hold back the moan as I arch my body towards him. His grip on my hip tightens and he suddenly pulls back, releasing me. His mouth keeps working from one breast to the other but oh so gently, as though he's worried he was being too rough before. In no state to question him about it, I fumble trying to pull him up to bring his body closer to where I want it. "Please Carter," I beg.

"Shh, I'm getting there, baby," he assures me as he leans back onto his knees. I open my mouth to complain about the absence of his body but I hear the tear of foil and know he'll be back in a second. The thought barely crosses my mind and he's back leaning over me taking my mouth with his. I gasp into his mouth as I feel him inch his way into me and pause for a moment as he fills me. His gentleness surprises me. He's not the ferocious Carter I have come to know and love. He's the guy whose kisses alone can push me to the brink of orgasm.

I squirm trying to make him move, his stillness is starting to torture me.

"I'm not going to last long if you keep squirming," he says sounding strained.

I still. "I...I need...mo..." The words die on my lips as

he starts to move and I suddenly lose myself in his movements and his kisses, getting closer and closer to the precipice with each one until I'm falling and the world around me shatters.

The world comes back into focus and Carter collapses beside me whilst pulling me over so I'm resting my head on his smooth muscular chest. Unable to stop myself I flick my tongue over his nipple, taking in his musky scent.

Carter's arm tightens over my side, stopping my ministrations. "If you don't want round two, I suggest you stop there." Having given his warning, he loosens his hold on me and I lift my head enough to look him in the eye.

Seeing him watch me, I flick my tongue out over his nipple once again. In less than heartbeat he has me in position on top of him ready for that second round he'd just promised.

Chapter Five

Frankie

I wake startled by the sound of a freight train charging through the wall behind my head. I sit up and glance around the room, slowly coming to my senses. It isn't a freight train coming to mow us down. It's Carter. *Snoring.*

A quick look at my watch tells me it's barely six in the morning. There is no chance I'll fall asleep now, especially when you combine the racket Carter is making next to me, and the fact that the sun is up and shining through the cracks between the slats in the blinds. Decision made, I head for the shower.

I walk back into the room dressed for a hot summer day in a floaty black dress, and listen to Carter's snoring for two seconds before I decide that I need to get away from that god-awful noise. Grabbing a pen and paper I write Carter a quick note.

Carter,

Running a couple of errands. I won't be long.

F. x

I drive my VW kombi-van to the farm, knowing the guys will be needing the van to transport the stock any day now. Figuring I can kill two birds with one stone, I walk through the field to the cemetery. I need some thinking time with my best friend and favourite stray.

I'm almost halfway across the field when I hear what sounds like a car back firing. The howl of pain that immediately follows tells me it's not a car. *It was Tony's howl!*

I sprint the rest of the way through the field, screaming in panic. "*Tony!*"

Moving purely on instinct, I vault over the fence without even thinking about it. The sound of a whimper coming from the direction of my family's plot confirms it must be Tony, I've never seen another dog around there. *It's our spot.*

Tony's black shape comes into view, lying on my

father's grave. Crouching down next to him, I immediately feel under his hind leg for a pulse. The steady beat under my fingers eases my concern until I pull my hand away to see that it's covered in blood. My exhilaration fades in a split second.

He cracks an eye open to look at me.

A plan was already forming in my head. "You're going to be okay, Tony. I'm going to fix you up."

He snarls at something over my shoulder, and I spin around, holding my arms out in a bid to block the view of whomever Tony is snarling at.

A man emerges from the tree line, a rifle in his hand. "I'd step away if I was you, little lady. He looks mighty vicious to me."

"You'd look vicious too if you'd just been shot," I snap back.

If I had any sense I wouldn't be yelling at a man who's pointing a rifle at me. Unfortunately, all I can think about is getting Tony to safety so I can look at his injuries.

"He's a wolf. He's deadly. He needs killing." He waves the gun. "Now step aside so I can finish the job."

Feeling Tony's menacing growl vibrating through the ground makes me think he's not helping the situation at all. I need to ease his tension. I turn and smile as I pat his head to comfort him.

Turning back to the man with the gun, I drop the smile.

"You will not point that gun anywhere near my dog. I'm taking him home to fix him up." A growl that would make Tony proud escapes my throat as I point at the man's rifle. "If I see you or your gun around here again, I'll stick your gun where the sun don't shine before I pull the trigger." Dismissing him, I turn back to Tony and crouch, putting my hands under him I ready myself to carry him. He rolls out of my reach and to his feet with a whimper.

I watch him wobble for a second before taking a hesitant step towards the fence, followed by another and another. He climbs through the gap as I climb over the fence. Neither of us look back at the man with the gun.

I glance down at Tony, limping heavily and leaving a nasty trail of blood behind him. Surely he won't make it on his own steam much longer.

After what feels like an eternity we reach the porch of the house. Tony enters and I push the door closed behind him before running through to the kitchen. The vet in me takes over. I push the paperwork- mainly bills - off the table, grabbing the empty ceramic fruit bowl and carefully placing it on the top of the fridge freezer. The last thing we need is a broken bowl for Tony to stand on and add to his injuries.

I turn as Tony slowly limps into the room. "Can you jump up here?" I pat the table. He takes a step forward and then stops, staring at me as if he's hesitating.

I berate myself out loud. "He's a freaking dog,

Frankie. He doesn't have a clue what you are saying." No sooner are the words out of my mouth than he jumps up onto the table just as I'd asked.

"Good boy, that's it. Now, let me see the damage." I gently lift his leg whilst running my other hand along his blood soaked fur, feeling for the wound. It's close to his femoral artery so I can feel his pulse as I brush over it. *Strong and steady.* His head snaps around and he gnashes his teeth at me, telling me that I have found the wound. I whip my hand out of the way before he manages to draw blood.

Trying to look as non-intimidating as possible, I hold my hands up. "I'm sorry. I'll try and be as gentle as possible, but it's going to hurt." I know he's an animal and won't understand my words but we have spent a lot of time together so he should know my body language and tone of voice well enough.

He suddenly starts to spasm before my eyes, like he's having a seizure of some sort. My mind runs through all the possibilities. *Could the blood loss cause a seizure? Low blood pressure could but his pulse felt strong and steady a minute ago.*

Quickly running into the front room, I grab the crocheted blanket off the back of the sofa. I need to warm him up and get the wound sutured immediately. Stepping back into the kitchen, I pause in the doorway stunned at the sight before me.

Tony is gone and in his place is a naked man covered in blood. The sight of the blood pulls me out of my stupor and I gingerly head for the guy who obviously needs medical attention. It isn't until he's standing before me that I realise just who Mr Naked is. It's Joey and Carter's boss, *Jesse*.

I stare at him in stunned silence but I have enough sense to close my mouth. I must look ridiculous; catching flies while he's bleeding to death in front of me. Questions run riot in my head, none of which I manage to ask out loud. *What the hell is he doing in my kitchen? Where is Tony?*

Jesse sits up, dangling his legs off the table's edge. "I thought I might be safer to treat." His pain is evident in the strain of his voice and the stiffness of his body.

"Safer to treat? You mean...you're...you're..." I lift my eyes to meet his, careful to not let them linger on other parts of his body for too long.

"A werewolf," he informs me at the same time as I whisper, "Tony."

I don't need him to confirm it. My answer is in his eyes. His eyes are indigo blue with a thin yellow outer ring - so similar to Tony's which have a thin indigo ring with a thick yellow outer ring like a flame. No wonder he put his shades on before I could see them yesterday. I would have made the connection instantly – if I believed in werewolves, that is.

"I'm a vet," I explain. "I treat animals. It would probably be easier if you were Tony."

"No." He shakes his head gravely. "I can't control him when I'm this injured. He could hurt you. He almost did, sorry about that." He lifts his hand towards my face only to drop it back to his side before our skin touches, obviously realising what he was about to do.

"He won't hurt me. *You* won't hurt me," I correct myself with a frown.

He looks at me, as though he can see right into my soul. "I can't take the risk. The bullet's silver and that's not a good thing for someone like me. Once we take that out of the equation, then we'll see if it's safe for me to change, okay?" His eyes plead for me to do as he says.

"Okay," I reply, throwing the blanket at him. "Here, cover up with that." I turn and look under the sink for Nonna's sewing basket and first aid kit, which I find right there on the shelf where it belongs. I place them on the table next to Jesse before turning to take in the room, wondering where I would find any alcohol. Nonna wasn't a drinker - she'd maybe have a sherry at Christmas but that wouldn't be any good for Jesse. Joey used to keep something in the freezer for the end of the week when the guys had a drink together. With me and Nonna not here I don't know if they still do that. I pull the freezer door open, praying that I'll find something...anything. My prayers are answered; I spot a full litre bottle of vodka, which I grab along with a chilled glass.

Filling the glass with vodka, I put it aside on the table before handing the bottle to Jesse. "If it doesn't help with the pain, at least the feel of it burning down your throat might be a distraction," I joke, trying to ease the tension in the room.

I wash my hands before leaning in close to the wound, which happens to be rather high up on his thigh. I suddenly blush when I notice how close my head is to his. I clear my throat, mentally berating myself for being unprofessional. *Focus dammit. The man is bleeding.* My eyes roam over the wound and I take in a deep breath of surprise.

"What is it? My leg doesn't feel like it's going to fall off just yet." Jesse tries to joke between his short sharp breaths of pain.

"This is so close to the femoral artery, a millimetre closer and you wouldn't have made it. Although..." I poke at the wound with my finger. The bleeding seems to have slowed down considerably; it's now just a trickle. The wound doesn't even look big enough for a bullet to have entered in the first place. I state as much out loud, "I'm not sure a bullet could have got in this hole. Unless... do you heal quick?"

"There's a bullet in there, trust me. We do heal quickly. Hell, I'd be all closed up by now if the bullet wasn't silver. Damn the person who discovered silver and

Werewolves don't mix," he bites out.

The wound is looking okay but he's getting paler by the second. He feels clammy to the touch and sweat is beading on his forehead. *Could silver affect him this badly?* I quickly tip out the first aid kit and pull the tweezers out of the pile of crap that first aid kits usually contain. His eyes connect with mine and with a swig of vodka he nods at me.

Taking that as an invitation I dig in. Unfortunately I mean that quite literally, because he's healing I have to make the hole bigger and clear away the flesh that has tried to close over the bullet. Jesse lets out a growl, and take it from me a wolf's growl sounds awfully strange coming out of a man's throat. Knowing he won't hurt me, I keep digging and pray I find the bullet soon. No sooner does the thought go through my head than the tweezers hit metal.

Gotcha!

I grip the bullet with the tweezers and pull it out in one short sharp tug. Blindly dumping the bullet and tweezers in the sink behind me, I press a gauze pad to the wound. Jesse is still growling, a continuous rumble that makes the table vibrate. I look up to see Tony's eyes staring down at me, even down to the shape of them. If I thought a growl was strange coming out of a human's throat, those wolves eyes on Jesse's face are terrifying.

"Don't be scared," he pleads, placing a hand on top of

mine.

I swallow. "I'm not."

His hand tightens on mine. "You're lying. I can smell your fear."

I pull my hand free. "Do you want to have a break for a few minutes? You can change if you want? That might be easier for us both." I can't stop the nervous rambling spewing from my mouth.

"Your fear will make the wolf more dangerous, I won't hurt you while I'm in human form," he says, I can tell he's trying to sound calm for my sake, but I can still hear the growl behind his words.

Knowing I need to get this over with as quickly as possible, I thread a needle and pull the gauze off the wound, before pouring the glass of vodka over the area to disinfect it. Jesse tenses and I look up to see him gazing down at me gritting his teeth. The stitches go in quick and easy. It doesn't take me long to tape a clean gauze pad on top of the wound and finish up by wrapping a bandage over the gauze and around the leg. "All done," I say, patting his knee.

I clear the table, putting the sewing basket and first aid kit back where they belong. I catch sight of Jesse with a quick sweep of my eyes around the room, looking more like himself. Taking a breath of relief I break the silence. "Will you be able make it upstairs to the bed?"

"Thanks for stitching me up but I'll be going home

now."

He doesn't look anywhere near well enough to leave, super healing or not and I tell him as much, "You are not going anywhere! You're my patient and you need to recoup for at least an hour or two before I'll even consider letting you out of my sight."

Jesse grins and shakes his head. "You're just like your mother. Giving orders whether you're more dominant or not, and you'll still be obeyed every time. What have I gotten myself into?"

My stomach clenches and my eyes widen. "You knew my mother?" I ask, completely stunned.

"Your father, too. I guess I have a lot of explaining to do." He glances around the room. "But before I get started do you have anything I could eat? Preferably meat. Healing takes a lot of energy and fighting the change took more out of me."

"There should be some bacon and sausages in the freezer outside. I'll go get them." I walk out the back door to Nonna's chest freezer on the back porch. It would easily fit in the kitchen but she always insisted the she didn't want the ungodly sight cramping up her kitchen. I open the chest and tap a loose fist against my heart in gratitude to the guys who must still be filling it with the meat cuts as they slaughter and sell the animals. It's crammed full. Grabbing a couple of steaks and a bundle of bacon rashers, I walk back into the kitchen to find Jesse hobbling around with Gram's crocheted blanket wrapped around his waist like a sarong. In my absence, he's managed to set two places at the table and is now scrambling some eggs in a bowl. *It would be a nice pleasing sight if he didn't look as white as a sheet and have a clammy sheen on his face and chest.*

"What are you doing? Sit down." I order.

Without a word of argument, he sits. I guess he was right about the order giving and obeying, or he was just too weak to argue.

Putting the steaks on a griddle pan, I ask him how he'd like his steak.

"Still running around in a field, but just cook it until the bacon is done," he says, without a hint of humour.

I quickly glance at him to see if he's as serious as he sounds. "You don't eat my cows do you?" I can't hold back the question thinking of the times I'd noticed dry blood around Tony's snout. I place the bacon in the pan with the steak and silently berate myself for asking such a stupid question. The guys would have told me if my cows had been getting killed.

"No, but I do eat the occasional fox that goes after your chickens," he says with a laugh.

"Oh, well... thanks." I look at the bowl of scrambled eggs trying to see whether they seem to be the right colour. *It does.* I hold it up to my nose and sniff.

"They're good. I'd be the first to smell them if they

weren't," he informs me, tapping his nose with a finger. "Just like I can smell that you and Carter had sex last night."

WHOA, that's out of left field. I feel myself blush at his words. "What?" I sniff myself and blush even more. *Idiot.* He has no right to make that comment. I shake my head and tell him as much. "It's none of your bloody business what Carter and I get up to." Turning my back on him, I pour the eggs in to a frying pan before flipping the bacon and steak over.

"Actually I'm his Alpha and I ordered him not to sleep with you, so Carter going against a direct order *is* very much *my* business," he says with a growl. A quick glance behind me makes it clear he isn't joking. The tension in his shoulders and the fists his hands have formed show his anger.

I stack the bacon and steak on a plate, add the eggs, and slide the plate across to Jesse. "I'd offer you some toast but it looks like the guys have eaten all the bread."

"This will be more than enough, thanks," Jesse replies, placing three rashers of bacon and a scoop of egg onto the plates he'd set out at the seat opposite him. "Eat," he orders, nodding toward the plate. I open my mouth to argue but he carries on talking before a word escapes. "Don't tell me you have already eaten today because you haven't. You never have breakfast unless it's cooked for you." He cuts a chunk of extremely rare steak — what is it they call it in a restaurant? Blue? — and places it in to his mouth.

I glance up, dumbfounded. *How does he know that?*

He swallows his steak and laughs. "I have been listening to your stomach grumble more and more this last month. It's no coincidence your Nonna isn't here to force you to eat." He pierces me with a dark look. "You're looking thinner every time I see you, too."

Oh my God. He's Tony. How could I have forgotten that? The things I've told him thinking he's a dog. I feel myself blush as I take a seat opposite him, remembering the time I told him about my first kiss. "It was so gross and sloppy, I would've been better off kissing you." I was only thirteen.

Jesse looks at me with a quirked brow.

There's no way I'm going to remind him about all the embarrassing memories floating through my head. Hopefully he has forgotten. I quickly fill my mouth with a forkful of egg as not to answer his questioning look.

A smile plays across Jesse's face and I know he's on the right path. "You're remembering all the embarrassing things you've told me over the years," he guesses.

Dammit! Am I that easy to read? I quickly change the subject, asking him one of the many questions I have going through my head. "Why did you order Carter not to sleep with me?"

He chews his last mouthful of bacon and places his

knife and fork neatly on the empty plate. "Let me start with your father. Things will make more sense that way."

Chapter Six

Frankie

I walk to the fridge for a bottle of water as I frown, unable to see how anything about my father can connect to Carter. "Fine, start with my father," I agree whilst pouring us both a glass of water.

Jesse reaches for his glass. "Thanks," he states before taking a mouthful. "Your father, Ant, was my Alpha."

Having heard him mention that he was Carter's Alpha not long ago, I jump to the assumption that it's a werewolf thing and interrupt him. "My father was a werewolf?"

"Yes." He gives me a challenging look but doesn't give

me chance to argue before carrying on. "It was back when I was barely old enough to be fighting in World War I. My—"

"Wait! Are you telling me you fought in World War I... that will make you..." I say trailing off, trying to work out the maths in my head.

"One hundred and sixteen, to be exact," he states like it's nothing unusual. "The werewolf gene extends our lives somewhat," he adds with a shrug, no doubt for my benefit.

"Huh..." I grunt, lost for words. He doesn't look a day older than thirty; I can't get my mind around him being over a hundred.

Getting a distant look in his eyes, he fills the silence as he carries on from where he'd left off. "My regiment was based in the Pacific Islands and one day we were attacked by what I thought at the time was a wild animal, it slaughtered us all. I lay there with laboured breathing thinking I was sure to die soon. Hoping with everything I had left that I would die before the Germans found me, I didn't want to become a prisoner of war. I must have fallen asleep because I awoke to find a man," he comes out of his trance to glance at the picture of my father on the kitchen wall. "Ant." He smiles upon saying his name. "Your father. I thought he was going to kill me, he held a knife to my throat but when his hand brushed my skin I felt something at the time I could only describe it as a jolt of energy."

Taking his eyes off the picture he smiles across the

table at me. "It was what you felt when we shook hands yesterday. A wolf recognising an Alpha." I open my mouth to deny it. *I'm not a werewolf.* But he shakes his head before I can interrupt him. "No you're not wolf yet, but you have one in you, it will arise sooner or later." He waves his hand in dismissal having seen I've once again opened my mouth to throw questions at him.

A wolf inside me? No way.

"Anyway. Where was I?" he asks himself out loud. "Ah, yes... The jolt of energy. Once I felt that, a smile crossed his face and he whispered, *'Well, I'll be...'* as he slid his knife back into its sheath on his belt. He picked me up in his arms and carried me away."

"Having fallen asleep again, I woke in a building with a small group of injured men, they all seemed to have a feel to them. It was like static electricity making the hairs on your arms stand up. I didn't know at the time but they were all werewolves; that's what I could feel. Werewolf energy."

I rub at my arms where the hairs were doing what he'd just said. I berate myself once again. *I'm not a werewolf. It's just the story making my hairs stand up.*

Unaware of my internal denial Jesse keeps talking. "Ant had been walking the battle fields hunting a rogue werewolf who was slaughtering everyone, and saving all who'd been attacked, caring for them while they healed and bringing them into his pack. Those, who survived anyway. Only seven, out of over twenty, made it through the change." Jesse's voice breaks and he clears his throat before talking again. "Ant got us on a boat and had us transported back here. God only knows how he managed that during a war but he did. His parents and his mate, Maria, were awaiting our arrival in a huge house that became the pack house. It still is."

"Do you still live there?" I ask, thinking how there is something that was part of my family still here and I had no idea about it.

He nods. "You're welcome anytime, if you'd like to see it," he says evidently guessing my train of thought.

"I'd love to, thank you," I say with a grateful smile.

He smiles. "In the beginning there was a lot of fighting between the new wolves and those that were here with Maria. Dominance fights to find out where everyone stood in the pack. It wasn't long until I became Ant's Beta and we became the closest of mates. Brothers."

"Once you were born we could all sense what you were, an Omega. Omegas are rare, a special kind of wolf that quite often don't live long lives. In terms of dominance they sit at the bottom of the pack and often become the scapegoat. That's dangerous in itself, but add their ability to soothe and calm an alpha to the mix and you've had it. Alphas will either deem you a threat or a weapon to use against other Alphas. We thought we could protect you but word got out, and one night Ant found an

Alpha in your nursery. He went ballistic tearing the Alpha to shreds right there beside your cot. Your mother was not happy; it was the last straw. The very next day he signed the house over to me on the condition that it stayed the pack house, which was fine by me. I didn't want a big house all to myself. I'd bought this little three-bedroom farm and found that too big and lonely. We're pack animals, we like company." I nod in agreement, knowing exactly how it feels to find a three-bedroom house lonely when one person is rattling around in it.

"So we swapped houses, he moved in here and I moved in the pack house."

"This…" I wave my arms around gesturing to the room, "was your farm?" I ask, surprised by the thought.

"It sure is, O'K Cattle Farm. O'K for O'Keefe. I thought if I found a mate, we could settle down have a nice little family if we were lucky enough to have kids."

I give him a questioning look.

"Chances of miscarriage are high for werewolves. If the embryo is more werewolf than human, the mother can't always carry to term. Human mothers aren't always strong enough. If the mother is a werewolf she has to be careful not to change during her pregnancy because that will automatically miscarry the baby. She can take energy from the pack to fight the call of the moon but that's not the only time we change. As you've seen tonight."

Needing to stretch my legs and get out from under

his knowing gaze, I take both our plates to the sink and start filling it with hot, soapy water.

"Have you heard enough for tonight, or do you want me to finish?" he asks from beside me. I jump; I hadn't even heard him move. He smiles at me and waves a tea towel in the air. "You wash, I'll dry."

I snatch the tea towel out of his hands, and point back at his chair. "You sit back down and tell me the rest, while I wash *and* dry." He watches me and for a moment I think he's going to snatch the tea towel back, but he takes a deep breath and does as I asked.

"Being South African, Maria, had some knowledge of Voodoo. Dark stuff. She had always insisted on it being the devil's magic, but while your father was moving the furniture in she took you out for the day and when you came back there was no trace of your wolf. We all knew only something dark could have buried your wolf, she must have taken you to someone who dealt with Voodoo, but no one ever asked her about it. Not even your father. I think like me, he was probably worried about the price a spell like that would have cost? And I'm not talking money."

"If she buried my wolf, why couldn't we all stay at the other house?" I question as I dry the clean plates.

"Because not only did she bury your wolf, that next day after you'd all moved in, as each of the pack members woke up, you were wiped from their memories. As far as they were concerned Maria and Ant had never had a child. They believed Ant and Maria wanted privacy and that's why we swapped houses. As your father's Beta, I was the only one that knew about it."

Placing the plates in the cupboard I turn and face Jesse. "Would that have been the price?"

"It might have been part of it. Your mother never did fall pregnant again, I think that may have been the sacrifice." He reaches out to stroke my forearm in a comforting gesture as I drop into the empty seat beside him. *My mother sacrificed future children for me.* The thought tears at my heart.

"Please. Tell me the rest," I plead, wanting to know as much about my parents as I can, no matter how painful it may be.

Taking me at my word, Jesse starts talking. "The night before your family were killed I met your father in the field near the cemetery fence. He told me he'd been invited on a full moon hunt in another Alpha's territory. Rick's territory. He said '*Rick knew about you and wanted to talk.*'" Jesse shakes his head sadly. "I told your father it wasn't a good idea, Rick wasn't trustable, if he knew about you he'd have his sights on using you as a weapon." He gently squeezes my hand with his and I glance down surprised to see our hands connected on the table. "He took Guisseppe because he was a hell of a good fighter and Maria insisted on going as well. I begged him to let me go, but he needed me to stay here and watch over you and Not, He knew if anything happened to him, I'd become Alpha and he didn't want the pack to lose two good Alphas in one night. I hated the plan, but Ant was Alpha and I couldn't go against his order. I promised I'd look after you no matter what, and that's what I did."

I feel a finger under my chin as he lifts my head slightly so we make eye contact and I watch as his eyes follow a tear down my cheek, before he wipes it away. "I saw how sad you were, at the funeral, and decided you needed a friend. What is better then a dog? Man's best friend." He shrugs slightly. "It seemed to be working out fine, until some of your friends left for university across the country and you hid away; it was as though I was the only friend you needed. As good as that is for a guy's ego, it wasn't healthy, so I sent Joey to work on the farm and hoped he would make friends with you. With a gentle push from Nonna, it worked. Unfortunately I found some werewolves from out of town, sniffing around at Nonna's funeral. It had me worried, knowing I can't watch you 24/7. I ordered Carter to watch you and unfortunately Carter's definition of watching you is slightly different to mine. He decided to become your boyfriend." He sighs. "Outside the diner yesterday, I ordered him not to sleep with you. I didn't want him to use you as another notch on his bedpost. Maybe I shouldn't have done that, I don't know." He shakes his head and looks at me with regret. "I was just trying to protect you."

I smile at him, hoping to ease his regret. "It's okay. Thank you." He had done so much for me and I had no idea about any of it. "For everything," I add. He looks tired and barely smiles back. He's been looking after me all these years, it's time I repay the favour and look after him, even if it's only for an hour or two. "Come on. Bed," I say getting up and pointing the way to the stairs.

He smiles, before standing. "Whatever you say Doc," he says as he follows my order.

I watch his movements as we walk up the stairs and I'm relieved to see that he seems to be moving better than he was before he ate. When we reach the top of the stairs I glance at Nonna's door knowing the room is bigger and would be much better for him, but decide against it knowing I've had enough pain for today. I grab some clean sheets out of the closet as we pass before opening my bedroom door. I'm suddenly hit with a musty smell, which isn't surprising since no-one has been in here for a month. My room doesn't look any different; it has the same wooden sleigh bed and bedside tables taking up most of the room and a wicker chair in the corner beside the window. I walk over to the window and crack it open to let some fresh air in before stripping the bed. Throwing the dusty sheets on the floor I spot Jesse sat in the chair. He must feel worse than he's letting on, having sat down without me ordering him to. Once I get the fresh sheets on the bed Jesse pulls off the home made sarong and climbs on the bed, pulling the sheet up to his waist to cover himself. Looking at his abs and chest makes me wish he'd pulled it up to his neck. Not that the sheet really matters, my mind can clearly conjure up what he's hiding under the sheet, since I was at eye level with it earlier. I have a boyfriend, I should not be perving on him I remind myself as I force my eyes up to his. He gives me a knowing grin and I feel my cheeks flame. I quickly turn to pull the curtains closed.

"You know, werewolves can see perfectly well in the dark." He laughs.

I grab the bundle of sheets off the floor and turn to the door not wanting to cause him to laugh at me any more. "I'm going to put the sheets in the wash and tidy up the kitchen while you rest."

"Wait! Can you just lie next to me for a while? An injured wolf likes to feel pack nearby." His pleading tone causes me to pause in the doorway.

I look at him over the mountain of sheets. "I'm not pack. I'm just... Me."

"You have a wolf in you, my wolf recognised it the other day. Remember the jolt of energy?" he reminds me.

I sigh and in that moment I make the decision to trust him. I've trusted Tony for as long as I remember, that shouldn't change just because I know he's not an ordinary wolf. I drop the sheets to the floor and climb on to the bed, lying down beside him with my back on top of the sheet. I stare at the ceiling thinking of everything Jesse had just told me about himself, my father, and even me. Things I had no idea about. My life has been turned upside down, yet I feel like I should believe every word he's told me, no matter how far fetched some of it sounds. After all I've seen some pretty unexplainable things with my own eyes today.

My arm brushes against Jesse's and I feel him physically relax at my touch. Who am I to take that away from him? I leave our arms touching and, if I'm honest with myself, the touch is a comfort for me too.

My mind becomes alert before my eyes and I snuggle into the bed. My body suddenly stiffens as I realise it doesn't feel like my sofa bed. Feeling Carter's arm tighten around my waist causes me to pause my uncertainty. I haven't shared my bed with anyone like this for a while, that's probably what's making it feel wrong.

I open my eyes and see that my uncertainty had nothing to do with the arm around my waist. I'm not facing the kitchen like I would be if I was at my apartment, instead I'm looking at a familiar painting of the beach, the one that's hung on my bedroom wall at the farm. The thought of the farm invokes memories to flood back... The gunshots. Tony. Jesse who's lying next to me... *naked!* I slip out from under his arm and cover him up with the sheet.

The sound of a man and woman arguing floats through the open window. I dash quickly down the stairs to quiet them down, before they wake Jesse up. The further away from window I get the less I can hear. It's not until I reach the bottom of the stairs that I pick up the conversation again.

"He's not stupid! He's bound to have Nate or Kelly there, even Carter would protect him from a challenge when he's injured. Let's just go home," she pleads in a whisper.

"Patty, I'm not challenging him. I'm going to kill him," a male voice says vehemently.

"It's suicidal" The woman - Patty, the male had called her - hisses.

"There isn't anyone there except him. I'm sure of it."

This guy is planning on killing Jesse? My patient. My father's friend. *Hell No!*

I tug open the front door with the intention to tell this guy how stupid he is for even considering killing Jesse, but before I open my mouth I feel a sharp pain in my stomach. As he steps back I realise it wasn't the entry I felt, it was the twist of the knife as he pulled it out. The man looks at me, eyes bulging in shock. I know behind my grimace of pain I'm mirroring his look. I put my hand to the wound to try to staunch the bleeding. *Seriously, what kind of person stabs someone before seeing whom they are actually stabbing?*

"You smelt like him," he says answering the question I thought I'd asked myself.

A fierce growl emanates from behind me; before I can turn to look at Jesse I see a blur of fur fly over me. The wolf lands on the shocked man and rips into his throat. I hear the woman screaming, something I can't quite make out, before the world fades away and darkness descends.

Something wet and rough rubs against my cheek bringing the world back into focus. I open my eyes to see Tony's snout in my face. "Hey," I say, it sounds slurred even to my own ears as the pain is ebbing away and a floating feeling is falling over me.

Tony whines over me.

My eyes close and I no longer have the energy to open them, not even to look at him to give him comfort. *I'm not hurting anymore. It's okay.*

The feel of teeth tearing into my stomach causes me alarm but there is nothing I can do, I can't move. Tony's eating me and I'm not even dead yet.

Chapter Seven

Carter

I turn on the bed to snuggle into the warm body beside me, to find it's no longer where it should be. I'm alone in bed. I listen to the apartment hoping to hear Frankie in the shower but my ears are greeted with silence. In a final hope I send my energy out to feel for her but there's no one here, no one but me. If I was in my own apartment I'd be worried she'd had regrets and done a runner but I'm in her apartment; she's probably just gone for milk or something.

As I lift the covers off and throw my legs over the side of the bed, a piece of paper slips to the floor. I pick it up and see it's a note from Frankie. Seeing the kiss she'd ended her note with washes away any worry of her possible regret that had been niggling at me. I shake my head in disbelief at the feelings I have for this girl - she's working her way into my heart and that's a first for me - before getting up and heading into the bathroom.

Once dressed and ready I look around the apartment and wonder what I can do with my time? My wolf is pushing at me to go hunt Frankie down. I'd normally put it down to the excitement of a chase but he's feeling unnecessarily anxious and I can't put my finger on the why. Without a second thought I follow his instinct and decide to track Frankie by following her scent. We know it intimately so on a dry summers day like today, we'll easily be able to follow it.

I trail her scent as far as the car park and stop in an empty spot with her apartment number painted on it. The other space with her number is occupied by her beloved Kawasaki Ninja. Knowing she uses the VW Kombi for the farm I put two and two together and decide to head to the farm.

As I'm approaching the entry road to the O'K Cattle Farm, the windows in my old rust bucket wound down as far as they can go, I'm well and truly regretting not staying in Frankie's apartment. Driving during summer in WA with no air-conditioning is hell, but I can't afford a new car and no matter how many times my mechanic replaces the gas and seals, it still doesn't fucking work. My nose picks up a familiar scent that instantly causes my wolf's hackles to rise. Blood. Jesse's blood. That scent alone is enough to have my gut churning in worry, but the sweet scent of Frankie's blowing in on the breeze has me instantly slamming on the breaks, jumping out the car and running through the small graveyard beside the road.

A number of visions flow through my mind as I vault over gravestones. Frankie, bleeding, with a manic Jesse ripping into her body is the worst one that my mind seems to be stuck on. The fact that I can't smell Frankie's blood doesn't help convince me she's okay. Jesse is obviously injured, he could easily loose his control and attack her. I pick up my speed pushing myself to reach them in time, all the while knowing if I do make it before he hurts her, I'm not dominant enough to stand up to Jesse. I'll only give him another body to rip apart before he turns to her. *Mine.*

I come to stop at the back of the graveyard; before me is a pool of Jesse's blood that tells me this is where the incident happened, whatever it may have been. I can see a trail of blood leading through the fence and into the paddock that leads to the O'K Cattle Farm beyond it. I take a step forward to follow the blood before pausing to pull out my phone. I immediately make a three-way call with the two people I know can give a manic Jesse, a run for his money - Kelly and Nate, two of the pack's best enforcers.

"Hello, " Nate answers first.

Within a second Kelly's voice joins the line. "Yo Carter, Nate, what's happening?"

"I've found some of Jesse's blood. A lot of it. My girlfriend Frankie's scent is here, too. I'm worried he'll attack her blinded by his pain. There's a trail I can follow but I'm not sure I can do anything except get myself killed." My body is wracked with pain as my wolf tries to force me to follow the trail; he wants to protect Frankie and doesn't care if we die doing it.

"Where are you?" Kelly demands in his New Zealand accent.

The power of the more dominant wolf's demand gets my wolf's attention and forces him to ignore his needs, which allows me to answer. "The cemetery. It looks like the blood leads to Frankie's farm, which is just across the paddock. Joey works there, I think."

"I've given Joey a lift there before. I'll go straight to the farm," Nate says before disconnecting from the call.

"I'm two minutes away, I'll come to you. Do not follow the trail until I get there," Kelly orders, his breathing changes and I know he's already running.

Chapter Eight

Jesse

The life fades out of Frankie's eyes and I do the only thing I can. I bite her, trying to provoke her wolf into surfacing. I step back and watch, hoping to see or feel a spark of something. What I see is terrifying, I haven't watched over her all this time for her to die now. To die at the hand of a pack member who was after me. *No!* The bastard had managed to hit her aorta; no amount of staunching the wound will help. She's bleeding to death. I bite her again. If I can get as much of my wolf DNA into her it might make her become a werewolf like it would a regular human.

"Shit! Jesse!" Nate bellows from behind me.

I freeze on the spot. Knowing how bad this will look I force my body to change, ignoring my wolf who whines at me in protest. He wants to keep biting Frankie. He needs her to survive. *Mate.* Every inch of my body burns as I push him back and pretend I didn't hear the word he just pushed through my head, the burning eases, turning to a tingle as I wiggle my fingers and toes. Not acknowledging the remaining pain I turn to find Nate cradling Frankie against his body. My wolf growls at the sight and I can't stop it from escaping my own throat.

Nate looks up at me with wide eyes.

"It's not what it looks like," I say with cracked voice that isn't quite human yet.

Nate glances down at Frankie and then back up to me. He doesn't say a word, just holds me there with his eyes, demanding an explanation.

I take a moment to thank the gods it's Nate who arrived first. He'll listen before acting, unlike the others who'd rather react and deal with explanations later. "She's Ant's daughter. Our old Alpha, Rossi." I use the surname hoping it will ring a bell, it's the name Ant mainly went by within the pack. Seeing a spark of recognition in Nate's eyes I continue, "I don't know where to start? Damn it..." My mind's moving from one thought to the next too quick for me to process.

"Start at the beginning." Nate's calm voice washes

over me. "We found your blood in the cemetery. Why were you there? What happened?"

My mind clears and I let the answers flow out of my mouth without thinking about them. "Before Rossi died he told me to watch out for her. I've been meeting up with her in my wolf form since she was seven years old. She calls me Tony after some story of her Nonna's." I wave hand in dismissal, knowing I'm going off track. "It's our day. I went to the cemetery like usual, but before she arrived a fucking bounty hunter came out of nowhere and shot me. He was using silver bullets." I shake my head at the memory of the hunter. His face memorised. I'll be hunting him down once we have deal with today's problems. "She helped me to the house and fixed me up. I had to change because I nearly went for her as she was feeling for the wound. She knew what I was and she didn't care, she carried on as though it was nothing." I swallow back the need to claim her as mine, knowing my wolf is over reacting in the moment.

"She fed me and forced me to lie down. I woke up when I heard the front door open." I point out the body a few metres away. "He was here to kill me but she answered the door and, blinded by his vengeance, he stabbed her."

Hearing the footfalls in the paddock behind me, I know my time is running out. More wolves are approaching and they are approaching fast. "I killed him and his mate. She was dying on me, Nate. I know she has a wolf in there; I felt her the other day and I was around when she was a pup in a crib. Her wolf wasn't taking over to bring her from the brink and I thought if I bit her it would provoke her out. It wasn't working - nothing is working." My voice breaks. "I thought if I got as much of my DNA in her as I could that might help. What else could I do?" I plead, hoping that he thinks of something I haven't.

"*You bastard!*" Carter shouts in my ear as I'm hit by a wall and plastered to the floor. I won't fight back, I know what he sees and what it's making him think. He hits me with a good right hook.

"*Carter, get off!* It's not what you think," Nate demands.

Kelly's head comes in to view over Carter's shoulder a second before Carter's weight disappears. I get up and brush the dirt off as I make my way over to Frankie. Nate's crouched over her once again. "How's she doing?" I ask. Not sure if I really want an honest answer.

"Her pulse is weak, she's almost gone. You did everything you could, Jesse," Nate says, no doubt trying to comfort me, but it's far from working. The guilt from biting her is raging through me.

I listen as Kelly manages to calm Carter down, taking Nate's word that I had been helping. We all listen in silence as Frankie's heart beats weakly, one last time.

Carter drops to the floor with his head buried in his

hands, a moment passes and he jumps up. "We need to do CPR," he states, trying to pry Frankie out of Nate's grasp. The sight before me makes me realise Carter really does have feelings for Frankie. She isn't just a notch on his bedpost after all.

"No! We listen and wait," I tell them.

"Wait for what? She's dead. She'll still be dead if we don't do anything. It's too late to even infect her." Carter punches the floor with his fist, leaving a cracked floorboard on the porch.

Looking up to the heavens I pray to Ant, hoping he's listening and he'll understand I've done all I can for his daughter. "Why do you think I bit her, Carter? It wasn't for the fun of it. She was born with the gene. We've just got to wait and pray it kicks in. If Rossi wasn't dead, he'd kill me for not stopping that bastard before he stabbed his daughter." I finish with a sigh. I want to kill myself. Dammit!

"*Frankie? No!*" Joey screams, as he runs full pelt through one of the paddocks.

Kelly stops him before he ploughs into us, pulling him into a warm embrace. "Shhh..." he murmurs as Joey sobs into his chest. Joey has always been one of the more submissive wolves but I've never seen him show his vulnerability infront of such dominant wolves.

"Rossi? You mean the old Alpha Rossi? This is his daughter?" Carter slaps his own forehead. "Of course!

Joey introduced her as Rosa Rossi, I didn't make the connection." Carter doesn't need an answer, but I nod regardless.

"Guys, she has a pulse again." Nate calls out from beside Frankie's body. "It's really weak but it's there. She's back, boys," he adds with a grin.

"Did you hear that Joey? She's gonna be ok. She's back." Kelly comforts Joey, patting him on the back.

I bend and feel Frankie's pulse for myself. It's not that I don't believe Nate or my ears, but sometimes you just need to feel it under your own fingers. My shoulders slump in relief as I feel it beat under my fingertips. Leaning over I place a kiss on her forehead. "Thank you," I whisper. "For everything," I add before standing. "Put Frankie in the bedroom with the door open. I'm going to go get cleaned up, call me the minute she wakes up," I tell them all as I walk in the direction of the cemetery. "Someone call Tracey, tell her she's needed," I state over my shoulder referring to the healer in our pack.

"Wait! Don't you want to be here we she wakes up?" Kelly questions.

"I don't want to scare her," I answer, before changing to wolf, knowing that will stave off any arguments about my decision. If Frankie wakes up remembering me attacking her, she may never want to be in the same room as me again. It's a huge sacrifice I'll have to make, my wolf already feels like he's lost any chance he had of having a mate, but it's worth it to have her alive. Nate and Kelly will protect her and Frankie will never have to see me again. *Ever!*

Chapter Nine

Frankie

I open my eyes to glimpse two dark brown, almost black eyes, watching me before the world falls away from me. The sound of birds tweeting brings me around to consciousness. Peeking open an eye I find myself looking at an attractive man, one I've never seen before sitting in my wicker chair, which has been pulled up next to the bed. I open my other eye to get a clearer view of him; he looks to be asleep so I leisurely take in the sight. His black hair is closely shaven to his head and his rounded face and broad nose fits with his muscular physique, his darker skin making him easily distinguishable as an islander. At a guess I'd put him in his late twenties. I shift on the bed to get into a more comfortable position and groan as pain courses through me. The man opens his eyes and stares at me, with concerned dark brown eyes that look vaguely familiar.

"Welcome back Darl'," he says, his New Zealand accent easily recognisable by his pronunciation of the first 'e' in welcome as an 'i', his face brightens with a genuine smile.

Knowing I'm in my room at the farm I try to sit up and look around the room to work out why I'm here, especially since I'm in the company of a stranger, no matter how at ease I feel with him. An agonising wave of pain rolls through my middle causing me to feel nauseous and evoking a moan from me as I curl in on myself.

"Trace..." the guy shouts, jumping up out of the chair. He pats my shoulder comfortingly. "Tracey'll be up in a sec, she's a nurse. She'll sort out the pain for ya." He looks at the door and it suddenly opens as a tall leggy blonde rushes in. I can't help but notice she has a remarkable resemblance to a Barbie doll, especially with the fuchsia pink tight tank top and cropped leggings she's wearing.

"Hey Kelly, what's wrong?" She looks at me, a huge smile gracing her face before she claps her hands together excitedly. "Ooh our patient is awake."

The guy, Kelly —that's what she'd called him — grimaces at her excitement and shakes his head. "Trace, can you give her something? She's in a bit of pain."

"A bit?" I question his under evaluation through gritted teeth.

Tracey reaches out and pats my arm. "It will be gone in a minute," she says as she picks up a needle and syringe filled with something clear off my dresser and jabs my arm with it. I pull my arm away from her and rub it watching the hole from the needle close as it heals before my eyes. Staring at my arm in shock causes me to be too late to question her about what the needle contained. I look up as the door closes shut behind her.

"I'm gonna go call Jesse, he wanted to know when you were awake. Do you want me to send someone else up?" Kelly asks as he steps towards the door.

The name causes everything to come flooding back; Tony laid on my fathers grave, Jesse bleeding all over the kitchen table, everything he told me about my father and me, the man stabbing me, Jesse eating him, and then eating me. "Jesse..." I whisper and I bring a hand up to my mouth in shock. "Where is Jesse?" I add, glancing at the closed door expecting him to walk in any second.

"It's okay, he can't hurt you. He's not here," Kelly reassures me.

I gasp in disbelief. "Hurt me? I know he won't hurt me."

"Don't you remember? He bit you! We thought you'd be scared of him."

"I remember," I confirm with a nod of my head. "Being eaten is something that's not easily forgotten. He bit me because he had to though; it was the only way he thought he could get my wolf to come out. I heard him tell her as much." I pause before adding, "Actually he did think of another way but he's not a rapist."

Kelly's mouth drops in astonishment. "That's not possible. He was in wolf form, you can't have heard him?"

"I don't know." I try to think back to the memory, but I can't see anything different. It was definitely Jesse's voice I was hearing. *I know it was.* At the time I didn't even think about him being a wolf. In my defence, I was just about dead. "It was him. He was saying sorry over and over, he was begging her to come forward. She was just... biding her time!"

"It sounds like you have the gift of hearing the wolf," says a voice from behind the door as it opens in front of Kelly. I look over his head to see a surfer looking guy, who you would expect to find at Cottesloe, not on a farm in Caversham. He looks tall, maybe six feet give or take an inch. His shoulder length wavy blonde hair is what gives him the surfy look, although his bare feet fit the theme too. The police uniform he's wearing certainly doesn't.

"I thought only Alphas could hear wolves while still in human form?" Kelly questions the newcomer.

He shrugs. "Me too, but I guess maybe the wolfborn can too." He glances across at me. "Hi, I'm Nate. I guess you'll be joining the pack now, since your wolf has finally decided to grace us with her presence?"

Kelly looks at me with curiosity in his eyes, but doesn't question my wolf hearing anymore. "Is it okay if I leave you with Nate?" he asks instead.

"I can go call Jesse, but Kelly hasn't slept all night so I thought I'd relieve him. I can get Tracey to come back up if you'd prefer her company?" Nate offers showing the gentleman behind the surfer.

His words about my wolf being present surprises me for an instant and I open my mouth to argue, before closing it again when I *feel* her, a churning inside me, it's somewhat similar to the butterflies you'd feel in your stomach only this is all over me. She's rippling just beneath the surface. "I guess if I'm going to have to join the pack, I might as well add you to list of those I know." I give him what I hope is a reassuring smile, as he steps into the room and Kelly leaves. He heads straight to the wicker chair, sitting with confidence as though it isn't the first time he's sat there. I'm suddenly hit by the smell of rain just before it arrives. I strain to see out the window, somewhat surprised not to be feeling pain; whatever Tracey gave me must have been good stuff. "Is it raining? It smells like there's going to be a storm," I ask.

Nate smiles. "No, the sky is clear tonight. That will be my scent you can smell, we all have our own scent. It's how we can tell who is nearby when we hunt. It might smell strong at first but in time you'll learn to ignore it unless you need it."

"Oh no, I love the smell of a storm coming. I find it quite calming." I blush, realising I'd just told him I love his smell. I look up at his eyes, hoping he hasn't caught onto my embarrassment and I'm stunned by how beautiful his eyes are, one is the colour of an emerald and the other's as blue as the sky at twilight. Words pour out of my mouth before I can stop them. "Your eyes are beautiful." I feel myself blush from head to toe, but I can't pull my eyes away from his.

"Thank you," he says with a genuine looking smile. "Not many people call them that. In fact I think you might be the first. I've had them called freaky and ugly, but never beautiful. Thank you."

I start to think of everything Jesse had said earlier and feel panic suddenly setting in. "Nate, Jesse said something about my dad. He kept me away from the pack because I'm an... O..." I break off as I try to remember the word he used.

"Omega," Nate offers.

"Yes, Omega. If I join the pack, will that cause problems for everyone? After all the trouble Jesse has gone to, keeping me safe all these years?" I start to ramble as my body trembles in panic and, if I'm honest, fear.

"Hey," Nate says in a calming voice, as he strokes my hand. A jet of energy flows from his hand through mine and my wolf becomes alert from where she's laid deep inside me. "There are plenty of us around, we'll make sure things don't get out of hand. No one will get near you without your say so," he says looking deep into my eye's. It's as if he's looking through me and directly at my wolf. "Alright?" he asks her.

With his words, she sends out a pulse of energy feeling for his wolf. She eases back into wherever she'd been resting before. She likes the feel of Nate, and urges me to trust him to keep us safe.

"What was that?" I ask, not quite sure what just happened.

"She's calmed down now," Nate states. "She was worried like you were. I just reassured her everyone will be safe." He removes his hand from mine and relaxes back into the chair. "You should rest now, it will help you heal."

Gently rolling over on the bed I close my eyes and try to sleep, an uneasiness running through me. I'm uncomfortable and I can't work out what's not quite right. This is the most comfortable mattress I've ever slept on so I know it's nothing to do with the bed. I slowly shuffle around on the bed trying to get more comfortable, putting it down to my injury even though it's no longer hurting. But it doesn't matter what position I lay in it doesn't feel any better.

"I think you need to feel a pack member next to you. Do you want me to call Carter? We sent him to Jesse's a few hours ago because he wouldn't sleep while he was here, he just sat watching you."

Carter. I hadn't even thought about him and he's been sat at my bedside. Guilt runs through me.

"Joey's asleep on the couch downstairs, I can get him instead if you'd like?" Nate suggests obviously remembering Joey and I are friends.

I sit up and look at Nate. It's what Jesse needed when he was hurt, he'd said he needed to feel my wolf and it worked for him; he relaxed instantly when we touched. "No, don't wake them, they need their sleep. Would you mind getting in with me?" I ask warily as I pat the bed next to me. I see him blush and immediately back track. "I understand, if you don't want to. We don't really know each other. I..."

Nate laughs. "It's not that. My wolf very much wants to lie there and comfort you. But you're naked under those sheets. I just thought you would feel more comfortable having him in the bed with you." He points to his uniform trousers and shirt, "I'd have to take these off," he adds.

"I don't mind, if you don't." The minute the words fall out my mouth, I know something inside me has changed. I'm flirting with an almost stranger and inviting him into bed with me while we are both practically naked.

Standing up with a nod he silently strips off his uniform, leaving him wearing tightly fitted black boxers that don't leave much to the imagination. Leaving his clothes neatly folded on the chair, he climbs in beside me, lying on his side facing me. I turn over and give him my back before wriggling back until he's spooning me. The movement causes pain to run through me in a wave, the injection obviously starting to wear off. I hold my breath until it passes while Nate places his arm over my side and holds me close, being careful not to disturb my wound. My body relaxes instantly. I feel almost weightless. His warmth, energy and scent a comfort to us, my wolf knows he'll protect us while we sleep.

"Is this okay?" I hear him ask, but being too close to sleep I don't reply.

Chapter Ten

Frankie

I'm chasing a fox through the bush, my mouth watering at the thought of how delicious it will taste. Nate moves beside me, slipping out of the bed and the dream fades away. Being too tired and just wanting to snuggle back down to sleep I don't stir or ask where he's going. It's not exactly any of my business; he probably has a girlfriend or wife to get back to. It's so strange thinking of how intimately we have just been sleeping when we don't know a thing about each other.

Hearing the door open, I lay still waiting for Nate to close it behind him.

"What the fuck is going on in here?" Carter shouts, causing me to flinch on the bed. I keep playing asleep as I listen to the sounds of Nate moving quickly across the room.

"Shh," Nate says. There's a ruffle of clothing before the door closes to and a thud sounds against the wall. "Calm down Carter. Let go of me or this will lead to a fight you won't win."

"You were getting dressed after being in bed with my girlfriend. What the hell do you expect me to do?" Carter demands.

"Don't you dare lecture me about sleeping around, not when you know you don't smell like you slept alone either. Frankie was hurt and couldn't settle - she needed pack. I asked her if she wanted me to call you or Joey but she didn't want to disturb either of you. We slept, that's all." Nate states, the fury clear in his voice.

They may have taken the argument out of the room, so not to wake me up, but I can hear every word even though they don't seem to be shouting. I guess good hearing is another perk to being a werewolf.

"I was stressed and Clarissa was at Jesse's," Carter says, his voice sounding distant during some of that making me think he's pacing.

"What?" Nate says with a sarcastic sounding laugh. "So your girlfriend can't sleep next to another guy to feel his wolf because she is hurt, healing and in need of the comfort, but you can have sex with another woman because you are stressed? You're a jerk, Carter. Frankie won't put up with it, her wolf isn't weak like Clarissa's."

I listen as someone stomps downstairs and whoever's outside the door takes a deep breath before the back door slams shut. The bedroom door opens as a car speeds away on the gravel road outside.

I smell sex and lavender before I see Carter come through the door. "Hey baby," he says as he walks over to the bed and sits where Nate had just been laid. He leans over to kiss me and I pull away before our lips make contact. *Is he seriously going to act like he's done nothing?* My wolf's energy runs through my veins making my anger stronger than it would normally be in a situation like this.

"You've had sex." I state with confidence, I can smell it after all.

His smile wavers. "No, I—" he starts to lie.

I stop him mid-sentence. "I can smell it, and I heard what was said between you and Nate too, so don't bother denying it. It just makes you look like a bigger jerk." I say crossing my arms and narrowing my eyes in annoyance.

He reaches his hand out to touch me. "Frankie..." he starts.

I pull away and get up out of bed. "No Carter, I don't want hear it. Just get out," I order. I walk across the room surprised to be steady on my feet, I was stabbed a couple of days ago and I feel better than I have in a long time. Opening the door I stride across the hall and into the bathroom, I haven't peed in a couple of days, granted I've not really had any liquid intake in that time either, but I'm still busting. After emptying my bladder I look into the mirror above the basin and notice I'm still naked. I sigh, deciding there is no need to be embarrassed, Carter has seen it all before. Thinking of Carter, I realise I'm not mad anymore - in fact I'm surprisingly calm about what I've just heard. I know I don't need a jerk like that in my life so I don't really care what Carter does now.

I open the glass door on the shower and lean in turning the tap to hot before stepping in. This shower is no power shower but it's hot, which is more than I can say for the shower in my shitty apartment. The heat on my shoulders and running down my back and over my chest feels amazing. It feels somewhat therapeutic, like I'm washing away the old me, and a whole new person is going to step out when I'm done. I peel the bandage off my wound to find nothing but a well healed scar. Granted it's a big jagged scar that looks like I've been a wolf's chew toy, but it doesn't have the pink angry look a fresh scar would. I run my finger over what is a souvenir to remember Jesse by. I take my time in the shower until the water turns cold; just as I turn the shower off and start to dry myself with the fluffy purple towel that I pull off the rail, there's a knock at the door.

"Are you ok in there, Frank?" Joey asks, worry clear in his voice as he calls me by my shortened name.

Grabbing the robe off the back of the door and tying it around myself, I unlock the door and pull it open, excited to see my friend again. I've missed Joey so much; it feels like a lifetime ago when we were sat watching True Blood the other night.

He pounces on me, pulling me into a big hug. "You were dead Frankie! I'm so glad you came back, I don't know what I'd do without you?" he says, almost squeezing the life out of me. The waver in his voice tells me he's getting emotional.

"Hey, don't get upset. I'm here and I'm not planning on going anywhere, okay?" I reassure him patting his back.

He relaxes and pulls back to look at me, holding my gaze for twenty seconds before glancing down at his feet and speaking. "You smell like Nate. Is that why Carter left so quick?"

It's not a question about Nate's smell on me; his werewolf senses make him certain of that. Which is something I'll have to talk to him about later. He's a werewolf and he never told me anything about it. "I told Carter to leave. He came up smelling of sex and lavender, according to Nate it was someone called Clarissa." I shrug my shoulders as I say her name, not really caring if the names correct or not, before walking out of the bathroom.

The smell of coffee and bacon hits me, making my mouth water. "Mmm... I'm starving and that smells so good," I tell Joey as I edge towards the stairs and closer to the smell of food.

"Hang on a sec, Frank." Joey demands.

My wolf stirs inside me as I stop and I hear a growl. I turn and notice belatedly that the growl was coming out of my own mouth. She isn't happy about Joey telling me to 'hang on'; it sounded too close to an order. I feel her power creeping down my arms and reaching out towards Joey, testing his dominance. No one has had time to give me a run down on all things wolf but I know I'm right in my assessment. I just know.

"Shit... I... I mean... I brought you some fresh clothes... they're on your bed," Joey manages to stammer out, no doubt hoping to turn this around and satisfy my wolf with his back tracking.

The smell of bacon and coffee gets stronger as someone opens the door at the foot of the stairs. "Everything okay, Darl'?" Kelly's concerned tone calls. "There's a bit of a power surge going on." I turn to his voice and see him looking past me, at Joey.

Pushing my wolf down, I tell her Joey wasn't meaning it as an order. She fights for a second and I worry she might just go through with her dominance war. I feel my eyes change and I see Kelly's eyes widen in shock at the sight. She glances up at Joey and he averts his eyes showing that he didn't mean it as an order. Pleased with his response she retreats back to the place she rests.

"We're fine, Kelly. It was a miscommunication, Jo was just suggesting I might want to get dressed before going down for food." I look down at the robe I'm wearing and blush in embarrassment; I wrap my arms around myself trying to hide from Kelly's eyes. "I guess it was a good idea," I say as I turn around to head back to my room before stopping on the landing and giving Joey a quick hug. "Thanks Jo."

I instantly spot my overnight bag on the white wicker chair next to the bed, taking the place where Nate's clothes had been neatly folded not long ago. As I sort through the clothes I know Joey had packed it. I can smell his sandalwood scent, which takes me by surprise. It's the first time I've used my sense of smell like that since releasing the wolf. I take a moment to test my other heightened senses out, I close my eyes and listen; I can hear Kelly and Joey talking downstairs, there is a woman's voice I don't recognise too. Not only can I hear them, but deep within me I can feel them. It's like I have an invisible rope tethering me to them. It has to be a pack thing. Maybe since my father was their Alpha and at one time I was part of the pack, I still am. Perhaps I was only ever hidden from them, like my wolf was hidden and buried from me. Reaching another rope I follow it to the end and find Carter; he feels angry and miserable. I reach out for another rope to see if I can feel all the pack members like that. I follow the first one I come across and find Jesse on the other end. He's only there for a second before he vanishes, leaving me overwhelmed with guilt. *His guilt.* I pull back from the invisible ropes and decide I should leave them alone. I shouldn't be intruding on other peoples' private feelings.

As I pull on the a red tank top, clean undies and a pair of denim shorts I come to the conclusion that it's a good job I'm not one of those girls that won't be seen in public without make up because Joey didn't bother to pack me any. I run my fingers through my hair, grateful for my short bob since Joey didn't think of packing a hairbrush either.

I quietly stride down the stairs and head straight for the kitchen and food. I open the door and the conversation in the room halts.

Kelly, who's stood over the stove frying some bacon calls out to me. "Hey, Darl', what do you fancy to eat?"

Before I can open my mouth to answer Joey places a coffee cup in my hands and answers for me. "Pancakes are her favourite."

"Pancakes it is then," Kelly says, throwing me a wink over his shoulder.

My eyes roam the room and fall on the female that must belong to the voice I heard, she has a familiar look to her and as I take in her features I can't quite put my finger on where I may have seen her before. Her long blonde wavy hair is loosely pulled back at the nape of her neck and her emerald green eyes are smiling at me having caught me looking.

"I'm Kate, Nate's twin sister. You must be Frankie?" she says, offering me a hand to shake. "Nice to meet you at last."

"Hi, I thought you looked familiar. I didn't know Nate had a twin," I say as I accept her offered hand. "Nice to meet you too," I add, trying not to resist as she pulls me into a hug. She's tall, at least four inches taller than my five foot four.

Kelly places a number of plates stacked with food on the table and we all take seats. The plate before me is full of pancakes, more than I could ever imagine eating. The others all have full breakfasts on them; bacon, eggs, tomatoes, sausage and mushrooms. We all dig in. The sound of four stomachs being filled is the only noise in the room. The pancakes are divine, the best I've ever tasted. I tell Kelly as much. "Oh, Kelly, these are delicious." I glance at Joey and give him a remorseful look, before speaking again. "I don't think I've ever tasted a pancake this good."

Joey smiles, making me think he can't be too insulted at the comment since his pancakes always held the number one spot before now.

Kelly leans over the table and lowers his voice to a whisper even though we can all still hear. "The secret ingredient is bacon fat. I cook them in the pan after frying the bacon," he admits with a proud smile.

Chapter Eleven

Carter

After storming out of Frankie's, knowing I'd been a complete dick and blown any chance I had with her, I find myself pacing back and forth outside the *Wolves Den,* our local bar, waiting for it to open. I can't quite believe how upset I am at losing Frankie. I knew I liked her more than any of the other women I've been with, but now I'm starting to think I may have fallen deeper than that. Dare I say it? *Love.* I let the word flow through my mind and decide... No. Love is not my thing, never has been.

Catching sight of my reflection in the window in the door, I'm filled with the urge to punch it. I want to do nothing more than give myself a good fucking beating. I pull my fist back ready to let it fly as the reflection disappears and Big Mac's face with brows furrowed in concern replaces it, having opened the door. I drop my fist. I wouldn't want to hit the Beta of the pack and suffer those consequences, no matter how tempting the thought of the pain is.

Big Mac steps back, allowing me to enter the building and find a stool at the bar. "Jesus Carter, it's early for you. Do you need to talk about it? I could feel your anger from out in the cellar, it won't do you any good." He pulls a glass down and pours two shots of whisky into it. "It won't do the person on the receiving end any good either."

"No, thanks, Big Mac. I just need a drink." He passes me the glass and I accept it with a small grateful smile. "Don't worry, it's me on the other side of the anger." I down the drink and slide the glass back to Big Mac. "Nate's right, I'm a jerk," I say to myself as Big Mac hands me a bottle so I can refill my own glass.

<hr>

Big Mac

I leave Carter with his thoughts as I get back to setting up the bar. I'm somewhat grateful that I'd let Carter in after sensing his anger outside. No one wants a werewolf that angry in a public space, no matter who he's angry at. Unless you want bloodshed and, no doubt, more pups. We already have a new female pup that's crawled out of the woodwork with potential to cause mayhem in our happy pack. That's not even taking her Omega status into account.

I think back to the time Frankie would have been born and struggle to place it. It's all a blur; I can remember there being trouble of some sort and Rossi selling the pack house to Jesse but I can't remember the cause of it. Rossi was still Alpha. Maria, Giuseppe and himself were always at the pack house; they just didn't live there. I can't remember a baby, not even talk of one. Shaking my head to clear mind of memories I can't find, I resign myself to the fact that my Alpha Jesse will explain everything soon enough since it seems he knew about Frankie all along. Word running through the pack grapevine is that Jesse, in wolf form, had been meeting up with her on a regular basis. It was a ballsy move, any werewolf meeting in wolf form with a child could easily lead to disaster but Jessie is Alpha for a reason. In fact he's one of the only werewolves I know whose human side is in full control of the wolf. Being a werewolf isn't easy, you are in a constant battle of wills with your wolf fighting over control. One outside argument weakening the human side even for a second means the wolf could prevail.

I drop my musings and plaster a smile on my face as I greet the customer who is walking through the door.

Chapter Twelve

Frankie

Being placed on twenty-four-seven watch is driving me crazy. I understand it's a must to keep everyone safe. If my wolf decides to take over and I start eating people it would not be fun – well, it might be for her. I've been assured that usually new pups don't release the wolf until the first full moon after their attack. They have all the heightened senses, speed and strength of a werewolf but they don't have the ability to slip into wolf form until they get the help from the full moon. Sometimes it takes more than one full moon before they can change form on command or with emotions like anger or rage, but since I was wolf born and she'd been suppressed for so long she's unpredictable.

Personally, I don't think Jesse's really worried about me losing control. My wolf seems pretty happy with me in the driving seat. To be honest I think he's more concerned about my Omega status and other wolves he and my father have been trying to protect me from all my life.

My main baby sitter is Kelly, he's been sleeping in the third bedroom which is a tiny box room, barely big enough to swing a cat in. I offered to sort out Nonna's room for him but he insisted it was fine, saying *'I only need a bed, and that one is perfectly fine.'* I'm certain the real reason behind him sleeping in there is because he doesn't want me to have to go through Nonna's things. He lost his wife, Gabby, two months ago and he hasn't stepped foot in their house since her death. He knows how painful a loved ones death is, and how real taking that step would make it.

We've fallen into a routine, Joey comes for breakfast before heading to work, which is handily on the farm, so he gets to come back to the house for lunch and dinner too. He often stays to watch TV on a night when the workday is over. Other guys working on the farm come in and out of the kitchen for lunch and coffee breaks, which makes me wonder why I'd stayed away so long. It's nowhere near as lonely as I'd imagined. If I need to go anywhere, Kelly comes too - he's like a second shadow.

As I walk back into the kitchen after waving Joey off

for work, Kelly strides into he room. "So Darl', where are we going today?" The tone of his voice tells me being housebound may be turning him a little crazy, too. We've been out on a couple of nice long motorbike rides, just to pass the time. We both have motorbikes and love nothing more than feeling the wind against our faces.

"I was wondering if you'd do me a favour?" I ask with a flutter of my eyelashes.

"Of course, anything," he replies instantly, no questions asked.

Brilliant.

He'd just given me his word that he will do anything and wolves never go back on their word.

"I want you to take me to Jesse," I say as I clear the table of our breakfast plates and place them in the dishwasher.

"I can't," he says with an edge of worry to his voice.

I smile smugly, feeling proud I've learnt something about wolf behaviour I can use to my advantage. "You just said you'd do anything. You have to."

He shakes his head, looking at me grimly. "Jesse ordered the whole pack to not take you to him. I'm sorry Frankie but I can't disobey him. He feels guilty about what he did to you." Kelly's eyes drop to my stomach referring to the bite mark that's hidden behind my grey scoop neck tee. "He thinks you hate him. He doesn't want you to have to see him."

My hands form fists by my side. "Damn him! He won't take my calls. He doesn't turn up as Tony anymore. I miss him." My vision blurs as my eyes well with tears. "He won't even let me feel him through the pack bonds. If he did he'd know I don't hate him. Surely he can't avoid me forever, he's my Alpha."

Kelly pulls me into his embrace giving me a gentle squeeze. "I'm sorry Darl'. You're right, but I still can't take you."

Suddenly hit with a light bulb moment I pull out of his arms. *He can't take me... but I can take him.* Pulling out my mobile phone I dial Joey's number, not bothering to search his name because I know the number better than I do my own.

"Joey can't disobey his order either," Kelly says, evidently recognising Joey's number and jumping to conclusions.

I grin at Kelly as Joey answers. "What's up Frank?"

"Hey, quick question. Is Jesse in the phone book?"

"Yes, wha—"

I cut him off mid sentence, having heard all I need to. "Thanks Joey, I love ya." I hang up not giving him time to question me.

I run to the pantry knowing the residential pages have always lived on the top shelf. Spotting them exactly where I thought they'd be I pull them down and, not bothering to move from the pantry, I flick through the pages straight to O'Keefe. There are seven O'Keefe's listed but Lady Luck is shining down on me because only one has the initial J. I type the address into the map app on my phone, before tapping on the arrow for the directions and up pops a map with a beautiful blue line showing me the way to go. *Jackpot.*

Glancing up I find Kelly frozen to the spot, staring at me with wide horror stricken eyes. "He's gonna to kill me. He'll think I disobeyed him."

I pat him on the back as I pass him in search of my leathers. "Don't stress. I'll tell him you didn't. I'll be leading the way on the bikes, so there will be no lie for him to smell and nothing for him to blame you for." I throw my jacket on and pass him his. "Now you can either come with me or stay here - it's your choice!"

Taking his jacket and settling it on his broad shoulders he smiles at me. "On Jesse's orders, wherever you go I must follow." Kelly gives me a wide grin.

Looking at the directions one last time, I snatch my bike keys off the hook beside the back door as I pass. I slip my phone into my pocket and kick off my sleek black Ninja ZX while I wait for Kelly to fire up his Boulevard M109RZ.

Chapter Thirteen

Frankie

Within fifteen minutes we're pulling up in front of Jesse's house. Not that I'd call it a house. A mansion is more like it. It's strange to think that I lived here once. My parents chose this house as their family home. I only wish I remembered it.

We park the bikes side by side next to a gorgeous grey Aston Martin DB9. Pulling my helmet off I hook it over the handle bars and take my jacket off before I overheat. Driving around wearing full leathers during a Western Australian summer is torture, but it can save your life. Kelly assures me as a werewolf my skin would heal pretty quick if I didn't wear them anymore but I'd rather not have to feel the pain I know I'd have if I tested the theory. I glance at Kelly as he pulls his helmet off without making a move to get off his bike.

"I'll stay here. Just in case he looks for someone to blame," Kelly says.

"Chicken shit," I call over my shoulder as I walk towards the large double doors at the front of the house. You'd easily be able to drive a large 4X4 through them, providing you had the skill to drive it up the twenty steps leading up to the verandah. The solid wooden doors each have a wolf carved into them, howling at the circular frosted window in the top of the door on the right. I run my hand along the wolf on the right feeling the exquisite ridges of the carved fur before I knock on the glass of the moon.

It opens almost immediately and I find myself engulfed in the lavender scent that I'd smelt on Carter the last time I saw him. The petite brunette standing in the doorway must be Clarissa. She's delicate looking with pretty chocolate brown eyes; she can't be much older than nineteen years old.

My wolf reaches out to gauge her wolf, finding no threat she settles back deep within me trusting that I can handle her on my own. Clarissa stands before me, staring. No welcome greeting. Nothing.

With Chicken Shit staying on his bike it's up to me to

gain entry. I offer my hand for her to shake. "Hi Clarissa, I'm Frankie. I need to see Jesse." I smile as she shakes my offered hand, hoping to ease her concern she's showing through a furrow between her thinly shaped brows.

"How do you know who I am?" she says, with a nervous edge to her voice.

"Your scent was on Carter last week. Nate referred to you by name."

She nods clearly accepting my explanation. "I'm sorry, but I can't let you in. Jesse ordered me not to," she says, the smug smile plastered on her face makes me think she is anything but sorry. It gives me the feeling that our dear Clarissa here doesn't like me very much. From what I've seen from her in the last couple of minutes I'm starting the think the feeling is going to be mutual.

I plaster a friendly smile on my face. "Is Jesse in?"

"Yes," she answers. The cautious tone of her voice would make anyone think I have a reputation of pulling the wool over ones eyes. I'm sure the trickery I played on Kelly and Joey earlier won't have gotten around the pack already.

"Well you're either going to move aside and let me pass or I'll move you out of my way." I give my shoulders a shrug. "I'm not bothered either way."

She gazes at me and presses her lips together tightly as she plants her feet in a wide stance making it clear she chose the latter. We are pretty well matched in height and weight but I need to get in that house. There is no way I will give up without a fight.

Not only do I feel her wolf come to the surface I can see it in the flicker of amber in her eyes. Her energy runs along my skin, coaxing my wolf out of her slumber. A smile crosses her face and I know she's felt my wolf as submissive. Being an Omega she's gentle and comes across as submissive but she'll stand up against any dominant wolf if she feels the need to. She won't cower like other true submissive wolves would. My wolf doesn't comprehend orders; that's what makes her so dangerous.

Reaching my hand out I push her, aiming to move her aside, but she stands her ground. Allowing my wolf to come forward I feel my eyes change shape slightly and a growl escapes my mouth. She gasps in surprise and her mouth falls open as she pins herself to the wall and allows me entry. I quickly step in trying to ignore my own surprise at my eyes changing shape. It's the first time my wolf has come so close to the surface since releasing her.

I hear Kelly's pounding footsteps behind me as he makes his way up the stairs. Leaving the door open for him, Clarissa steps away from the door still making sure to give me a wide berth. "Carter won't stay faithful to you," she says in a scathing tone.

"Carter and I aren't together anymore. You are very much welcome to him," I state, not bothering to look at her. I couldn't care less what she thinks. I look around the large entrance hall and focus on the reason I came here in the first place. Jesse. "Jesse, are you going to come and see me or am I going to have to search every room for you?" I stand waiting for a reply for a solid minute before I decide to take action. "Ready or not here I come," I mutter under my breath.

Kelly gives an amused laugh behind me. "Fancy a game of pool, Clarissa?"

I hear Clarissa's flirtatious tone as she replies, "I'll whoop your arse." I can't help but picture the fluttering eyelashes she's probably throwing his way as I glance around deciding where to start with my hunt for Jesse.

Through a glass sliding door directly in front of me there's a paved courtyard with a large outdoor table placed in the centre. I've never seen a courtyard in the middle of a house before, you'd think it would look out of place but it doesn't. In fact it looks so welcoming I can imagine having some wonderful family meals out there. Seeing there is no one out there I look in the room on my left and find an equally empty formal dining room.

Walking into the room on the right I find Clarissa setting up the pool table, as Kelly stands chalking his cue. There's a sofa along the wall to the right the doorway, facing the pool table, and a bar in the back left corner of the room with three stools in front of it. To the left of the bar there's a closed, heavy wooden door. I knock on the door hoping it's an office and try turning the handle but find it's locked. Hearing no one shout from inside I turn to go find another room to look in.

"He's in there but he doesn't want to see you," Clarissa informs me as she takes her shot hitting a red ball straight into the middle pocket. "Just face facts, one of the males in the pack doesn't want you."

Facing the door once again, I plead with him. "Please, Jesse. Open the door and talk to me."

"I'm sorry, Frankie. I made a promise. I can't," he says through the door, his voice sounds so close making me think he must be standing right behind the door. My wolf reaches out to feel his energy, but there's nothing; the door is too heavy to feel it through. She's craving his energy and, if I'm honest, I'm craving having him near me. I've seen him as Tony on such a regular basis, not seeing him is leaving a big gaping hole inside me.

"Is Clarissa right? Do you not want me…Do you not want me in your pack?" I ask, before holding my breath as I await his answer. His answer doesn't come and I can't bear the silence any longer. Silence to a question like that is an answer in itself. "I don't know what I've done wrong, but I'm sorry." Laying my hand on his door, I take a deep breath knowing I really don't want to give him the only option I can think of. "I'm sorry I've been so much trouble. I'll find another pack, another Alpha might take me in."

The door flies open and Jesse's eucalyptus scent hits with so much force it takes my breath away. "*No!*" he orders as he reaches a finger out and wipes tears that I didn't know I had from my cheeks. He tugs me into his office and wraps his strong arms around me. "I'm sorry," he apologises into my hair. "I promised you, you wouldn't have to look at me again. Not after what I did to you, but I can't bear to lose you to another pack. I can't let you go."

Pulling my head off his chest, I look up at him, with my head tilted to one side and my brows knitted together in confusion. "What you did?"

Releasing me he turns and closes the door. I wrap my arms around myself to wash away the cold from the loss of his arms. Jesse turns back around, his eyes trained on my midriff. "Tracey told me about the horrendous scar I left you with. It's bad enough leaving you with the memories of the bite. Memories can fade but a physical scar will always be there to refresh those memories. I'm so sorry."

I watch as his eyes well up, my own eyes widening in shock at his explanation.

Lifting my tank top I expose the scar he's talking about. A gasp escapes Jesse's mouth and I place my hand on my scar, stroking it gently, trying to show him the love I feel towards it. The reminder it represents.

His water filled eyes are still focused on my stomach, one blink will send tears falling down his cheeks.

I drop my shirt and lift his chin with my hand, bringing his eyes in contact with mine. Grabbing his hand with my free one I place it on the scar; he stands with his shoulders as stiff as the door behind him. My eyes roam across his pale face taking in his haunted look before they land to look directly into his eyes so he can see the truth I'm speaking as he hears it.

"This isn't an horrendous reminder of a horrible act. It's a beautiful souvenir of you saving my life." I belatedly add the "Thank you" I've been waiting to say since I'd realised what he'd done.

His shoulders drop as the tension leaves his body, finally letting go of the guilt he'd been drowning in. Kneeling down he kisses the beautiful souvenir, leaving me with a wonderful memory. I run my hands through his hair and hug his head to my stomach. Our scents become overwhelming as they mingle together making a whole new scent. My wolf reaches out for his. I feel his wolf start to reciprocate before Jesse pulls back, cutting our contact, and looks up at me. Not liking the silence or the serious look on his face, I speak, "I sat at the cemetery everyday hoping Tony would show up. I missed you."

Standing up with a sigh he crosses the room to his desk. "I'm sorry," he says grabbing a glass filled with amber liquid and downing it before opening a drawer in a filing cabinet behind his desk and pulling out a bottle of the amber liquid. "Do you want a glass?" he offers looking across the room at me.

I shake my head. "No, thanks. I'm driving."

He pulls out another glass and pours a generous

amount into both glasses before holding one out towards me. "You've not had any alcohol since your change." I shake my head in answer, even though it was more of a statement than a question. "Your metabolism's completely changed, it won't stay in your system long enough to have you drink driving."

Reaching out I take the glass tentatively. As our hands touch my wolf's energy dances along my skin. I place the glass down on the desk without taking a sip and before I can really think about what I'm doing I pin Jesse to the wall and plant my lips on his, kissing, tasting. Jesse is frozen against the wall, not kissing me back but the smell of his arousal keeps me kissing him. Wanting more than a one sided kiss I nip at his bottom lip, hoping to tempt him into kissing me back.

He releases a growl and spins us around, effectively pinning me to the wall. He repays me with a nip of his own, telling me he is the one in control here. The Alpha. He pulls his mouth away from mine, but not before lapping at the blood he'd drawn from my lip. Turning his back on me he walks back to his desk, as if nothing had happened. "Things are going to get tense in the pack for a while after we've introduced you, but it needs to be done," he states, more to himself than me, as he picks up his mobile phone off his desk and starts typing on it, making me think he must be texting someone.

Standing where he left me against the wall, I watch

the muscles in his back flex under the tight t-shirt he's wearing as he leans over and places his phone back on his desk. I wonder if I should just leave since I've told him what I came to say.

Jesse turns to look at me and I feel myself blush as I quickly look away, knowing he caught me watching him. "She's a flirtatious little wolf," he says. The smile in his voice has me looking back at him just as quickly as I'd looked away. "I have a feeling she's going to be testing many of our men. Just be careful, Frankie, because they don't all have as much control as I do," he adds, turning serious. "I nearly lost it. That nip could have led to far worse things. I don't want you ending up hurt or in a position you can't handle." Filling his drink once again he picks it up and downs it in one.

Pushing myself off the wall, I walk over to his desk and reach for my drink. I take a mouthful, hoping to settle my nerves that suddenly feel on edge. "My wolf was testing you?"

"Your wolf likes mine. It could be for a number of reasons but it's more than likely it will be the power of an Alpha that she likes. That's usually the case when it comes to females being attracted to me," he states. I don't miss the sadness in his tone. "Because my wolf let all that just happen," he points to the wall where we'd pinned each other. "I'd say he likes her too."

My heart starts racing with his words. *His wolf likes*

my wolf. I tell myself to calm down. He didn't say *he* likes me.

He must see something in my face because he quickly picks up where he left off. "It doesn't mean you have to like me or I you. Our wolves are looking for their mate. Sometimes the wolf and human choose the same mate, other times they don't."

"Does that mean I could end up with two mates?" I ask, still unsure about how these things work.

Jesse laughs short and sharp. "No. They'd tear each other apart. I've witnessed the aftermath when someone chooses a mate because of their wolf, only to then change their mind and go for the human choice," he states staring off into the distance, before giving his head a slight shake. "No one comes out of that unscathed."

"What if she chooses someone I really don't like? Will I be stuck with them?" I can't help picturing myself stuck in a relationship with someone grotesque.

Jesse's brows furrow. "No. Whichever choice you make whether it be the wolf's or the human's, your other half will learn to love them. Your tastes will be similar but she'll be more influenced by the male's power than, say, his caring nature. Whereas you'll probably favour someone who is romantic, not necessarily someone with the power to protect you."

I watch as he refills both our glasses and think to myself; if I chose Jesse he'd fit both of our requirements easily. "I'm sorry she tested you, I didn't hurt you did I?" I ask, still watching the glass, knowing the bite he gave me was harder having drawn blood and I had hardly felt it.

He's around the desk and standing in front of me, tilting my chin with a finger before I even realise he's moved. "You didn't hurt me, Frankie. You turned me on." His words are punctuated by his scent getting stronger with each one. "It took every ounce of will power to pull away when I did."

I flick my eyes away from his too quickly to see anything in his. I don't know if it's my wolf or the alcohol loosening my tongue but I find myself asking the next question before I can stop myself. "Do you want me?"

Suddenly the room is heavy with silence. I realise belatedly how much I want him to say yes. "I'm sorry, I shouldn't have asked that." I say, with a shake of my head.

Unable to take the silence any more, I turn to leave and feel Jesse grab my upper arms, pulling me back towards him. He leans into me and presses his lips gently against mine, kissing me passionately, returning the kiss like I'd wanted him to earlier. My head suddenly spinning I fist my hands in his light grey shirt.

Jesse ends the kiss pulling back mere inches, just enough to look in my eyes without going cross eyed. "I want you, Frankie, more than I have ever wanted anyone. But you're just getting used to your wolf. You need time and space to weigh up your options and know that when you make the choice it's the right one for you." He pauses and I nod. "Just remember I'm one of those options," he adds before kissing me, full of passion once again.

I vaguely recognise the sound of the door bursting open but I don't care enough to pull away, not wanting the kiss to end.

"Boss, the—" is all Carter manages to say before his words turn into a growl. Carter's scent of fresh grass fills the room.

Jesse pulls back and I try to move away from him but he holds me firmly in place with his hands on my back. "Are the pack arriving?" he asks Carter over my shoulder.

"Yes," Carter says sounding defeated, before the sound of the door closing alerts me to his exit.

I turn to look at the closed door, feeling awful for what must be going through Carter's mind. We may not be together anymore but the sadness in his voice was enough to know how much he regretted what he had thrown away.

Jesse steps away from me. "Go, talk to him," he says reading my mind with a flat, monotone voice. I glimpse his sad, downturned features before he turns to his desk, ignoring me as though I'd already left.

Knowing our moment is over I leave the room and close the door behind me trying to ignore the ache in my chest.

Chapter Fourteen

Jesse

Listening to the door close I sit in my chair and take deep calming breaths as I run my hands through my short hair. My wolf's fighting for control, wanting to call Frankie back in and demand her to be his mate. I push him down, reminding him of what happened last time we chose a mate. *"Where is she now?"* I ask the wolf silently.

"Dead!"

The word rings out in my head. Not knowing if it was me or the wolf that said it I carry the on with our silent conversation, *"We don't want Frankie dead. Let her go."*

The wolf inside me settles down and I sigh in relief

while I can, knowing the threat will only placate him for so long.

Even though I told Frankie I'd give her time to make her decision, I hope she'll be quick about it. Being an Omega will always be dangerous for her and her mate but once she is mated some wolves will feel less threatened by her; they'll feel that the mate will hold her in check. When a new female joins a pack there is always tension until she puts the males into their place, making it clear she is either interested or not. So, if and when she mates with the lucky male, the tension in the pack will ease. The fact that she is born to two werewolf parents, one having been wolf born like herself, also adds to her appeal. She is more likely to carry a child to full term and even have a wolf born child herself as she carries a stronger werewolf gene than she does human genes. When a regular werewolf has a child it's a lucky dip as to which gene is the strongest, wolf or human. They can easily miscarry if the female wolf tries to shift during her pregnancy. The moon's call can be fought if The Alpha wishes to share his power to the pregnant pack member, helping her hold her human form. If her emotions cause her to shift that's a whole other story. It often happens too quickly for The Alpha to have chance to help.

I try to clear my mind. Why the hell am I thinking about children? I've never been interested in having a family. I watched the struggle Rossi went through protecting his family and look at the outcome of that; Frankie is the only one left. My attraction to Frankie has nothing to do with whether she can or can't carry a child to term. As much as I know her wolf will give me a run for my money - she'll push the boundaries at every chance. I tell myself to quit thinking about it; she probably won't even choose me, there are plenty of honourable contenders in our pack.

Chapter Fifteen

Letting go of the door handle I look up to find the room before me full of strangers. I glance around in search of Carter, feeling the need to explain what he'd just walked in on. It doesn't take me long to spot him on the sofa plastered all over Clarissa. Turning back to the door I'd just closed I plan to tell Jesse to *stuff my options*, but I catch Nate's scent. Having not seen him since the night he'd lay with me when I was healing I turn my gaze back on the room searching the faces for him. I find Kelly and Joey talking to three other guys near the big bay window that looks out on the drive. Kate's standing at the bar with

Tracey, who had been my nurse, and another girl I haven't yet met.

Seeing me, Kate waves me over. "Hey Frankie, this is Gemma," she says introducing the tall blonde.

"Hi," I say as I walk over to them.

Gemma offers her hand in a shake and I take it. "Hello, it's lovely to meet you. I was close friends with your mum." She swallows hard, as though she's becoming overwhelmed with emotion. "I'm sorry. You look so much like her, you have her chocolate brown eyes. The last time I saw her she'd had her hair cut in a similar style to how yours is today. I miss her a great deal."

Seeing her struggling with her emotions I pull her into a hug. It's somewhat comforting to think that this woman cared about my mum and, going by her reaction to meeting me, I'd say she still cares even though my mum is no longer here. "I miss her too. I wish I could remember her more clearly."

She steps back from the hug. "Maybe I could tell you about her sometime? The things we got up to; she was never one to shy away from trouble."

"I would love that," I say with a grateful smile. Reaching out she pats me on the arm and mentions the bathroom before walking off, probably in the direction of the bathroom.

Feeling someone's eyes boring into my back I turn and find Nate standing in the doorway, staring back at me.

I let a big grin cross my face and practically skip over to him. Stopping in front of him I rise on my tiptoes and gently kiss him on the cheek.

Nate reaches his hand up and touches where I had just kissed him. "What was that for?" he asks, eyes wide in surprise.

"I didn't get to thank you for laying with me the other night," I say, hoping he can see the gratitude in my eyes. "Thank you," I add quickly.

A huge smile plays across his face as his scent, that wonderful smell of rain, gets stronger. "Anytime," he says with a wink.

"I might hold you to that. I haven't slept so well since," I flirt back with a wicked grin on my face. This darn wolf has a lot to answer to; I never flirt. The words *you do now,* resonate through my head.

"For fucks sake." Carter growls. "Here's a tip for you Frank, if you go in the kitchen you'll find some guys you haven't met yet, I'm sure they'd be more than willing to make out with you, too."

"*Carter!*" Kelly chastises. "She pecked him on the cheek. If anyone is making out, it's you and Clarissa. You've been dry humping on that sofa for the last five minutes."

Grateful for Kelly jumping in and sticking up for me, I shoot him a small smile as I catch his eye.

Carter smirks before opening his mouth to speak and

I suddenly wish Kelly had kept quiet. "You've already had your fill of her. What else would you be doing while you've been guarding her twenty-four-seven this last fortnight?"

"I'm the only one that was willing to take guard duty. She was your girlfriend and you didn't offer because you didn't wanna lose out on your casual sex time with the bike there," Kelly spits the last few words angrily pointing at Clarissa, labeling her the bike he'd been talking about.

Carter stands up, loosens the collar on his polo shirt and cracks his knuckles. "Clarissa might be a bike, but Frankie isn't far off it herself. I just found her in Jesse's office with her tongue down his throat," he states, glaring at anyone who makes eye contact with him.

Jesse's office door flies open and he storms out, his energy full of rage; so much rage. It burns against my skin. Looking at the grimaces on the faces around the room, I'm not the only one feeling it. Jesse's eyes level on Carter, taking his energy with them and hitting Carter full force. "That's enough, Carter," Jesse demands, his voice full of authority.

Carter collapses on to his knees with the weight of Jesse's order and rage.

Jesse's body takes a formal stance, feet shoulder width apart as he looks around the room, making sure to make eye contact with everyone as his eyes fall upon them. He reminds me of a sergeant, making me picture him in his army fatigues in the past. "Everyone's here," he states.

The room is full of heavy silence; the sound of a pin dropping would be deafening.

"Frankie, come here," Jesse says softly. The command behind his words can't be missed as he holds his hand out towards me.

So much for easing me into the pack gently.

I watch my feet as I make my way over to him and take his offered hand. The moment our hands make contact my wolf's energy dances along my skin, recognising her Alpha. Everyone in the room gasps, having felt my energy and knowing what it means.

I pray to whoever may be listening my wolf doesn't take things too far, like she did in the office earlier. *Not in front of an audience like this.* I try pulling my hand back but Jesse holds on tight, putting a halt to my plan to take the temptation of him away from her.

"That's not possible. She feels like pack." Clarissa breaks the silence. "But she's not. We haven't voted her in... There hasn't been a ceremony."

"You can all feel her energy; she *is* pack. I brought you all here to be introduced to the newest member of our pack, who has actually been in the pack for the last twenty-four years," Jesse states.

"Boss, how is that possible? She hasn't even had her first change yet," a big guy who's stood by the door asks with a puzzled expression on his face, which really doesn't suit the biker look he has going on with his leather cut.

"Meet Rosa Rossi. Our last Alpha Pair's, Rossi and Maria, daughter." Jesse waves his hand in my direction, as though he'd just made me visible by some magic trick.

Seeing everyone's eyes turn to me, I look down at my feet uneasily as I mutter, "Frankie. I go by Frankie." I hate being the centre of attention but I don't want them calling me by a name I've never gone by. Jesse gives my hand a gentle, comforting squeeze, reminding me that I'm not alone. I glance up with a smile and catch sight of a few people nodding their heads, accepting Jesse's explanation as truth.

"How do you know it's her? She could be lying," Clarissa says, pushing her way through the crowd of people and coming to the front.

"Clarissa, are you forgetting I'm Alpha? I can't be lied to." He drops my hand, allowing his hands to fall to his side and form fists. "If you'd met her mother you'd know it isn't a lie. Frankie is Maria's double." Leaving Clarissa to mull it over, he addresses the room in a booming voice. "The reason you can all feel her so strongly is because she has a lot of pack blood in her veins - her father was the original Alpha of our pack. His blood *began* our pack. It may be my pack now but his blood is still pack blood." His eyes flick to me and then back to the pack. "I've been watching over Frankie since she was seven, when her parents were murdered. Rossi's last order was to protect her from anyone who might recognise her for how special she is. That's what I've tried to do all these years."

"If she's so special why haven't you claimed her as your own? If what Carter said was true and you were kissing just now, surely she's yours? You're Alpha, you can have anyone," Clarissa argues once again. I'm starting to feel like she really doesn't like me.

Jesse looks at Clarissa with raised eyebrows. "Do you really think I'm such a bad a person I'd use the fact that I'm Alpha to force someone to be my mate?"

"You've done it before," snaps a tall woman with a long, slim face and short, choppy red hair, her nostrils flaring and teeth bared in anger.

Jesse sighs, his shoulders drooping in guilt. "Yes, I have Mary." The room fills with whispers, everyone no doubt as curious as I am about the revelation. "You and I both know how that turned out."

"You ripped them apart," she spits accusingly.

He releases a growl, clearly unhappy with her accusation. "I've learnt from my mistakes," he admits; his voice breaking with emotion, a slack expression on his face.

Mary steps in front of Jesse and cups his check with her hand, forcing him to look at her with his wet dull eyes. "She was my best friend, Jesse, I miss her. But it's no excuse to speak to you like I just did, I'm sorry." She drops her hand from his face. "You're a good Alpha, I've seen you change since that day. All I've done is open old wounds."

She drops to her knees and turns her head to a side, offering her neck to him.

Glancing around the room Jesse takes in a deep breath and his shoulders straighten, as though he's made a decision about something. "Stand," he demands, sounding tired with no real authority behind the words. Authority or not, Mary stands without argument. Jesse leans in towards her offered neck, he doesn't need to bend down with her being tall. Being so close to them I watch his teeth become sharper a second before he strikes her neck. He steps back revealing a clean bite on her neck.

I gasp in horror at the sight of the blood. Blood that's running down her neck.

Her hands go to her neck to staunch the bleeding and she suddenly sits on the floor, most probably dizzy from the blood loss.

I take an impulsive step forward to help her only to find someone behind me, a hand gripping my arm and holding me in place.

"She'll heal," Nate whispers in my ear, in a warning tone. I startle at the sound of his voice. I hadn't seen him move from where I'd left him by the door.

Wiping the blood from his mouth with the back of his hand, Jesse lets his eyes roam around the room, making contact with every single pack member. "We are lucky to have such a large number of females in our pack, but they choose their mates. Nobody in *my* pack uses dominance to force mates. Ever," he orders, the authoritative tone making the order ring loud and clear. "*I* won't allow it."

A nod of approval runs through the room, taking any lingering tension with it. Nate slowly releases his hold on my arm but stays close, the feel of his body warm against my back. His energy makes goosebumps ripple along the back of my neck.

Mary's still sitting on the floor with a hand to her neck The blood flow seems to have eased but I daren't take my eyes off her just in case. So I don't pay much attention to anything Jesse is saying, just hearing a word and name now and then. The mention of the full moon catches my attention, tuning back in just in time to hear him tell everyone to meet here at four in the afternoon on Saturday. *My first full moon.*

He turns his eyes on me, and Nate behind me. "Frankie, Nate, Carter and Kelly, I want you four here at noon." I nod my agreement.

"Sure thing," Kelly agrees from across the room.

The room starts to fill with chatter as everyone falls back into the relaxed casual get together that the room had been filled with before Jesse exited his office.

I stand and watch as Jesse bends down to say something into Mary's ear. I strain my ears but can't catch a word of it through the noise in the room. Kelly's cheery voice pulls my attention away from the pair before me.

"Hey Nate, do you fancy a thrashing?" he asks as he

racks up the balls on the pool table.

"I'd love to wipe that smile off your face." Nate replies from over the top of my head, brushing the small of my back with his hand as he moves to step around me. My wolfs energy flares over him, causing him to freeze in place. Our energies mixing together feels good, too good. I don't want to move and break the spell. No, that's a lie, I want to move, to spin around and run my hand over every inch of the body my energy's roaming over. I lick my lips as I'm overcome with the urge to taste him. Nate's scent flares and I suddenly realise he can probably smell my arousal. My embarrassment gives me the strength to fight my wolf and step away from Nate, breaking the contact and sexual tension between us.

"I'll beat the winner," I say glancing around the room, hoping no one else is aware of what just happened between Nate and I. If my wolf keeps acting like a hussy she's going to earn me that name Carter called me earlier. *Bike.*

Kelly laughs. "You're on, Darl'. Just don't cry when you lose."

"Oh, fighting words, Kelly," I tease holding a hand to my chest in mock pain. "Fighting words." I take slow steady steps in the direction of the pool table as I try to ignore Nate's eyes burning into my back and my body's need to turn back to him.

Chapter Sixteen

Frankie

Sitting on the bay window bench gives me a good view of the table and I watch as Nate sinks six of his balls in a row. Kelly takes his shot, sinking five, and I realise I need to prepare myself for losing abysmally when it's my turn. Taking my eyes off the table I glance out the window and watch some of the other members leaving, making sure no one knocks into my baby. It looks completely different in the makeshift car park. No longer just the three vehicles like when I'd arrived, there are more than two dozen cars haphazardly parked out there now. There's no order about it and makes me wonder how anyone will get out.

I see a tall, slim guy, wearing a pair of khaki shorts and a leather cut that makes me think he's a bikie, although the fact that I can't see any patches from where I'm sitting make me think he might just be a wannabe. Even Prospects have a prospect patch. The big burly bikie, who questioned Jesse during the meeting, is standing beside the wannabe, his shiny bald head glowing in the moonlight. They both walk around my bike, admiring it, giving me a look at the back of Mr Bald and Burly's cut and the patch that's on it - a howling wolf. He's wearing a black t-shirt under his cut paired with jeans. When I had a good look at his face earlier I would have put him at mid-thirty's but werewolves don't age at the same rate as human's do, our aging process is dramatically slower. Jesse is well over one hundred yet he doesn't look a day over thirty-five.

Mr Wannabe reaches a hand out, stroking my baby, causing me to jump up. "Kelly, who's the guy with his mitts all over my baby?" I point out the window, wishing for the guy to turn and see my death stare.

"Colin," Kelly answers, the tone of his voice making me think he's not very well liked in the pack. "The other guy's Big Mac. He won't touch, he has a baby of his own," he adds before turning back to the table and sinking the black. "Woohoo, I whooped your ar—" His cheer's suddenly cut short as the white ball rebounds and drops into another pocket. "Aw, fuck."

Feeling the need to protect my baby, I head over to Kate who's still behind the bar, pouring vodka into half a dozen shot glasses. "Hi Frankie, are you joining us for some shots?" she asks, nodding in the direction of the glasses.

"Yeah, why not?" I shrug. "But first I need a cloth. Is there a clean micro-fibre one behind there somewhere?" I ask, leaning over the bar to try and see for myself.

Ducking down under the bar, Kate drops out of sight. I hear the crinkling of some plastic wrapping before she jumps up and hands me a brand new blue micro-fibre cloth. "There you go."

Perfect, I think to myself as I take it. "Thanks, I'll be back in a sec."

Glancing out the window one last time to check if my bike is still being manhandled as I make my way to the door, I see it is. I stride down the steps two at a time and come to a stop in front of Colin, waiting until he acknowledges me with the cloth held out towards him.

Colin notices the cloth first, which is no surprise since I'm practically holding it under his nose. He glances from the cloth to me, and then back to the cloth again, nothing but a puzzled expression on his face.

I wiggle it at him. "Here, take it. You'll need it to wipe your grubby fingerprints off my baby." I shrug at his blank expression. "Or you could use it to stop your nose bleeding all over my baby. Either way, it's your choice," I say, losing patience quickly.

Reaching his fingers up, he touches his nose hesitantly. "My nose... isn't bleeding," he states in an uncertain tone.

Mr Burly, Big Mac - Kelly had called him, laughs a hearty belly laugh, clearly amused by Colin's complete stupidity.

"No, it's not." I growl, hoping to make my intent clear with my next sentence. "But it will be if you don't wipe my bike down." I try to put as much authority into my threat as I can, which is a mean feat for someone who comes across as a submissive wolf.

Snatching the cloth with a grunt he gets on with wiping my bike down, finally heeding my warning.

Big Mac turns to me, a grin taking over his face as he offers me his hand to shake. "You're my kinda girl. Your baby is gorgeous, I've always loved the ZX."

I take his hand and hold my breath, hoping my wolf doesn't react to him like she has some of the other men when I've had physical contact with them. I release his hand and a huge breath when she does absolutely nothing. The last thing I need is for her make me look like more of hussy than she already has. I take in the *President* patch on the front of his cut and realise he's not only in an MC, he's the President of one. Having spotted a beautiful Harley and a motor cross style bike when I'd looked out the window earlier I take a guess as to which is his. "It looks like she's got a fight on her hands with your Harley for the top beauty award."

He laughs. "My Hillary may just be the winner there. Biased or not."

"Big Mac, is your place open?" Colin interrupts us, glaring in my direction.

A rumbling growl vibrates through my chest. My wolf isn't overly impressed with the look Colin's giving me. *If looks could kill, I'd be dead and buried.*

"Sure is! That's why I employ all species," Big Mac says, stepping in between the two of us, clearly having picked up on my mood. Grabbing Colin by the arm, he pulls him towards their bikes. "Come on, I'm heading there too." He looks back at me over his shoulder. "It was nice meeting you, Frankie."

"You too," I shout after him. I watch as the two bikes drive off down the dirt road, wanting to be sure Colin doesn't decide to take his anger and hatred towards me out on my bike. Swiping the cloth off the seat of my bike where Colin had left it, I can't help but notice he'd done a pretty good job.

Chapter Seventeen

Jesse

Relief flows through me as the pack nods their agreement to my terms regarding female pack members. I learnt from my mistakes a long time ago and I will not sit idly by watching someone else live through the same terror. I move the meeting onto more general things like territory patrols and our hunt during this coming weekend's full moon.

As everyone falls back into relaxed chatter between themselves, I duck down and speak into Mary's ear. "Come, we'll get you cleaned up."

She takes my offered hand without argument.

"Thanks, Jesse."

Once she's steady on her feet I lead her out of the room towards the ground floor bathroom. I feel Frankie's wolfs energy flare up and the scent of her arousal invades my nostrils. I sense Nate's wolf react and force myself to carry on walking, all the while reminding myself this is what I wanted. I wanted her to weigh up her options. *"It doesn't mean we have to like it,"* my wolf reminds me.

"You really meant what you said back there," Mary says beside me, sounding surprised. "You have learnt from your mistakes."

"I have. It's killing me to not go back in there and fight my way through the contenders, and into her heart, but I will not let history repeat itself. I will not see her dead and definitely not by my hand. Not like... Cl...Claire," I stumble over the name I haven't uttered in over thirty years.

"Frankie seems like a smart girl, she'll see past all the other males and find the only real contender in the pack," Mary says with a consoling pat on my back as I reach out to open the bathroom door.

I check in the cabinet under the sink to ensure there is a spare shirt for Mary since hers is covered in blood. I usually have plenty of spare clothes in all the cupboards and rooms for pack members to use. The house is, after all, the pack house and any pack member will always be welcome. Seeing everything she'll need I wave her in and exit the room myself. "You should find everything you need to clean yourself up in the cabinet," I state before pulling the door closed behind me.

I brace myself for any kind of flirting Frankie's wolf may be doing before I slip back into the poolroom. I'm surprised to find everyone quickly moving away from the window and no Frankie in sight. I lean against the wall just beside the entrance and open my mouth to ask what everyone is doing when the front door opens and Frankie walks in. Kelly meets her in the doorway of the room blocking my view of her and hers of mine.

"That's the first time I've seen Colin knocked down a peg or two," Kelly chuckles, handing Frankie the cue. "I took your first shot. You're stripes."

Frankie swaps the cue for a blue micro-fibre cloth. "Thanks, Kelly."

What the hell is she doing with a cloth? And what has it got to do with Colin? Is he another contender for her mate? I feel the tension flow into my body at the thought but try to remain propped against the wall as casually as I can. "How did you knock down Colin?"

"She made him clean his finger prints off her bike," Kelly says waving the cloth around as evidence. "I think we should frame this cloth," he adds as the room erupts into laughter.

I suppress my own laughter at the thought as I watch Frankie weigh up the table, preparing to take her shot.

Kelly had sunk three of her balls in the shot he took. A smile graces her beautiful round face as she spots the eleven hanging over the corner pocket. She lines up and hits the white ball with enough force to make it bounce back and not follow the eleven into the pocket. She hits the fourteen into a middle pocket but, unfortunately, the white follows suit, entering the pocket too. "Damn," she mutters under her breath, probably to herself even though we can all hear her clearly.

Nate steps up and slowly circles the table weighing up his options with a brow furrowed in concentration. He has three balls and the eight left. His brow suddenly relaxes, indicating that he's come to a decision. His three balls go down without any effort but the eight is another story. It rebounds out of the pocket to a chorus of *"Aww"* throughout the room.

A quick glance around the room has me finding Carter and Clarissa all over each other on the sofa, which is no surprise really. Those two have been on and off for months, which is one of the reasons why I was so pissed at Carter for sleeping with Frankie. Turning my eyes from them I spot Joey and Mick sat in the window seat, deep in conversation. They are an unlikely friendship, Joey being a farmer and Mike being a pilot. You wouldn't think the two would have much in common but Mike is one of the nicer dominant wolves; he isn't one to throw his dominance around. He likes to keep the more submissive wolves happy.

I can hear Tracey, Kate and Niki giggling at the bar and I can't help but smile hearing it. It's nice to feel my pack members happy. My eyes turn back to the table just as Frankie is leaning over the table directly in font of me, giving me a clear view at her ample cleavage. I'd let my eyes linger if I couldn't see Tim directly behind her, staring at her arse, a number of wicked thoughts written on his face. I release a threatening growl. Both my wolf and I are unhappy with his thoughts. I hear the telltale sound of Frankie miscueing but don't take my eyes off Tim. He looks up, making eye contact for a second, before dropping his eyes to the floor in submission. A slow threatening rumble is still coming from my throat in warning. I've had my wolf on such a short lead in regards to Frankie I can't pull him back now. He feels the need to assert his dominance. It's taking everything from me to stay where I am. He'd challenge Tim in a heartbeat if I let him, regardless of Tim's apparent submission.

The pressure of someone's hand on my forearm, followed by a calming wave of energy, flows through me causing my wolf to step back and relax, allowing the human to come to the forefront. I glance down at the hand in question.

"Can I have a quiet word?" Frankie's voice says right in front of me. I look up wondering where she had come from, she'd been at the other side of the pool table only moments ago, and find her smiling shyly at me.

I clear my throat before speaking, feeling somewhat out of sorts. I have a sudden flash back to being drunk when I was a teenager and realise that's exactly what this feels like. Being inebriated. "Yeah, let's go somewhere quieter," I state distractedly, trying to get a grip on myself, knowing I can't be drunk. A werewolf's metabolism won't allow it.

Frankie's hand drops away and I turn, leading the way through the dining room and into the kitchen. With the physical contact cut my mind becomes less foggy and I realise what had just happened. She used her Omega influence on me. As I turn to ask her about it, I catch such a look of wonder on her face as she takes in the granite surfaces and the slate floors that I can't bring myself to break the spell she's clearly under. Pulling a pan down from the cupboard I fill it with milk and put it on the gas stove top.

I lean a hip against the counter and watch as Frankie runs a finger over the intricate swirls that are carved into the cupboard door before her. "Do you like it?" I ask.

She looks up, eyes wide in surprise no doubt, to find me watching her. She smiles. "It's beautiful. So perfect, it must of taken hours to just carve one of theses doors." She looks around the whole room taking in the dozen matching doors.

I nod. "About five days a door. The billiard table took

me three months, I was glad when that was finished."

She rubs the carvings, seeming to appreciate them all the more hearing my words.

I turn back to the milk, and stir it making sure it doesn't burn to the bottom of the pan. Once I can see it's reached the right heat I add my secret ingredients and the room fills with the wonderful smell of hot chocolate. I look over my shoulder at Frankie. "Do you want one?" I ask, nodding towards the saucepan.

"Yes please," she answers with a nod, settling herself against the worktop opposite me.

Reaching for two mugs out of the cupboard beside the range hood, I fill them with the steaming liquid and hand one across to Frankie. I watch as she blows on it and takes a tentative sip.

"Mmm... Cinnamon?" she questions trying to pick out the extra ingredients I sprinkled in.

I nod in answer, taking a sip of my own drink. I'm always taken back to my childhood when I make hot chocolate; it's my grandmother's recipe after all. Why wouldn't I be taken back to the times I shared a hot chocolate with her in her small kitchen with the canary yellow cabinets hanging on the walls. I drink half a mug before I pull myself out of my memories and into the present. "You wanted to talk? Is something wrong?" I ask, suddenly remembering there was a reason we came in here in the first place that had nothing to do with hot chocolates.

Frankie startles at the sound of my voice, having obviously been in her own world enjoying her drink. She looks at me with a blank expression, clearly having no idea what I'm talking about, or maybe she is struggling to arrive back in the present from wherever she may have been visiting just then.

I jump in with an apology, hoping to refresh her mind. "Look, I'm sorry about how I reacted in there." I nod towards the door, signaling to where we'd been before we came in here. "Tim should be allowed to show his appreciation of you. I just... I didn't like the look on his face. I've been protecting you from the likes of him for years. It's going to take a while to be able to watch it calmly," I say, hoping to explain my reaction sufficiently.

She shakes her head and her sparkling chocolate brown eyes widen in surprise. "No. That didn't bother me. In fact, I didn't like the wicked thoughts he had plastered on his face either. I didn't really need to talk." A blush flows over her face, making her look even more beautiful. "I just thought you'd maybe appreciate the distance," she admits her blush deepening. "Although now we are here there is something I'd like to ask. It's about my 24/7 shadow." She pulls a face as the words leave her mouth and I know what she wants to ask.

The tension that had left my body with her earlier touch suddenly floods back in, causing my spine to stiffen.

I place my mug on the side before I crush it in my hand. "Has Kelly done something wrong?"

"*No!*" she denies quickly. "I just don't think it's fair that he gave up his life to guard me."

Realisation hits me; she's worrying about things that had been said earlier. "If it's about what he said to Carter earlier... he only said that to stick up for you." I glance around the room and listen to ensure no one else is around to hear, before dropping my voice to a whisper just to be sure. "The thing is, I think he needs the company. He hasn't been this happy since Gabby died."

"Oh," she says, as a grave expression crosses her face, which tells me Kelly has told her about Gabby and her death in the time they've spent together.

The sound of someone attempting to sing ABBA's '*Dancing Queen*' flows through the open door to the lounge. I catch Frankie look in the direction of the sound, leaning towards it in curiosity, causing a smile to cross my face. "It sounds like the party has moved to the lounge and, unfortunately, Niki has pulled out the Singstar." Giving a small chuckle she turns her attention once again to me. Feeling the need to get back on subject I drop my smile and let the seriousness fall back over me. "If it's bothering you having Kelly as a shadow, we can stop it. In fact, I'd rather go back to keeping my own eye on you, anyway."

"*You* keeping an eye on me?" The puzzled expression she gives me causes me to laugh.

"Do you really think you've been wandering around all these years without someone watching over you?" I step towards her before she can answer and turn her in the direction of the door leading to the lounge, the opposite direction from where we entered the room. "Let's go join the party!" I order, hoping she doesn't question me about my comment.

Chapter Eighteen

Frankie

We enter the lounge room to find Niki handing her microphone to Kelly. Nate picks up another off the floor and stands beside him. A song starts and I recognise it immediately, *'Don't go breaking my heart'*. The cheers and laughter running around, coming from everyone, makes me think I'm not the only one to recognise the song. Standing in front of a huge projector screen pulled down from the ceiling, Nate opens his mouth and sings Elton John's part, leaving Kelly to be Kiki Dee. I gasp in surprise at how good they are. I was expecting them to sound as bad as Niki had.

Between the singers and us are two large L shaped sofas which is where everyone else is sitting, laughing at the pair's overacting. In the middle of the room between the sofas is a magnificent coffee table. As we get closer I can see the most exquisite carving I've ever seen under a glass table top; a pack of wolves creeping up on a herd of deer in a forest. I flick my eyes to Jesse, who's taking a seat on the sofa, a question in my eyes. *Did he do this?*

He nods in answer. Wanting to feel the carvings my hand reaches out and rubs the glass of its own accord as I sit in an empty spot on the sofa, my mind imagining the ridges of the wolves fur like I'd felt on the front doors earlier.

"It's nice isn't it?" Clarissa's question pulls me out of the trance I'd fallen into over the scene on the table. *My God! Is Clarissa actually starting a nice conversation with me?*

"Breathtaking." is the only word worthy to describe it. Taking my eyes off the table I turn to Jesse again. "How long did it take?"

"Two months," he says looking down at the table in question, a slight blush marring his cheeks.

Tracey looks between the two of us and down at the table before reaching out from the sofa where she's sitting to rub her hand on the glass, almost mirroring my actions. "Did you do this?" she asks gazing at Jesse with an emotion I can't quite put my finger on.

All eyes in the room flit from the table to Jesse, astonishment clear on their faces with the wide eyes and dropped jaws. *Did no one know that all these carvings around the house were done by his hand?*

Jesse glances up and, seeing everyone's eyes on him, his blush brightens. "Yes. Anything made of wood in this house is probably carved by me. It's what I do. I took up carpentry after I was turned in World War I."

"What? That makes you..." Clarissa pauses, probably trying to work out his age. "Old," she adds, clearly giving up on the math. "I've never come onto you, have I?" Showing her concern over the question she pulls a bottle of vodka out of Carter's hand beside her and chugs a mouthful, before passing the bottle to Tim.

"No, Clarissa. There's no need to panic, you haven't made a move on this Grandad," Jesse jokes, making us all laugh, Clarissa sighing in relief causes Jesse to join in with the laughter.

Tim holds up the now empty vodka bottle. "Anyone fancy playing spin the bottle?"

"How old are you, Tim? We're not in high school," Nate admonishes, taking a seat on the sofa.

"Aw, go on," Niki begs, before biting her lip. Kate and Tracey nod along in agreement, holding their breath in hope.

"Older than you, Nate." Tim grins. "A war behind the boss though," he admits, shoulders slumping in disappointment.

"Ew, Carter, you're not old like these two are you?" Clarissa asks wringing her hands in her lap.

"No, Clarissa. I'm the age I look, you're safe with me," Carter answers before pulling her into his lap for a kiss.

"Come on, don't be a killjoy, Nate," Kelly says, causing all eyes to fall on him questioningly, knowing he's only recently lost his wife; and worse, mate. "Oh, come on, it's only a bit of fun."

A chorus of "I'm in," flies around the room.

"I have things to do, but have fun," Jesse says, standing and moving towards the door.

I yawn and glance at my watch. "Oh wow, look at the time. I'm going to head home," I say, standing up. Kelly suddenly jumps up from his spot on the floor against the side of the sofa, as though he plans to leave too. "You're alright, Kelly. I've spoken to Jesse and he's freed you from twenty-four-seven guard duty." I walk to the door and shout over my shoulder. "Have some fun, Kelly. Hell, you deserve it for putting up with me all this time."

I reach my hand out for the handle but the door bursts open before I make contact with it. Leaving me face to face with Jesse who has three full bottles of spirits held to his chest with one arm.

He spins me around with his free arm. "If I have to suffer this, it's only fair you do too." He hands me a bottle of Jack Daniels. "Here, have a mouthful of this. It might help."

I look at the bottle for a second before taking it and cracking the lid. It can't hurt, that's for sure.

We all settle in on the sofas, Kate and Niki both taking seats on the floor beside Kelly and Joey. Tim places the bottle on the centre of the table and quickly twists it, making it spin on the spot. We all watch with rapt attention.

Excitement runs through me. I haven't played this game since I was fourteen. I shudder as I remember the kiss I'd had with a pimple faced boy, wearing braces. I can't even remember his name, just his sweat. Even the memory of it almost makes me gag.

The bottle stops, pointing at Clarissa. "Ugh, you're old enough to be my Grandad," she says, before giving Tim a quick peck on the lips, much to his dismay.

Clarissa sends the bottle spinning and Kelly chooses that moment to get up and head into the kitchen, which means, food will be coming soon. My stomach grumbles at the thought. It suddenly dawns on me that I'm going to miss his cooking when he's not shadowing me anymore. He's such an amazing chef. I wonder if he'd move in permanently if I asked? It would solve my issue with the house being too quiet without Nonna.

Although Kelly had wanted us all to play, I'm pretty sure him going into the kitchen is his way of escaping the game. I knew he wouldn't want to be kissing someone that isn't his mate.

The bottle stops its rotation, pointing at Tim. "No way! You fixed it, you were the last one to touch it," Clarissa complains, clearly unhappy with the outcome. "I'm spinning again," she states as she leans forward giving the bottle another spin, all the while glaring at Tim. I don't blame her really. I wouldn't want to kiss him once, let alone twice. Don't get me wrong. He's a good looking guy; a tall, dark and handsome poster boy in fact. He just oozes creep factor, definitely the kind of person you don't want to come across in a dark alley. I hold my breath as the bottle starts to slow and see it lands on Carter. She crawls into his lap and they immediately start with the tonsil tennis, nothing we haven't been watching them do all night.

"Pizza will be ready in fifteen," Kelly announces popping his head through the door before disappearing into the kitchen once again.

"Carter, come up for air man or forfeit your spin," Tim states as he shoves Carter's shoulder, causing him and Clarissa to bang teeth.

Clarissa breaks away and rubs her teeth with a finger. "Ow, Tim," she whines.

Ignoring Clarissa, Carter takes his spin and we all watch it with rapt attention. "Oh no. No way. Not after you've been all over Clarissa," Tracey quickly declines, shaking her head frantically as the bottle comes to a stop on her.

"Just give him a peck on the cheek and move on, you won't catch anything. I want a spin," Niki demands. With a huff Tracey does as she's told and we once again watch the bottle do its thing.

Her cheeks turn beetroot red as the bottle stops pointing at none other than Jesse. I'm starting to think this girl has it bad for our Alpha. Leaning over the coffee table she kisses him with a ferocity that would even give Carter and Clarissa a run for their money. The poor girl is full of passion, making it more than clear how she feels about Jesse. Being sat next to Jesse gives me a clear view and I can see it isn't all one sided, Jesse is kissing her back and allowing the opened mouthed kiss. Tracey's energy flows out of her in waves, her excitement is almost palpable. She pulls away and averts her eyes to the floor as she sits back looking even more flushed.

We all watch as Jesse's spin seems to be never ending. It spins around and around, and doesn't seem to be slowing. "Me, me, me," Niki chants under her breath.

Clarissa spins her head to glance at Niki, giving her an *'are you crazy?'* look with her raised eyebrows. "Aren't you bothered that he's old enough to be your grandfather?"

"Hell no, that just means he has more experience," Niki says, raising her own eyebrows at Clarissa. "It's not like he looks his age. He's fucking hot." She glances across at Jesse as he clears his throat, no doubt in embarrassment at being talked about like that. "Sorry, but it's true." She shrugs.

His bottle finally comes to a stop the neck pointing directly at me. A huge grin crosses his face and I immediately snatch a bottle of Jack's out of Nate's hands just as he'd brought it to his lips. *Dutch courage and all that jazz.*

"Ready for a good show guys?" Jesse asks the others, knowing exactly how our wolves react to each other. Our moment in his office earlier today flashes through my mind and I feel a blush cross my face as I swallow the mouthful of Jacks and hand the bottle back to Nate. Jesse settles back into the cushions of the sofa and crooks a finger at me, telling me to come to him.

My wolf's energy dances along my skin, seeing the playfulness in his eyes. I turn towards him and close my eyes as our lips touch. We start slow. Barely touching.

He doesn't push for more. He's giving my wolf and I control, allowing us to take this as far as we'd like.

Having him hand the reins to me gives me the courage to lean in closer, pressing my lips to his more forcefully. I want to consume him. My hands grip into his shirtfront, pulling him closer. I hear the sound of material ripping, but I don't care. I don't let it deter me. Wanting to melt into him, to merge with him and become one, I explore his mouth. Every inch of it. I'm vaguely aware of myself moving, crawling into his lap, but his hands running down my back and stopping in a death grip on my arse distract me from thoughts about my own movements.

The rumble of a growl vibrates through his chest under my hands. It reminds me of the purring of a cat. We, my wolf and I, love the fact that we're the reason he's making that sound.

Something hard hits me on the head with such force it jerks me forward, causing my teeth to bite into Jesse's lip. The taste of blood and the horrendous pain soaring through my skull's pulling my wolf to the surface. I force myself to pull away from Jesse and turn to see who'd hit me with the bottle of Jack's. The taste of Jack's running down my face and into my mouth makes it clear that's exactly what hit me.

Tracey is towering over us, the now broken bottle pulled back ready to strike again.

The room around us fades and my focus is solely on her. I see her arm move a fraction and all I can do to protect myself is throw my hands up to cover my face, the jagged glass cutting into my wrist. *If I'm not already dying of blood loss from my head, the wrist might just do the trick*, I think before reacting to her actions. I blindly grab for her wrist and manage to capture it with my uninjured arm. I don't let the warm blood running down my arm distract me; I can worry about that later. I need to get that bottle out of her hands before she can cause more damage.

Grabbing the bottle I wince in pain as it slices into my fingers but I grip it hard, not caring about the pain, and give it a good tug hoping to loosen her hold. It works; she releases her hold on the bottle and her shoulders slump with the defeat.

My adrenalin kicks in.

Dropping the bottle to the floor, I push her across the room stopping only when I have her pinned against the wall. *"What the hell do you think you're doing!"* I growl in her face, spit flying everywhere.

"He's our Alpha, he's mine. You've only just released your wolf. He deserves someone who knows how to be an Alpha's mate, not some tart that flirts with any male she lays her eyes on," she snaps back. She has guts I'll give her that, but she loses any respect I have for her the second she drops her eyes to the floor, breaking eye contact with me. Letting us both know exactly how submissive she actually is. Being an Omega I feel submissive to other pack members, no one should feel the need to drop their eyes to me.

I squeeze her upper arms in my hands, not caring about any bruises I may be causing. "It was a game, we weren't declaring our love to each other. Hell, *you* even kissed him!" Getting angrier by the second, my chest rumbles with the constant growl behind my words. My wolf wants out. She wants to stand her ground and teach this bitch a lesson.

A heavy hand drops onto my shoulder. *Jesse*. His energy strokes my wolf, calming her. "Frankie, go sit down before you bleed to death. Let someone look at your wounds. I'll deal with Tracey. Okay?"

Tracey looks up at his words, her eyes falling on mine. I stare into her eyes, not wanting to leave her thinking she's more dominant. She drops her eyes once again before I can even count to five.

"Don't ever try that again!" I snarl leaving the 'or you'll be dead' as a silent threat.

She gulps and nods, all the while keeping her eyes downcast.

Happy with her reaction, I turn around to follow Jesse's previous order and the floor comes up to meet me before everything turns black.

Chapter Nineteen

Jesse

As Frankie turns to face me, my heart jumps into my chest seeing her eyes roll back and her body drop like a ten tonne weight. "*Fuck!*" I call out, reaching out and catching her dead weight in my arms. I'd told her to sit down for a reason, it wasn't so I could fight her battles for her. *Stubborn females.* I hoist her up, an arm under her knees and another around her back, and head for my bedroom without a word to any of the others.

I feel Kate following me up the stairs but I don't question it. I'm sure Frankie would prefer another female to clean her up. Laying Frankie on the bed I turn to face

Kate.

She pulls her long blonde waves back into a hair tie. "I'll make sure she's comfortable and clean. Make sure they save me some pizza," she says.

I give her a grateful smile. We both know there would be no worries about the pizza being eaten. Kelly lives to feed us, he'd make her a whole fresh one if there wasn't any left for Kate. "Thanks, Kate. I'll come back as soon as I've dealt with Tracey." I shake my head. "I don't know what she was thinking."

"Jesse, I know you. You're going to blame yourself, thinking you must have done something to make her think she had a chance with you." Kate reaches a hand out and gives my arm a comforting squeeze. "You've done nothing of the sort. The things she said about you being hers... She's batshit crazy." She releases a nervous laugh.

"We definitely need to keep a close eye on her. I dread to think what she'll do next time." I glance back at Frankie unconscious on the bed. *There won't be a next time.* "I should have stepped in and done something."

Kate walks to the bathroom and starts running the tap, no doubt filling the sink to clean the blood and liquor off Frankie. "No, if you'd have jumped in and taken charge Frankie would have looked weak. Hell, there were a few of us fighting the urge to jump in. Me included. She needed to deal with it herself and she did a damn good job in the end." She speaks from the bathroom not bothering to raise her voice as I can hear her easily with my enhanced hearing.

I nod to myself, knowing she's right. "You're right," I admit. I glance at Frankie laid out on my bed one last time before walking towards the door. "I won't be long," I say to both of them as I leave the room.

I walk back into the lounge to find everyone sat glaring at Tracey, who is sitting on the sofa in the same place she'd been before it all started. "What were you thinking?" Niki asks. Tracy doesn't even acknowledge the question, fiddling with the hem of her floral skirt as she stares at the floor in a trance.

"I'd like to know the answer to that, too." Tracey jumps at the sound of my voice, lifting her eyes to mine for a second before snapping them back to the ground in submission.

"I... It's like I said to Frankie." She raises her eyes and straightens her shoulders, showing no embarrassment over her actions. "You deserve better than her as a mate."

"You said *'He's mine.'* That sounds like you're staking a claim on our Alpha to me." Nate says.

Tracey gulps and her shoulders drop slightly, cowering under the anger in his voice. She glances up at me. "I'd be yours in a heartbeat if you wanted me," she begs. Her heart is as clear as day on her sleeve.

Part of me wants to comfort her as I let her down gently but I wonder if she'll look too deeply into that. The memory of Frankie crumpling before me flashes in my mind, bringing my anger to the surface. "Tracey, you've been a member of this pack for a long time. If I was interested don't you think I would have made a move by now?"

"I..." Her sentence dies off as she shrugs.

"I'm an Alpha. If I want something I go for it." I pause, not really wanting to say my next words but knowing I have to if I want to get my point cross. "It's taking all my will power not to stake my claim on Frankie, but I want her to choose me. Not feel forced to be with me. She knows I want her; that's the only thing allowing me to hang on to my will power." I turn and stride out of the room.

I hear Tracey's apology follow me out of the room. "I'm sorry, Jesse."

"You owe Frankie that apology, not me," I call back as I take the stairs two at a time. My wolf anxious to get back to the person he wants as his mate.

Chapter Twenty

Frankie

I open my eyes to a dark, silent room. It only takes a second for my eyes to adjust thanks to my wolf's vision. I glance around to find myself on a four poster bed. Reaching my arm out I touch the one closest to me, feeling the intricate carvings in heavy wood under my fingertips. The feel of the cool satin sheets against my skin suddenly brings me to the realisation that I'm naked beneath them. *How did I end up naked?* I rack my brain trying to remember something to explain it.

There's a movement beside me, alerting me to the fact that I'm not actually alone in the bed. I can feel the loss of the body heat from the person on my left hand side. Questions of who this could be run through my head causing panic to settle in. I slide back away on the bed and pull the cover closer to conceal my nakedness.

Jesse's raspy voice caresses me through the darkness. "I won't let anyone near you Frankie. You're safe."

Jesse.

Relaxing, I settle back down and turn to face his back. Believing every word he'd said while wondering who I should be worried about. A vision of Tracey rearing back with a broken bottle in her hand flashes through my mind reminding me of the events that led up to this moment. "Tracey," I growl.

"You dealt with her pretty well. She'd be an idiot to try anything like that again." Jesse's gruff voice confirms my memories of the incident. He turns over and opens his eyes.

My breath catches in my throat. If I thought his eyes were beautiful in the daylight, they are magnificent at night. They glow just like a flame in the dark. "You're beautiful." The words leave my mouth before I can even think about whether to stop them or not. I allow my body to move towards him, wanting him to know that I want him.

"*No!*" he orders, holding me in place at my side of the bed with a hand on each shoulder. "I don't have that much self control. Please don't kiss me." His whole body's rigid, as though it's taking everything for him to hold me back. The sadness in his eyes is the only thing helping me through his rejection. He doesn't really want to stop me. He moves faster than my eyes can track and he's suddenly looking at me from beside the open bedroom door. "No one will bother you in here, you're safe. Sleep well."

Watching the door close behind him I raise my voice out of habit, forgetting he'll hear me even if I whisper. "Please stay." I concentrate on my hearing, listening for signs of movement behind the door. *There's nothing. He must still be there.*

I start thinking Jesse must have gone without making any noise when his voice finally comes through the door, sounding as cold as ice again. "You need to weigh up your options before you choose a mate. There are plenty of male wolves in the pack; some you haven't even met yet."

Tears roll down my cheeks at his words. He spoke as though it doesn't even hurt him to push me away. I know he can hear me sniffle but I can't stop myself. I want him to know how much this hurts me. "Why do you insist on pushing me towards other men? Why can't you just accept me... claim me?"

He sighs deeply and I hear a thud against the wall. "Because hearts are fragile, Frankie. It's painful when the one you chose chooses another, not to mention dangerous." He pauses for a second and I wipe away my tears with the back of my hand. "You heard what Mary said earlier? I ripped my last mate apart. I won't let that happen again, not to you." The sound of his footsteps walking away causes my heart to hurt even more than I thought it could.

Letting my head fall back on the pillow, I take a deep breath to calm myself. Jesse's scent invades my sinuses causing my mind and emotions to race. Anger burns inside me, making my wolf pace beneath my skin. She's just as angry as I am. I can't help but let a manic laugh out. He doesn't want to rip me apart. Can he not see that he already is? It's just not physical. Hell! I'd take physical over this; at least it would be over quickly. Unable to lie here any longer I slide my legs on the satin sheets and hang them off the bed wrapping the top sheet around myself. Switching on the lamp on the bedside table, my eyes fall on the intricate vines carved into the bedposts which my fingers had previously traced in the dark. I run my fingers along them once again, following their path with my eyes. *How can Jesse show so much love in his work and yet not care enough to see he's hurting me?*

I need to get out of this house. I pull my hand away from the bedpost and glance around the room. Spotting my clothes in a neat pile on top of the dresser, I jump up and grab them before heading through the open bathroom door.

Looking at my reflection in the mirror I ignore the red puffy rings around my eyes that give away the fact that I've been crying and tip my head to the side to look for the spot where the bottle had connected. There isn't a mark. Running my hand through my hair I feel for any sign of injury and come across nothing. *It's healed.* Someone had cleaned me up really well, having only missed a small amount of dried blood in my hairline.

Seeing a clean towel folded on the vanity top, I decide to get a quick shower. I don't want my head to sweat in my helmet on the way home and cause the blood to stain it.

Knowing my phone and keys were in my jacket, which should be downstairs where I had left it earlier, I turn off the lamp and I leave the bedroom in darkness. The abrupt change in light makes me wish I'd kept the light on but I pull open the door and I'm surprised to find the hallway doesn't get any brighter. There are no windows at all, making the hall pitch black. The only sign of light I can see is what is showing under a door further down the hall.

I take a tentative step and my foot accesses something in front of the doorway. I hear a grunt and a shadow of a figure slowly rises from the floor. "Who is it?" I ask in a panic, imaging it being Murderous Tracey or even Sleazy Tim.

"It's me, Nate."

Nate's voice calms me instantly and I feel out for his energy allowing it run along my skin. Why hadn't I thought to do that a second ago? "What are you doing on the floor?"

"Jesse came and asked me to sit guard, I must have dozed off. What are you doing leaving?" I hear him move and see the hands of his watch glow in the dark, having lifted his arm to look at his watch. "It's 3am."

Where do I start? "I just... Need to leave," I mutter as I walk past him, not giving him a chance to reply, all the while hoping I'm heading in the right direction of the stairs. A small smile comes to my face as I think how lucky I am that it's not Kelly, I'd never get away from him. He'd just follow me on his bike. If Nate jumps in a car to follow me I can easily lose him. Finding the stairs I hop down them and hear Nate following behind me. Not stopping, I grab my jacket off the rack by the front door and dash outside.

"Frankie, I don't know what happened between you and Jesse but he's just as pissed as you are. Please don't leave."

Seeing my bike, exactly where I'd left it with the helmet hanging on the handlebars, I take sure strides across to it, knowing my escape is close. "Nothing happened Nate, that's the problem," I snap, not even feeling weird about let my feelings for Jesse be perfectly clear for Nate to see. Pulling my helmet on I kick the bike off and speed down the gravel driveway, not caring that everyone in the house would have heard me leave. *It's too late for anyone to follow.*

Chapter Twenty One

Frankie

Enjoying the feel of the wind in my face through my open visor, blowing the cobwebs and any remaining anger towards Jesse away, I ride until the sun starts to rise. I finally pull to a stop at the cemetery, wanting to delay my arrival at the farm for a little longer. Running my hand over my father's name on his gravestone I briefly wonder what it would be like if he was still here and still Alpha. Would Jesse still be pushing me away? Maybe he wouldn't even be interested in me, having not had to protect me all those years. I let out a sigh as sadness rolls over me, knowing I'll never know those answers.

I straddle my bike once again and ride it the few metres to the farm. I should really go back to my apartment; I haven't been back since I was stabbed. The bed will still be pulled out how Carter had left it that morning. I hope it doesn't stick open. I contemplate heading in that direction for a second before deciding I wouldn't be able to last the drive into town, especially not after my body relaxed at my pit stop. I need sleep.

As I pull on to the drive I spot Kelly's bike parked where he usually leaves it; he must have come home after I left Jesse's, thinking I'd be here. Parking my bike next to his, I pull off my helmet and shake my hair out as I brace myself for the Spanish inquisition I'll get the second I step in the door. After taking one last grounding breath I open the door and enter the silent house. I pause for a second, expecting Kelly to jump out at me in the dark, but to my surprise there is no sign of him.

Heading straight for my room I tip toe up the stairs trying not to wake him if he's still sleeping. I throw off my clothes and climb into bed.

"She's here... No, she's gone straight to her room... Okay, I will." I hear Kelly's voice through the thin walls as I drift off to sleep. He's no doubt on the phone to Jesse.

The smell of bacon and sausages rouses me from my slumber. Knowing how satisfying Kelly's breakfasts are, I pull on some clean clothes and dash downstairs. My stomach grumbling I barge into the kitchen, praising

Kelly, "smelling good." I come to a sudden stop at finding Carter cooking on the stove.

"Are you talking about me or the food?" Carter glances back at me over his shoulder, giving me a cheeky grin.

"Carter, what are you doing here?" I ask, sounding as puzzled as I feel. I'm in two minds about whether I should throw him out or eat his food first. It might not be Kelly's breakfast, but it sure does smell good and I'm starving. The healing last night must have taken more out of me than I thought. Come to think of it, the last thing I ate was yesterday's breakfast.

"Cooking you breakfast. That healing will have taken a lot of energy out of you. I bet you're starving," he answers, sounding perky, which is somewhat confusing to me since we haven't been on talking terms lately.

He was on point and I'm not exactly feeling like raking up the past. If he can be here and act like none of it happened so can I. "Where's Kelly?" I ask, wondering if he'd actually stopped guarding me. Surely he wouldn't just leave without saying goodbye, unless he thinks I don't want him here? Or worse, what if what I thought was a friendship between us was actually just a job to him?

"There's another Alpha sniffing around town and Kelly's a brilliant tracker. Jesse asked him to find out where they're staying." Carter says whilst piling two plates high with food.

Overcome by a wave of dizziness, I slump down in the nearest chair at the table. Carter gives me a weary look as he places a plate of food in front of me. "Eat. You'll feel better in no time." Ignoring my glare at the order he sits down and starts tucking into his own plate of food.

It only takes me swallowing a few mouthfuls to start feeling better and allow my mind to function properly enough to come up with some questions. "Why are you here though? Yesterday Jesse said I didn't need guarding anymore."

"He doesn't know what this Alpha wants. He's come into Jesse's territory without asking or telling him. That's a huge *'no no'* for werewolves or any supernatural being," he admits with a shake of his head before taking another forkful of food. He waits until he's chewed and swallowed his mouthful before going on. "Jesse's worried that Rick might have caught wind of you. So I'm sorry, but you'll have to suffer a shadow for a little longer."

I watch as Carter goes back to his food without a care in the world. *Rick.* The name runs through my head as panic flows through me and the hackles rise on my wolf. "Rick? Rick as in the Alpha that killed my parents?" I ask as a flood of emotions flow through my body; panic and fear - that he may kill someone else I care about, and anger - that he had killed my parents and is still alive. Part of me wants to march out of the door so I can go and find him myself; to kill him myself. But I'm not suicidal, there is no way I could go up against an Alpha and survive.

"He told you about that?" Carter asks, the note of surprise in his voice matching his raised eyebrows. I nod. "Yes, it's that same Rick." No doubt catching onto my panic he places a comforting hand on top of mine, giving it a little squeeze. "Don't worry. He won't get anywhere near you. I won't let him."

Looking at the emotion in his eyes I can see that he really does care about me. *Why would he have slept around if he cared so much?*

He speaks once again before I can ask my question aloud. "I'm really sorry, about everything. Nate was right; I am a jerk. I know it's no excuse but once I felt your wolf when you were asleep, I knew I wouldn't have been good enough for her," he says, answering my unspoken question.

I shake my head. "You're wrong Carter. It wasn't until you came in after I'd heard every word that went on between you and Nate and you acted like nothing had happened." I give him a sad smile. "That's when *she* decided you didn't deserve us." I turn my hand over under his and stroke at his fingers comfortingly. "She let me come after you when you left Jesse's office, wanting to give you another chance but you were already playing tonsil tennis with Clarissa."

We waste the day away watching TV and chatting, while I try my hardest not to stress about what is going on with Kelly, Jesse and Rick. I can't help but see what attracted me to Carter in the first place. It's not just his devilish good looks; he's caring and smart too. My wolf is content in his company. Nate arrives mid afternoon and we move onto the porch to enjoy the afternoon sun with a couple of board games.

After a game of Scrabble, Carter leaves Nate and I playing Battleships to pick up a takeaway for dinner. None of us can be bothered to cook after such a relaxing day. We play two games before realizing Carter has been gone a lot longer than he should have. Pulling my phone out of my back pocket, I enter his number. We both hear it playing its tune in the kitchen. The bloody idiot must have left it there earlier.

Nate glances out to the field before closing his eyes to listen to his surroundings. "I'm going to go check the drive and field to see if I can see any sign of him. Okay?" I nod and he jumps up and walks down the porch steps. "If anything happens, just holler. I won't be far," he says, giving me a concerned look over his shoulder, conflict over needing to stay and needing to leave clear in his eyes.

"There's a shotgun in the pantry. I'll be fine," I say, hoping to ease some of the worry I can feel coming from him.

With a nod and one last worried glance he walks around the house and out of sight. Nate's only gone a matter of minutes before I hear Carter's phone ring again, someone else obviously trying to contact him. It stops and my phone starts ringing immediately. Jesse's voice comes out of the speaker before I even have a chance to say 'hello'. "Put Nate on, and tell Carter to answer his damn phone."

"Hello to you too," I say sarcastically, wasting time hoping one of them gets back before I have to tell him I'm alone.

"I haven't got time for hello. Put one of them on the phone *now!*" The growl in his voice makes his rage clear.

I gulp, knowing I've wasted all the time I can. "I can't Jesse, they aren't here." I pause for a second before deciding it's safer to carry on talking and not give him a chance to yell at me. "Carter went to pick up a takeaway. He didn't come back, so Nate left two minutes ago to check the drive and field to see if there's any sign of him."

"Fuck!"

Hearing the gravel on the drive crunching underfoot I ran to the kitchen window to see who it is.

"Kelly lost Rick's trail. He sent him on a wild goose chase. We think he might be coming for you," Jesse states, voice wavering with concern.

"He's here. And he's not alone." I gulp, trying to swallow down the terror that's rising within me. I have no chance of getting away from them. I can hear Jesse's voice but it's just a sound; I can't discern the words through the shock I'm feeling from seeing Rick walking towards me. I've never seen Rick before but I can tell who he is by the air of power he's carrying with him and by the way the men with him are all fanned out behind him allowing him to lead them to their destination - one on either side just slightly behind, flanking him. They're most probably his Second and Third. There are more in a row behind them, but I can't tear my eyes of their Alpha - Rick. *This man killed my parents.*

"How many?" Jesse's panicked voice pulls me out of my state of shock and back to the call.

I spin on the spot, not sure what to do or where to go. "Rick, and seven others on foot plus one driving a transit van, moving at a crawl behind them."

"He wouldn't come with uneven numbers, there must be one in the back of the van too."

I look back out the window and watch as the van comes to a stop and the driver gets out, I watch them, on tenterhooks as they gather around the van's side door. The driver opens it and a guy fluidly jumps out. The driver and the guy who I've appointed as Rick's Third reach into the open van and drag two unconscious bodies out, dumping them unceremoniously on the ground. *Nate and Carter.*

"Oh my God," I whisper into the empty room, forgetting I have Jesse on the phone until I hear his calm voice in my ear.

"Frankie, talk to me. What is it?"

"They've done something to Nate and Carter. They just dragged them out the van. I can't tell if they're dead or unconscious. They're not moving."

"*Shit!* Frankie, you need to run and find somewhere to hide. I'm on my way," he orders before hanging up.

"I can't hide from a pack of werewolves, they'll sniff me out," I say to myself. Running across the room to the pantry, I tug the door open and try to still my fingers from their shaking as I roll the combination on the gun safe. I finally get the right sequence and pull out the gun with a handful of cartridges. I stuff them in a small shoulder bag that's hanging on a hook by the back door. I know shotgun cartridges won't kill them, but it will at least slow them down.

Knowing that hiding would be impossible, I decide confrontation is the best and the only option I have until Jesse arrives. I walk out of the kitchen door with the gun hanging at my side and the sound of my feet on the gravel catches their attention. I lock my eyes on Rick and don't dare let them stray.

He takes a sharp intake of breath. "Wow. You are definitely Maria's daughter."

The sound of my mother's name coming off his lips causes anger to flow through me. "I wouldn't know. I don't remember what she looks like. You *killed* her!"

"You've got her sharp tongue as well as her looks." He lets out a menacing laugh. "She'd be stood there with a shotgun too." With each word he's slowly getting closer to me. His guys stop, leaving him to walk the final ten metres alone. "I didn't want to kill her, I told her they could all live if only she'd come home with me. But no, she thought they could take on my whole pack; six against more than twenty. We both know the outcome to that." His smirk makes me want to smack it off his face. One minute he's ten metres away from me, the next he's centimetres away.

I jump back, and feel strong arms wrap around me from behind, bringing me tight against a hard male body and holding me in place. A satisfied smile spreads across Rick's face. All that talk about my mother was just a distraction so I wouldn't hear his guy coming up behind me. He tugs the gun out my hand and throws it to the side, I watch helplessly as it skids across the gravel and comes to a stop about five metres away. "Stick her in the van, Gary."

Doing as he was told, Gary lifts me in his hold so my feet are no longer on the floor, and drags me to the van. My kicking and screaming don't hinder him a bit or loosen his grip. He stumbles over Carter's body - my thrashing body probably blocked his view, and we tumble to the floor. He quickly loses his grip and I come face to face with Carter on the floor His eyes open and he pops up, making me think he was pretending to be unconscious; at least for the last minute or two, biding his time.

"*Run!*" Carter bellows.

I don't wait to be told twice. I run.

RELEASING THE WOLF

The telltale sound of fighting surrounds me - males grunting in exertion, bodies slamming together. I daren't look back to see who's fighting or how they are fairing; it'll slow me down. I run as fast as my legs will take me, heading towards the cemetery, knowing it like the back of my hand. There are plenty of tree roots and head stones to slow down my pursuer whom I can hear gaining on me. My wolf's pacing inside me, pushing me to run faster, but my human body can't move as fast as she wants me to. Her wolf body is faster. It can get us out of here in no time. *I need to be in wolf form.*

The thought is barely through my mind when I feel my body shift. Bones breaking. My face elongating. It hurts like hell, but I don't have time to dwell on it. I need to focus on getting out of here. I can't slow my stride.

My four paws hit the dirt, as I hear a growl coming from in front of me. Looking up I see a familiar wolf fly over me. *Tony. Jesse.* Hearing the impact of his body colliding with my pursuer causes me to dig my paws in and spin around.

I can't tear my eyes away as I watch Jesse sinking his teeth into the abdomen of the guy still in human form, blood pouring everywhere from the rip in his stomach. I take a step forward wanting to rip into the prize of Jesse's hunt. My instincts hold me back from following through on the thought; Jesse hasn't invited me to join him.

"Frankie! Run!" Jesse's voice rings inside my head.

"Follow my scent back to my house. Rick won't go there, you'll be safe."

The thought of Carter fighting runs through my head, should I really be leaving them to fight? I have teeth and claws. I could fight too. *"What about Nate and Carter? They're out numbered,"* I thought hoping he'd hear me, the sight of Nate unconscious on the gravel drive clear in my mind. I can't leave.

"We're okay. Kelly, Big Mac, Tim and a couple of others are here," Nate's voice informs me once again in my head. *Does the whole pack hear everything when we're in wolf form?* I shake my head to rid myself of that worrying thought. It's not important right now.

Knowing there are plenty of our guys dealing with Rick and his men, I take one last look at Jesse, who nudges the lifeless male on the floor. Not even a whimper escapes the body. With the amount of damage I can see across his body, I know he won't be getting up. Jesse, having no doubt come to the same conclusion, flicks his eyes to me. *"Run!"* he orders before running off through the trees and out of sight towards the farm.

I follow the order, knowing my presence would only hinder their fight. I'd only be running on instinct with no idea how to really fight. I break through a line of trees and step onto the driveway with Jesse's great big mansion at the end of it. As I slow my pace I'm overcome by an horrendous pain deep inside my chest, taking my legs from under me. A chorus of howls come from the direction of my house. A howl escapes my own snout, and I'm suddenly aware that someone is dead. *One of ours is dead.* I don't know how I know it, but I do. Panicking, I quickly feel through the rope-like pack bonds inside me. I find Kelly immediately, followed by Jesse, Carter, Nate, Big Mac and Tim, too. Finding the severed bond my panic increases tenfold, there's nothing to tell me who it belonged to. Drowning in sadness, I turn and flee back to the farm. I need to know who's gone.

Skidding to a halt on the gravel, I take in the scene before me. It's horrific. There are lifeless bodies scattered around the drive. Trails of blood are everywhere. The van is no longer in sight, which is a telltale sign that at least one of the bad guys got away. A quick glance and count of the bodies confirms Rick escaped with at least two of his men. Our guys are all standing around a figure on the floor, their clothes tattered and torn from the fight. I'm vaguely aware that Nate and Jesse are both naked and in human form but I'm too focused on the body to really care about their state of undress. Jesse is leaning over the body - *Our dead.* I catch a familiar scent on the breeze and don't believe my own senses. *It can't be.*

Reaching down the pack bonds my worst fears are confirmed, and my heart breaks into a million pieces. *Joey's dead.*

I lose sense of the moment and I'm suddenly in

human form pushing my way through the circle of men. I crouch beside Joey's limp body and take in the sight of him. I flash back to the first day I met him, seeing that carefree sixteen year old trying to persuade Nonna to give him a job.

I gently rub the blood off his face with the tips of my fingers, not wanting it to mar his beautiful face. My eyes blur with tears as I realise I'll never see his charming smile again. I need to hold him. Jesse's hand on my shoulder stops me lifting Joey into my lap. I glare at him over my shoulder anger flowing through me.

"I'm sorry, sweetheart, But..." He points to Joey's neck. I follow his finger with my eyes and only have enough time to turn to the side before losing my breakfast. Joey's head is no longer attached to his body. I vomit until I'm left dry retching. I put my head in my hands not wanting to see the sight before me again. Unfortunately, it's ingrained behind my eyelids and it can't be unseen. I sob uncontrollably in my hands as I feel a blanket cover my shoulders and let whomever it is lead me into the house and place me on the sofa, leaving me to hug the blanket tightly around my body for comfort as I fight to get the sight of Joey's body out of my head.

The cushion beside me dips, pulling me out of my trance and I look up to find Carter holding a cup out to me. "Here, drink this."

Not caring to argue I do as I'm told and take a sip.

"Ugh, too much sugar, " I complain as I pull a face. It's so sweet he must have put the whole canister of sugar in my mug. I'm surprised it isn't more of a syrupy texture.

"Sugar's good for shock." He raises a brow and gives me a determined look, which makes me think he won't let me get away with just having the one sip.

Forcing myself to swallow another mouthful I know I won't be able to drink anymore. "Thanks Carter, but I can't stand tea." The tears come back twofold. Joey would have known to bring me coffee, not tea. Joey knows me better then anyone. *Joey knew me.* Seeing my distress Carter pulls me into his side with and arm around my shoulder. I don't fight him, I need the comfort he's offering. I let him sit back pulling me along with him and I sink into his side.

Chapter Twenty Two

Frankie

Having fallen asleep, it's dark when I open my eyes again to find I'm still lying on the sofa against Carter's side. The loud snore coming from him tells me he's asleep. Hearing voices in the kitchen, I decide to go and find out what is happening. I move slowly so as not to wake Carter and remember I'm wrapped in a blanket and naked beneath it. Having some modesty I tiptoe upstairs, avoiding the steps that I know creak, reminding me of the many times Joey had crept up on me by avoiding them too? *What am I going to do without him?* I feel the tears well up again but fight not to let them fall. I can't break down again; I need to know what happened. Joey is a submissive wolf, he would've never been sent into a fight. How the hell did he get caught up in all of this? Once in my bedroom I pull out some underwear, jeans and a blue tank top from the dresser and throw them on before heading back down the stairs.

"Frankie!" Carter yells, his voice shrill in panic. I run down the stairs hitting all the squeaky steps deliberately so he will hear me. He pulls the door at the bottom of the stairs open as my feet hit the last step and steps up to me taking my face in his hands. The relief in his blue eyes is hard to miss so close to mine. "Don't do that to me again," he begs before pulling me to his chest. "Please," he whispers into my hair.

I push his chest to escape his tight embrace. "I can't... breathe." He reluctantly releases me and I see through the open door; Jesse, Nate, Kelly, Tim and Big Mac have all moved from the kitchen to the lounge. Their faces all show concern in either the furrow of their brow or a grimace. "I only went to put clothes on." My words don't change the looks on their faces.

"I thought someone had taken you," Carter says as I step around him. He didn't need to say the name, we all knew he was talking about Rick.

"Do you really think someone could sneak in and out with you lot here? They wouldn't make it a metre up the drive," I state with a sad smile on my face, remembering the mess that was on my drive not long ago. "Is it still there... the... bodies?"

"No, it's been cleaned up. You can walk out there now and you wouldn't know anything had happened," Jesse says, stepping forwards.

I walk towards him and stop a little in front of him. "It can't be unseen," I whisper to myself more than anyone else. "How did it happen?"

Jesse reaches his hand out and wipes a tear from my cheek. "We don't know. That's what we've been discussing," he says, knowing exactly what I'd meant. "I'd left him at my house, I told him I was sending you back and he should wait for you." He shakes his head as though he's trying to make something fall into place. "I can only guess that he thought he knew a short cut. That he thought he could get here quicker to help you. Unfortunately, he ran straight into Rick."

"He had no chance, it wouldn't matter which of Rick's men he'd run into. They were all much more dominant than him." I state as the dam bursts once again, and the tears flow down my cheeks.

Jesse tugs me into his embrace. "I'm sorry Frankie." He strokes my hair and holds me against him while I cry on his chest in silence.

After what feels like hours but must have only been minutes, Big Mac's deep baritone breaks the silence. "I need to go to the bar, is that okay, Boss?"

"No problem. I don't think he'll be back tonight. It will take him a while to think up a new plan and find some strong wolves to replace the ones we took out," Jesse states over the top of my head. The feel of his voice vibrating through his chest is surprisingly comforting and I allow myself to take the security his arms offer.

I listen to Big Mac's footsteps as he walks out through the kitchen before leaning my head back to look up into Jesse's face. "You think he'll be back?" I ask nervously. I'd assumed he would give up after failing today.

"He wants you, Frankie. He's wanted you for a long time and he won't give up until he gets what he wants, or dies trying." I bite my lip in worry. Jesse gently pops it out with a thumb on my chin. "He'll die trying because I'm not letting him take you anywhere. Okay?"

I glance around at the others who are still standing around the lounge watching our conversation. Their serious faces tell me that they agree with Jesse wholeheartedly. The five dominant wolves before me will lay their lives on the line to save me. I nod my agreement to Jesse's question and decide to break the tension that I can feel building up in the air. "What's for tea, Kelly? I'm famished." The guys all laugh and the tension that had been almost suffocating a moment ago fizzles away to nothing.

"I best go see what we've got then," Kelly says before glancing at Jesse. "How many am I cooking for, Boss?"

After giving the top of my head a gentle kiss, Jesse slowly releases me from his embrace. I miss the comfort of his arms immediately. The stiffness in his own body as he pulls away tells me I'm not the only one reluctant to lose the comfort. "Carter, Tim and I are leaving. I'd appreciate it if you two would stay with Frankie tonight?"

"Of course," Nate says with a nod. At the same time Kelly says, "No worries."

"Does that mean I've got my shadow back?" I grumble, knowing that's what they'll expect. As much as it was driving me insane to have a shadow only a day ago, it's somewhat comforting to know I'll have two strong werewolves with me if Rick decides to come back. Not that I want them to know that's how I feel.

Jesse gives me a sad smile. "Unfortunately it does."

"That's okay, I don't think I can live without Kelly's cooking anyway," I say with a smile, not quite joking like the others think I am. Jesse is the only one who doesn't laugh, knowing I'm not one to eat unless it's put in front of me. I quickly change the subject hoping to remove the anger from Jesse's eyes. "Thanks for fighting for me."

"You're one of us. Pack. You'll never be left to fight on your own. If you need us, we'll be there," Jesse states flatly before turning on his heel and leaving the kitchen the same way Big Mac had, Tim following behind.

Carter follows too, only to stop before me and take my hands in his. "I love you, Frankie. I'll fight for you until my dying day."

Seeing that he meant every word he'd said I pull a hand out of his and caress his cheek with the back of my fingers. "Don't make promises like that because I can't face losing you as well."

"I'll just have to make sure I win then," He says, grinning wildly before dropping my hand and leaving the room.

I sigh, sitting down on the sofa a little heavier than I had planned to as I listen to Kelly clanging pots and pans around in the kitchen.

"You and Carter are back together," Nate blurts out of the blue.

I frown, wondering where the hell he'd gotten that idea from? "No. As far as I know he's still with Clarissa. We just came to an..." I try to think of the right phrase to use, "understanding this morning. This morning... It feels like days ago," I say with a shake of my head. It really does feel like a lifetime ago.

"It has been a long few hours, that's for sure." He sounds as exhausted as I feel. Having seemingly read my mind he sits beside me and picking a cushion up, he places it on his lap before gently patting it with his hand. "Here, close your eyes for a few minutes before the food's ready." I oblige, laying my head down, my eyes suddenly heavy as I breathe in his calming scent. I've always loved the smell of rain. His hand gently stroking my hair helps me drift into a light slumber.

"Grubs up." Kelly's voice causes me to suddenly jump out of Nate's lap. "You know, I'm starting to feel left out. I seem to missing out on all these hugs."

I follow him back not the kitchen and watch as he places three plates of burger and chips on the table. I wait for him to straighten up before I grab him in a huge bear hug.

He laughs into my hair. "Thanks, now eat up. I don't want my hard work going to waste," he says as he pulls away after only hugging me back for a few seconds.

"I'm glad you're alive, Kelly. You were the first one I found when I felt ...Joey." I couldn't bear to say the words dead aloud. Thinking them is hard enough. "I found you all, then found the severed connection but...I didn't know who it was. Not until I smelt him as I approached. I don't want to feel that pain again. Especially not for either of you two," I admit as I look from Kelly to Nate, who had joined us in the kitchen, letting them see the truth in my eyes even though they'd be able to hear it in my words.

I pick up my plate and turn heading for the lounge. "Let's eat on the sofa, I need comfort tonight." They both follow, Nate taking a seat next to me on the sofa once again and Kelly sitting in the armchair. We all tuck in and, after a few minutes, something about earlier comes to mind. "Nate, how did you hear what I said to Jesse in the cemetery?" I ask, referring to when both Jesse and I were in wolf form and talking in each other's minds.

"You said it to me, not Jesse," he informs me, a sparkle in his eyes and a smile hidden behind a forkful of food.

"No. Jesse had just told me to leave but I was concerned about you and Carter. Last time I saw you, you were unconscious on the floor," I say hoping to explain myself, thinking he'd gotten mixed up.

He shakes his head and finishes the food in his mouth before talking. "When you thought about me being unconscious, did you picture it?"

I think back to the moment and try to remember whether I had. I vaguely remember the vision that flashed through my mind. "Yes, I did," I answer excitedly. "Why?"

Both Nate and Kelly seem to smile and nod, clearly seeing something I don't. "That's how talking in wolf form works. You have to picture who you want to talk to, otherwise the whole pack would be talking at the same time. It would be confusing and noisy, we wouldn't hear what anyone was saying," Kelly states, while Nate chews on another mouthful of burger.

I think about how overwhelming that could be. "I'll have to remember that next time. I wouldn't want to say something to the wrong person," I say, imagining how embarrassing things could be in an instance like that.

"Hey. How did you shift anyways?" Kelly asks suddenly. Being a new wolf I shouldn't be able to shift until the first full moon calls my wolf out of me. Some new wolves are known to come out before then but it doesn't happen often, even in dire circumstances like yesterday.

I take a moment to eat some of my burger while I think about when I changed into my wolf. "I don't really know." I shake my head. "I heard the guy gaining on me and my wolf was pushing me to run faster, but we both knew my human body couldn't go fast enough." I close my eyes as I live through the moment again in my mind. "One second I was thinking I'd be able to get away in wolf form, and the next I'd shifted and had four paws on the floor." I open my eyes and glance up at Kelly. "Does it hurt that much every time?"

He nods and Nate answers my question from beside me. "You'll learn to live with the pain, if that's any consolation."

"Not really." We all laugh and focus on finishing our meals in a comfortable silence.

Nate clears the plates as I bring some bedding down for him to make a bed up on the sofa while Kelly has a run around the property to check there is no one out there that shouldn't be. It's not long before we all retire to bed after ensuring the doors are locked.

Chapter Twenty Three

Frankie

A knock on the door wakes me from a deep sleep but I don't bother jumping out of bed knowing it will only be Joey and he has keys to let himself in. I allow myself drift back to sleep. Nate's concerned shout brings me to reality and has me bounding out of bed before I'm reminded that Joey won't be letting himself in ever again.

After throwing yesterday's clothes back on I dart through my bedroom door and I'm halfway down the stairs when I hear Nate call out to me. "Frankie, there's someone at the door. He's saying he's an old friend." I've never heard Nate sound so skeptical.

"I'm on my way," I call back loud enough so that the other person - presuming he's human - would also hear me, wondering all the way through the house who the hell it could be? I don't have any friends.

Arriving at the front door I find Nate in the doorway, effectively blocking my view. I hadn't previously thought of Nate as a big guy but seeing him fill a door way makes him look extremely intimidating. I tap him on the back and he moves to the side just enough to give me a five centimetre view between him and the door jamb.

"*Gareth!*" I call out in excitement, a little too loud for Nate's super sensitive ears. He flinches beside me. I haven't seen Gareth since high school, he moved across the country to go to university, so I can't help but be excited.

Nate turns his head to look at me without moving his body even a centimetre. "You know him?"

I bat at his arm. "Yes, move out of the way."

He moves grudgingly. "I'll be right in here. If you need me, shout," he says, hooking a thumb over his shoulder and pointing to the lounge before leaving Gareth and I to our reunion on the doorstep.

Throwing myself at Gareth I have a second's concern that he won't catch me. His arms tightening around my lower back chases the silly concern away and I enjoy the bear hug he was always famous for in school.

"Wow, what's with the bouncer?" he asks, causing me

to laugh wholeheartedly for the first time since yesterday's horror.

Having no idea what to tell him I stick as close to the truth as I can. "A jerk tried to kidnap me yesterday, my friends are being a little over protective today."

"Jesus, Frankie. It looks like I came at the right time. Do you have room for an extra bouncer?" he asks while pointing to his suitcase, which I hadn't seen standing at his feet until now.

Stepping aside, I gesture for him to come in. "I'm sure we can squeeze you in somewhere." Walking into the lounge, Nate gives me a filthy look from his position leaning against the kitchen doorjamb. "Make yourself comfy, I'm going to go get some drinks," I say gesturing to the armchair, before heading for the kitchen knowing from Nate's look he has something to say to me. Stepping back, he allows me entry and I close the door behind me. Kelly steps up holding a tray of drinks out towards me, clearly having heard my offer of drinks. "Do you mind taking them, Kelly? Nate has something he wants to say to me."

Taking a quick glance at Nate's face, Kelly nods. "No problem."

"Be nice," I say before clicking open the door behind me and moving aside for Kelly to pass.

"I always am." True to his word I hear him offer Gareth a drink and introduce himself as my lodger before closing the door once again and turning my attention back to Nate.

I open my mouth to prompt him only to close it again as he opens his own. "What do you think you're doing?" He pauses, and I once again open my mouth only to close it again as he carries on. "He's human, it's too dangerous for him to stay here. Not while Rick is still breathing." Calling him angry would be an understatement: he's livid.

"You heard Jesse, he doesn't think Rick will come back until he's thought of a new plan and has better back up. We'll be fine for a few days at least," I say, hoping both Jesse and I are right. "He'll need to be with his pack tonight anyway, because of the full moon," I add hastily.

"Okay, a few days. But you need to tell Jesse about this tonight and see what he thinks," he grumbles, clearly not able to argue with my logic.

Smiling, I give him a quick hug before pecking him on the cheek. "Thank you."

Friends once again, we join Kelly and Gareth back in lounge. Seeing Kelly sitting casually in the armchair I join Gareth on the sofa. Nate chooses to stand in a corner, playing intimidating bouncer once again, instead of sitting on the footstool next to Kelly. Gareth, completely unfazed by Nate's actions, stands and offers him his hand. "I'm Gareth, we seemed to miss introductions earlier." Being a bouncer himself I'm not completely surprised. I'm sure if he knew Nate was a werewolf he'd be more cautious.

Nate shakes his hand and gives him a gruff, "Nate," before leaning back against the wall dismissing Gareth.

I wait for Gareth to get comfortable once again before speaking. "Come on then, let us have it. What's the real reason you're here?" I ask. He glances at Kelly and Nate warily, making me think whatever he has to say he doesn't want to say it in front of strangers. "If it's personal they can leave, but if it's about me it's okay. I don't keep secrets from my friends."

Taking me at my word he nods. "Danny and Mel broke up," he says as though it tells me everything. *It tells me nothing.* I know who Danny and Mel are but why I need to know they've broken up beats me. My returning silence and blank look makes him explain in more detail. "Danny thinks he has a chance with you now Mel is out the picture. He's coming here. I thought I'd better come first and warn you."

My hands start to shake and I take a deep breath. "When will he be arriving?"

Gareth reaches out and gives my hand a comforting squeeze, not even aware it's exactly what I need. Sometimes humans need the comfort of touch too. "He'll be here tomorrow, or Monday. He's gonna be pissed when he gets here and finds out I've spoiled his surprise."

"It doesn't take much, he's always pissed at something." I retort with a laugh, remembering all the times he'd lost his temper in the past at the smallest things.

"Who is this Danny?" Nate says, sounding deadly calm and showing his concern by making his way across the room, perching on the arm of the sofa next to me before placing an arm over my shoulders.

I shake my head, not believing how hectic and complicated my life has become in the last few weeks. *When am I going to catch a break?* "He's someone I dated back in high school, he dumped me for his ex, Mel. They went to Uni in Melbourne with Gareth. He's aggressive at the drop of a hat."

"He's going to get here expecting to stay and by the looks of it, there isn't going to be enough room. I can book a hotel if you want?" Gareth offers, showing how well he knows Danny. I bite my lip unsure what to do for the best.

"No, you're okay. He can have my room," Kelly offers.

"You are not leaving Frankie here with this guy. I don't like the sound of him," Nate states standing up and clenching his fists at his sides, practically forgetting Gareth, a human, is even in the room.

"I didn't say anything about leaving her. I'm sleeping on Frankie's floor," Kelly states.

I flick my eyes to Kelly wanting to see if he's joking, but by the serious look on his face I can tell he isn't. "That'll piss him off even more."

"Tough shit," Nate states with a shrug as Kelly says, "more fun for me," while flashing me a mischievous grin.

Another knock on the door causes us all to jump, which shows how distracted we all were. None of the werewolves picked up on the sound of someone approaching. We all look around the room, eyes flitting from one to another, trying to decide who should answer the door. Nate gives Kelly a nod and he makes his way to the front door. We sit in silence, focusing on the click of the door opening, and the room fills with the smell of a hot summers day, allowing both Nate and I to relax. It's Kate. Kate is Nate's twin sister and we both know she is nothing to worry about. Out of the corner of my eye, I see Gareth edge forward on his seat, straining his ears to hear anything Kelly and the person at the door could be saying.

We hear a commotion as Kate barges past Kelly and storms into the lounge. "You guys should be at Jesse's. He's getting tetchy, and today is not a good day for tetchy w—" Kate stops mid-sentence the instant she spots Gareth perched on the edge of his seat.

"Wankers... not a good day for tetchy wankers. Not after the kidnapping yesterday." Nate quickly finishes Kate's sentence before Gareth can question what her W word was going to be. It was quick thinking from Nate; it just looks like she doesn't want to swear in front of company.

I glance at the clock as I see Kelly lift his arm to look at the watch on his wrist. One-thirty, no wonder he's tetchy, he wanted us there by noon. "Shit! Gareth, I totally forgot we've got…" I pause to scan my mind for a suitable excuse. "Tickets for a nature show," I blurt saying the first thing that comes to mind. It's somewhat close to the truth. "We were going to stay at Jesse's house tonight. The show ends late and he lives practically next door to the venue. Do you mind if you are on your own tonight? There's plenty of food in."

Gareth relaxes back into the sofa. "No, not at all. I can feel the jet lag creeping in anyway, I'll be asleep soon."

"Thanks Gareth," I say, giving him a kiss on the cheek before running upstairs and packing a little bag to ensure I have some clean clothes for tomorrow. I grab some clean bedding out of the small linen cupboard on the landing as I pass for Gareth. Arriving back downstairs I can hear Kelly showing Gareth where everything is in the kitchen and how it all works.

I quickly swap Nate's used bedding with the clean stuff and place it in the laundry basket beside the washing machine in the corner of the kitchen. Entering the lounge once again, behind Gareth and Kelly, I catch the moment Kate gives Gareth a longing look. She quickly glances from him to me and a slow knowing smile crosses my face. Kate is interested in the Teddy Bear.

"What are you grinning at?" Nate asks giving me a nudge with his elbow, having evidently seen my smile.

"Nothing," I lie, not wanting to give Nate any more reasons to dislike Gareth more than he already does. I remember a little belatedly I'm surrounded by wolves who'll know I'm lying.

Kate steps forward and pushes me out of the house. "You're lying, but we don't have time to discuss it. Jesse was already close to having a coronary when I left, I dread to think what state he'll be in now."

Kelly leaves on his bike. Kate following behind him in the car she must have arrived in. I turn to grab my helmet and keys to find Nate blocking my way back to the house. "You can ride with me," he says, spinning me around by my shoulders.

"What? Why?"

Nate sighs. "You're safer in a vehicle with someone as protection." I personally think they don't want me going AWOL in the middle of the night again. But doing as I'm told I slide into Nate's dual cab Nissan Patrol. Nate flicks on the radio and I hum along, forcing myself not to sing, no matter how much I love it. I'm completely tone deaf and I've been told on more than one occasion that I should never, ever sing in the vicinity of another person, especially a hot and sexy person.

We arrive one vehicle after the other, like a little convoy. I spot Clarissa pacing before the front doors and stopping once she sees us, causing me to think she can't have recognised the sound of our vehicles as she would have easily heard us coming. We pull to a stop and exit the car.

"Thank God you're here. Jesse is wound so tight I had to leave, I couldn't bear being in the building with him. It must be the full moon."

I glance at the others and see them all doing the same thing. No one is quite brave enough to face Jesse's wrath. I sigh. "It's my fault we're late, I'll go. I need to tell him about Danny and Gareth too."

"Are you sure?" Nate asks with a raised brow. "I'll come with you if you want?"

I laugh at his frown of concern. "Thanks Nate, but I'm not scared of the big bad wolf."

"You should be." I hear Clarissa mutter under her breath as I walk in the front door, my skin immediately tingling with Jesse's power hanging in the air. No wonder she couldn't stand being inside. Following his energy I find him pacing his office. His anger hits me full force as I step over the threshold. He looks up hearing the hiss of pain escape my lips and immediately tones down his energy. It's still an uncomfortable tingling against my skin but it's no longer a searing pain.

Chapter Twenty Four

Jesse

Hearing a hiss of pain pulls me out of my pacing, causing me to look up from the carpet I'm currently staring daggers at. Seeing Frankie's wince of pain, I ground myself with a deep breath and pull my anger back. I shouldn't be making others suffer because I'm angry; angry with myself because Rick got so close to taking her yesterday. I cross the room and come to a stop before Frankie, now standing in front of my desk. The sight of her safe before me helps reduce my anger slightly. As noon struck and they weren't here so many scenarios ran through my mind. None of them ended well for Frankie, or myself come to think of it. I couldn't bear to lose her and hate to think what it would do to me. Thankfully, the full moon will keep her here for the next twenty-four hours, protected.

I'm reaching forward and tucking a loose strand of hair behind her ear before I can even think about whether I should be doing it. I need to touch her, to feel her under my fingertips so I know that she's really here, safe and not just an illusion my mind has conjured up. I've spent so long watching her from a distance I'm starting to think I've made her up, just a figment of my imagination. I drop my hand from her face, allowing it to brush her hand on the way past. Our energies flare for a second with the contact, allowing my wolf to finally relax for the first time since I heard her scared voice on the phone yesterday.

"I'm sorry we're late, it's my fault. An old friend turned up on my doorstep with a suitcase. To cut a long story short, he came to warn me that an ex is going to be turning up in the next couple of days, expecting me to welcome him with open arms," she says, her worry shows in the way she's wrapping her arms around herself.

"You're not looking forward to him arriving?" I question, unsure whether she's worried about her ex's arrival or my reaction to it.

Looking up at me she shakes her head and bites her lip in worry. "Danny's my ex for a reason, he's got a nasty temper. I'm worried he's going to cause trouble for us all.

I've already brought so much trouble to your front door in the last couple of weeks, I don't want to add to it," she says, the sadness in her voice pulls at my heart. She blames herself for Joey's death and doesn't want anyone else to get hurt.

Unable to bear hearing the sadness in her voice any longer I take her hand in mine and try to comfort her. "We'll deal with what ever knocks on the door together. We're Pack. Isn't that how it's meant to be in a family?"

She smiles, not quite the beautiful full smile I'm used to seeing but a smile nonetheless. "Thank you." Tears well in Frankie's eyes and I pull her close, resting her head against my shoulder. She soon relaxes, sinking into me. I enjoy the moment, stroking her back as I hold her against me. I've felt her cuddled up against me as a wolf but to feel her sink into me and trust me to keep her safe in human form feels perfect. I want more of this.

I shouldn't have allowed her to feel the brunt of my anger. She didn't deserve it. "I'm sorry I was so angry when you came in," I say, feeling the need to apologise. "I've been on edge since I heard your fear through the phone yesterday. The full moon isn't helping the situation much."

"Not to mention the sexual tension," Frankie grunts, making me laugh. "Deny it all you like, I know you feel it too. You have to."

"I'm not denying anything. I find it highly amusing, how stubborn you are. Your father used to complain about your mother's stubbornness all the time and I'm starting to understand why." I feel my smile broaden and wonder if I can ever remember smiling like this before? Or felt this happy? I know I've felt at my happiest in wolf form with her at the cemetery, but here and now, in human form this is so much more.

Mate. My wolf allows the word to float through my mind. A mate should make you feel happy. He may be allowing us to sit back and wait for her to choose us, but I don't think he'll be willing to wait much longer. He's already claimed her in his mind. Hell, I won't be able to bear the distance much longer. She's ours. *Our mate.*

Hearing Frankie moan about sexual tension, and seeing her pout at my amusement, I'm guessing her patience is on its way out too.

I allow the words to flow before I lose my nerve, "I'll make a deal with you."

Frankie pulls back slightly, to look up and into my eyes. The quizzically raised brow says *"spit it out,"* loud and clear.

"You'll meet most of the pack tonight." Frankie nods and I carry on before my nerve completely slips and I chicken out. "We usually have a big get together a couple of days after. It'll be at Big Mac's bar on Monday this month. Any you don't meet tonight, you'll meet then."

Nodding again, Frankie sighs and gives me an impatient look.

"*If,* after you've met everyone tomorrow, you haven't found anyone, or your wolf hasn't found anyone, that interests either of you as much as I evidently do I'll stop pushing you away. But remember, this can't be taken lightly. I can't go through what happened with Claire again." The name feels foreign coming out of my mouth. The face of the woman it belonged to clear in my mind's eye, as if she was stood right before me.

Frankie's hand wiping a tear off my cheek pulls me away from my past and to my possible future that's so close to my grasp, standing in my arms. "Thank you. I promise I will never put you through that. Ever," she says before reaching up on her tiptoes and brushing her lips gently against mine in a promise. The combination of her chaste kiss and promise is more than enough to fill the room with our mixed scents.

The thought that I could have her forever, if only I'd give in, runs through my mind. Tempting me to do just that and claim her right now.

Frankie steps back breaking the hold of my arms and the thought running through my head. Dropping my arms I allow her the space to step away. "I best go and tell everyone it's safe to enter. They're all on the drive not daring to come in and face your wrath, as Clarissa put it," she states before turning and reaching for the door handle. She flashes me a beautiful smile over her shoulder as she pulls the door open causing a mirrored reflection of the same smile to break out on my own face.

Sitting back down at my desk I contemplate the deal I've just made with Frankie and all the horrifying outcomes it could lead to. I'm not denying it could lead to a happy ending but I've always been a glass half empty person. I reach into the top drawer and pull my best bottle of whisky out as a heavy knock sounds on the door. Placing the bottle on the desk I pull out two glasses. "Come in," I call out in answer.

The door opens, revealing the last person I expect it to be. Nate. I fill two glasses placing one in front of the chair on the other side of my desk and take a sip out of the other while gesturing for Nate to take a seat. The furrow of Nate's brow gives me warning that he has something on his mind. Something he must be deeply worried about if the emotions flowing through the pack bond from him have anything to say about it. Nate has never been one that can be made to talk; he'll talk when he's good and ready, no sooner. Knowing Nate has been on the other side of this kind of conversation many times before, since I'm the same in that aspect, I sit back, savouring the flavour of my drink as I wait for Nate to talk.

After a minute of thought he finally speaks. "I'm concerned about this Danny guy. I don't like the thought of him staying in the same house as Frankie. I'm not keen on Gareth staying either, although he does seem like a genuine, nice guy. They are both human and it's not a good idea to have them here in the middle of all this stuff with Rick."

I contemplate Nate's concerns as I watch him pick up his glass and swallow half of its contents. "They're both staying at Frankie's?" I ask unable to keep my voice free of worry.

"We left Gareth there just now. He's sleeping on the sofa, and Kelly said Danny can have his bed because he'll crash on Frankie's floor... Didn't she tell you?" Nate asks tentatively.

I sigh, pushing down the anger that's once again starting to build, knowing Nate doesn't deserve to feel the brunt of it. The saying *"Don't shoot the messenger,"* flit's through my mind. "She told me they were in town, or arriving soon in Danny's case. But the fact that they are staying at hers must have slipped her mind," I say, punctuating it with a grunt before picking up my glass and downing its contents. I watch Nate as I refill my both our glasses, knowing he's my biggest competition in winning Frankie's affection, no matter what I told Frankie about her needing to meet the whole pack before she comes to a decision. This caring guy before me is exactly what Frankie is attracted to. That's why she was such good friends with Joey all those years. It sounds like her friend Gareth is cut from the same cloth. Whereas I have the same brutality Danny seems to have. She's clearly attracted to that also, but how much of that is her and how much is her wolf?

Her wolf was dormant when she was with Danny, she'll have still had some influence, dormant or not but how much is the question.

Nate's voice pulls me out of my musings. "I know this is none of my business, but Carter overheard your deal with Frankie. Why are you pushing her away? She obviously wants you, we've all seen and felt it." Nate's voice is gentle but the tension in his shoulders and fists formed on his lap show me exactly how angry he is.

"I know how she feels about me, but I've also seen how she looks at you."

Nate looks across at me with wide surprised eyes. "Me?"

His complete shock causes me to laugh. "Yes. You." I shake my head in disbelief. How can he not see it? "You, Nate, seem to be my biggest competition." I sigh, not really wanting to admit this but knowing I need to say the words out loud at least to Nate. "I just want her to be happy. If it's you that gives her that, then I'd rather she picks you. You know what happened to the last mate I chose." I shake my head vigorously, not even wanting to contemplate that outcome happening with Frankie. "I don't want that happening to Frankie. I couldn't live with myself. Not a second time, and certainly not if it was Frankie." I finish my drink at the thought and Nate does the same so I top up our glasses once again.

"What are we going to do about Danny?" Nate asks

getting back to the subject clearly playing on his mind.

I take a moment to mull over the problem Danny poses. Nate, being the patient man he is, waits quietly knowing I'll talk when I'm good and ready, just like he had earlier. If it was Carter sat opposite me, he'd be repeating himself left and right and I wouldn't be able to think about anything other than Carter's repetitive voice getting on my last nerve. "Kelly's going to be in Frankie's room at night, which would be the time Danny would be thinking of making moves on her, so she'll be safe in that aspect." The frown he gives me at my words tells me he isn't convinced she's safe. "You've got to remember she's a werewolf now. He's just a human. Frankie'll be able to handle him, even if he gets aggressive."

Nate purses his lips in thought. "I don't know. I think she might care for him too much to stop him if he gets out of hand. You know, like the domestic violence cases that are often on the news." His words make me question whether he's over thinking things or I'm under thinking them for a second, before I'm brought to my senses as my wolf gives me a huff in annoyance. *Do I really think of her as a weakling?*

"You've felt her wolf, she isn't that weak. You saw how she reacted to Carter and Clarissa," I suggest, relaying what my wolf had just told me with his huff.

"That example might not be such a good one. They've been getting a lot closer since Joey's death. Did you hear him tell her he loved her yesterday? She pretty much said it back to him. Well, as close as she could without actually saying the three words aloud. Carter's even called things off with Clarissa in the hopes of getting Frankie back." The two have never had much of a friendship between them but the venom in his voice surprises me. I make a mental note to keep an eye on the two of them.

"Don't worry about Carter, he'll do something stupid soon enough. That's what Carter does best." Nate nods in agreement at my words. I stand and head for the door, seeing Nate out the corner of my eye follow my lead. "Lets go wait for the moon to take control," I suggest as I pull open the door. I've always enjoyed watching my wolves lose control to the moon, looking and feeling - through the pack bonds - their freest. Other days, even when they are running you can always see the fight between human and wolf either in their eyes or the set of their body. The pull of the moon takes all the fight away. As Alpha I can never lose the fight so it's a blessing to watch my wolves be free and feel it through the pack bonds.

Chapter Twenty Five

Frankie

Sitting on the window bench in front of the pool table, I pretend to watch the game Kelly and Carter have going on but really, all my instincts are focusing on the heavy wooden door on the wall opposite me, trying my hardest to acquire X-ray vision from the moment Nate shut the door behind him. It doesn't matter how hard I strain my ears I'm not hearing anything through the door. I don't know why Nate and Jesse talking privately worries me so much, no doubt they do it all the time since Nate is a strong wolf, high up in the pack. I sigh. *Who the hell am I trying to kid?* I have a feeling they are talking about me behind that heavy wooden door, that's what's bothering me. Nate's been on edge ever since I'd invited Gareth into my home. Deciding to give up I turn my attention back to the game in front of me only to snap my head back to the door as Jesse's energy pulses through the room. The sight of Jesse walking out of the room with a smile on his face as he glances back at Nate who's following behind him, makes my heart skip a beat. I watch as they stop at the bar and Kate - who's playing barmaid as usual - pours them both a drink.

Hearing a bikes engine I turn to look out the window and watch as a Colin's motor cross bike pulls up alongside Ben's bike. He removes his helmet and places it on the seat, before lighting a cigarette and standing back to admire Ben's beauty of a bike.

Once again turning back to the game I find two glasses held directly in front of my face. One of amber liquid which smells of Whisky, the other's scent tells me it's Captain Morgan's spiced rum with coke. Glancing past the glasses and up into Jesse's face I give him a puzzled look as he hands me the Morgan's. "How did you know that's what I drink?"

His smile transforms into a playful grin. "If I tell you that, I'd have to kill you!"

Raising the glass to my mouth I catch onto his 'spy' reference and silently berate myself, he's been following me around for years, of course he would know what I drink. I swallow a mouthful of the heaven in a glass and wonder, not for the first time whether Kate is a professional barmaid because she gets these drinks just right.

"How are you feeling? Is your wolf still calm and collected, or edging to get out?" Jesse asks a slight frown furrowing his brow.

Taking a moment I feel deep inside myself and find her laid happily, with no hurry to get out. "Calm and collected," I answer my voice high in surprise.

"Most new werewolves would have changed by now, that's why I had insisted on you coming in early." He flicks his eyes to the window and points to the cars. " It looks like some of the other pack members are getting edgy."

I watch a steady stream of cars pulling up to a stop and people jumping out of them. None of them seem to be coming into the house, though. I spot Mary exit a blue Ford Falcon with two guys, I haven't met yet. My eyes widen in shock as they strip off their clothes and place them in the car before closing the door. From my view of them I can't see a sign that they are embarrassed about their nakedness in the slightest. Within a matter of minutes I'm watching three wolves standing beside the Ford Falcon. Their shift hadn't looked painful. At this distance and with the windows as a sound barrier, it had looked magical. I know different, I've felt the pain of a shift and it's far from painless. I glance at Jesse who is still standing next to me, watching the wolves intently.

No doubt feeling my eyes on him, he speaks without taking his eyes off the newly changed wolves. "I love watching the change. Look how free they are now," he says sounding wistful. Following his eyes Watch the three wolves and smile. He's right, they look free, so free it's making me feel like joining the and experiencing it for myself.

"Boss, Can I guard Frankie tonight? Carter's question pulls my attention away for the wolves outside and back into the room.

Jesse turns to face Carter who is twirling his pool cue in his hands nervously. "I was going to ask Nate to stick with her." He shrugs his shoulders. "But if you want to do it, I've got no objections."

Carter's smile doubles in size at Jesse's words. " Let me know when you're ready to shift, Frankie," he says to me before turning back to his game.

I watch him break the balls on the table and turn back to the window letting my eyes roam around the drive for three wolves. They're nowhere to be seen but the sight of new cars arriving keeps my attention outside. I feel Jesse lean against the edge of the wall I'm leaning against, his leg brushing my shoulder causing my wolf to sit up and pay attention to his energy running along my side. Together we watch the pack mates arrive and shift, not bothering to talk. We can hear the others laughing and joking as they play pool behind us, the number of voices going down as they each decide it's time for them to shift.

"Alright guys, I'm going out to join the fun. Anyone fancy coming with me?" Kate announces to the room.

Niki and Clarissa both jump off the stools they'd been occupying by the bar and answer in unison. "I'm in." The three girls leave and I take a good look at the guys. Nate and Kelly both seem calm and collected but by the way Carter is fiddling with his cue, chalking it's tip until there is nothing left of the chalk block in his hand.

Unable to sit and watch Carter's anxiety rise anymore, I speak up. "Okay Carter, you don't look like you can hold out much longer so lead the way." He gives me a grateful smile, hangs his cue in the rack on the wall and turns an expectant look on me.

"Wait outside, Frankie will be right out," Jesse says from his position against the wall beside me. After a subtle nod Carter dashes out of the room. Jesse offers me his hand. "Come on, you can shift upstairs so you don't have to get naked in front of everyone."

I follow Jesse up the stairs and come to a stop as he opens the door to a room and gestures for me to go in with a wave of his hand. "Are you shifting because you need to, or because Carter needs to," he asks as he follows me into the room. I can hear his footsteps on the soft carpet and feel his energy tickling my back. Teasing.

I smile, as I turn to face him. He caught me. "I'm

changing for Carter. Although I want to experience that freedom everyone else is and don't really see the point in waiting any longer."

The smile drops off his face and his shoulders slump. "It looks like you do have the ability your mother had."

"You aren't happy. Why?" I ask, my curiosity getting the better of me. I should really be shifting. Carter is probably wondering what's taking me so long.

Jesse sighs deeply. "I was hoping you wouldn't have the immunity to the moon, your mother had. Your Omega abilities are already a big enough temptation for Rick to have his eyes set on you. I'm afraid your immunity to the moon will make him even more determined to have you. He won't be the only one either. It's just gotten ten times more dangerous for you."

Unable to bare the sight of the sadness on his face, I step closer to him before reaching up and placing my hand on his cheek. His stubble rough under my fingertips. "You've kept me safe all these years. Just you, on your own. The pack know about me now, you've got them to help protect me too. So it doesn't all fall on your shoulders anymore." I stroke my fingers across his cheek andante his hair, enjoying the softness between my fingers. "I know I've complained about having a shadow, but I will be happy with ten shadows if it helps you." I've not taken my eyes from his from the moment I started talking, hoping he can see how much I believe in him and how well he can protect me. Releasing my fingers from his hair, I drop my hand back to my side.

He laughs. "I'll remind you of that when you complain about being guarded, next." The smile that accompanied his laugh drops from his face and is replaced with a frown. "I just want you to have as normal a life as possible. I don't want you to feel imprisoned with an escort twenty-four/seven, but I can't think of any other way to keep you safe." Jesse reaches up and strokes my cheek with the back of his index finger. "I just can't bare the thought of anything happening to you. I'm sorry."

The need to be free from all of this worry flows over me. Does Jesse feel like this all the time? No wonder he watches the other wolves enjoy their freedom so intently. "Come have some fun, change with me." It sounds too much like an order, even to my own ears. I wince ready for his anger to hit me. It doesn't come.

"I'd love to but I have to wait until the last wolf changes. Kelly and Nate are still down stairs, and Big Mac hasn't even arrived yet. He'll still be handing the bar over to his bar manager." He gives me a smile and takes my hand in his, giving it a gentle squeeze. "I can come and find you when shift. If you'd like that?"

I give him a grateful smile at his offer. "I'll look forward to it." Jesse steps back with a nod and leaves the room closing the door behind him.

Hearing the click of the door, I remove my cloths and

fold them, placing them in a neat pile on the bed, ensuring my underwear is tucked tightly into my jeans pocket before I step away. *Okay, how do we do this?* I ask addressing my wolf in my head. I feel her stretch leisurely in answer, clearly in no hurry help me out. Taking a deep breath I think back to the one and only other time I've done this. It was a life and death situation, that seemed to happen on instinct. I needed to be a wolf. I don't have that need right now. I crouch on all fours, thinking being in the position a wolf would be in can't hurt, and focus on how much I want to be a wolf. How much I want to feel the freedom my pack mates are feeling. I'm aware of each and everyone of them through the pack bonds. Reaching down a random one I find Kate, she's happy. Exhilarated even. Reaching another one I come to the ragged end of Joey's severed bond. A deep sadness runs through me and my chest hurts at the loss. My wolf charges out of me, wanting to be free of the pain and sadness too.

Standing on all fours, my skin covered in fur I look at the closed door briefly wondering how to let Jesse know I've shifted, when it opens. I tilt my head to a side giving him a curious look, like I've seen him do many times over the years, wondering how he knew I was ready.

Obviously knowing how to read wolf body language and therefore understanding my curiosity, he places a hand over the centre of his chest. "I felt your shift in the bonds." Walking past me, and to the bed he picks up my clothes. His movement sends his delectable scent to invade my nostrils, its the strongest I've ever smelt it, making me realise my sense of smell is stronger in wolf form than it is in my human body. "I'll put them in the shed at the border of the forest, that way you won't have to walk too far naked. You will probably fall asleep out there in wolf form and wake human," he informs me.

I'll fall asleep in wolf form and waked up as a human. Naked! Why had no one thought to warn me about this until now. I let out a whimper at the thought and Jesse reaches down to ruffle the fur on my head playfully. "Just remember we're all in the same boat. Some of us have just had longer to get used to it."

And some are just perverts and enjoy it. I retort to myself, thinking I'd love him to be able to hear me.

Jesse laughs. "Yeah, well, maybe Tim," he admits, having evidently heard me. He leads me downstairs, through the house and to a glass door letting me out into a small yard surrounded by a forest.

I stand, listening to all the wolves in the forest there's so much to hear, playful yapping, happy howling. It's beautiful, the sight and sounds. I watch Jesse walk to a shed in the righthand corner of the yard, disappearing inside and reappearing minus my clothes. He runs a hand over the length of my back as he passes me on his way back into the house.

"I'll leave the door open. If anything happens go to

my office and push the door closed behind yourself. Nobody in wolf form will be able to open the door. Once you're wolf on a full moon you can't change back until the moon releases you." I smile inwardly, knowing he is still thinking of ways to protect me - even from his own pack.

Mate. My wolf sends the word through my mind and I have the briefest second to consider how right she is, he'll make the perfect mate for some lucky lady, before I feel a snout nudge at my rear.

I spin around, crouching in a defensive stance readying myself to pounce at whoever was just sniffing my arse. The wolf in question is grey with a white marking on his front right paw, it looks like almost like a sock. He faces me with no intimidation or threat in his body. I don't know how, but deep down I know it's Carter.

"Come on, Frankie, it's what wolves do. We sniff each others arses." Carter's voice rings in my head. I don't know if what he's saying is true, but I know I'm not feeling any urge to sniff his arse.

The scent of the trees catch my attention and I suddenly notice how sensitive my senses have become. I can smell everything. The eucalyptus trees, the palms, the soil, the wolves - all of the ones that have crossed this path and others floating in on the breeze.

"Come on," Carter says before running into the forest, causing my instincts to kick in and chase him.

I push myself to go faster. Harder. Until I'm gaining

on my prey. I nip at his hind legs managing to trip him up. He rolls across the floor and before he can get back to his feet, I run off in another direction now playing the part of the prey. We play like this for a while trading places as one of us trips up the other before I run into a clearing, bumping into Clarissa, Kate and a grey wolf whose energy and scent I don't recognise, telling me I've probably never met him before. Jesse had said I would meet some new wolves tonight.

Carter breaks through the tree line behind me and comes to a stop before crashing into my arse. Clarissa instantly pounces at him, playfully nipping at him before sprinting off in to the tree line opposite us. Carter steps around me and following his instincts, he ready's himself to chase her and I watch the conflict in his body as he decides whether he should play or not. The muscles in his hind legs tighten and I know the decision to play won out, a second before he bounds off after her. I give it to Clarissa, she was true to her word. She'd cornered me earlier today after I'd come out of Jesse's office, leaning in close to me and barely whispering ensuring no-one else could hear her. "Carter may have called things off with me, but it won't last I'll have him back by the end of the day." It definitely seems like she's going to get her way.

Kate yaps and runs off into the trees, the grey wolf snapping at her heels. Leaving me to enjoy the peace and quiet of the forest, along with the beauty it holds.

I spin on my heel as the crunch of leaves behind me breaks the peace I've been bathing in. Expecting it to be Carter or one of the other guys, I'm surprised to find myself confronted with a large brown wolf I've never met before. The way he's stalking towards me tell's me its anything but friendly playfulness he's interested in. Seeing something bright pink peak out from under his pelvis tells me he has only one thing on his mind and I have no interest in that. I back away from him until I bump into another wolf, once again I spin around, just far enough to have a wolf on either side of me. So I can see them both, the brown wolf and the newcomer that has a mix of browns and greys. *Colin.* I can tell it's him by the unique feel of his energy against my fur and his scent reaching my nostrils.

Another brown coloured wolf strides menacingly through the trees before me, halting the escape plan running through my mind. I look from one wolf to the other and lift my hind leg readying myself to escape through the only wolf free space there is behind me.

"That's not going to work, sweet cheeks." A voice runs through my mind and I turn in a circle trying to work out which wolf the voice belongs to. A grey and white wolf walks into the clearing from the place I was going to make my escape and I know I'm screwed. I've got no chance of escaping from four wolves.

"I'm having her first," Colin says confusing me. Can't

we only talk to those we want to hear? Who is he talking to and why can I hear him? *"No. I was the one that talked Clarissa into getting that useless waste of space out the way. I earn't the right for first dibs."* Colin's voice rings out in my head once again making me realise I'm only hearing is part of the conversation. Could he be so excited that he's forgetting to block me out or does he not care what I hear?

"Carter I could really do with a guard right now," I think focusing on picturing Carter, with everything I have, hoping he'll get my message. The wolves before me growl at each other, obviously having a fight of wills. I take the moment to wrack my brain to come up with something that will get me out of this predicament. I let out a howl hoping someone will hear it and sense my distress through the bonds. I strain my ears to listen for a replying howl but all I hear is playful upping in the distance.

I catch sight of a grey and white blur as the wolf pounces on my behind, trying to mate me. Panic races through me as I realise that's what they all want. *They are all wanting to mate me.* I kick my hind legs out trying to buck him off. He repositions himself. *"Carter!"* I scream in my mind.

Feeling Nate's shift through the bonds, I call out to him knowing he'll here me now that he's a wolf. *"Nate. Help me."*

Relief flows through me as his voice floats through

my mind. *"I'm on my way. Fight."*

Chapter Twenty Six

Frankie

Having Nate on his way gives me the confidence I need, to know I'll be free from these idiots soon. No one is going to mate me without my consent. I do as I'm told and buck my back legs trying to kick off the grey and white wolf. For an instant I'm reminded of a game I used to play as a kid *'Buckaroo'*, I believe it was called.

The feel of sharp teeth biting into my back wipes the game from my mind. I try to kick my legs again but his teeth in my back strengthens the hold he has on me, making me unable to lift my legs under the weight of his body.

A blur of cream flies past me as the weight of the grey and white wolf leaves me. Nate, the cream wolf snaps at the other wolf who he'd thrown across the clearing, trying to get him to submit. The wolf gets to his feet and snaps back. Remembering there were another three wolves here I turn to find them, knowing Nate can't possibly take them all on at once, on his own.

The grey wolf is nowhere in sight, no doubt having known he'd already lost his chance and deciding it was better to flee. Colin and the big brown wolf turn their attention from the two wolves fighting and I see a spark in the brown wolf's eye as he now obviously realises he still has a chance to get what he came here for. I watch his hind legs bend as he pounces towards me, digging my paws in I brace for the impact, knowing he isn't at the right angle to jump straight on my back. He'll be wanting to take me down and reposition us first. A black and tan wolf comes flying out of trees between us and taking the impact of the big brown wolf. *Tim.*

I jump to the side to avoid the rolling wolves on the floor and turn to face the only threat left. Colin. Knowing I'm more dominant than him from our confrontation in front of my bike the other day I don't give him the chance to run. I pounce on him, my snout open in a snarl ready to sink my teeth into his flesh. There's no resistance, I'd expected the skin to be tough and hard to break but it's like a knife going through butter. The warm blood, pouring from the wound is surprisingly nice. I rip a chunk of flesh away and bite into him again before the sound of someone approaching catches my attention, releasing my prey from my teeth I snap at the newcomer. *This is my food.* Seeing Tony stood before me, I stop mid snap. Leaving Colin where he lays, I drop to the floor as flat as I can possibly get to show my submission to Jesse and dropped the floor as flat as I could possibly get to show my submission to Jesse, My Alpha.

"Get up Frankie, it's over. I'll deal with them now." His voice almost vibrates as it flows through my head. He brushes his head against mine as I do as I'm told and get up, before turning to face the others who had been round up, even the grey wolf who'd ran away was cowering before Jesse. Nate and Tim, both snarling at the group of wolves. *"Nate, do not let Frankie out of your sight."* Jesse's voice rings in my head and it makes me appreciate him even more. He didn't have to let me hear his words, but he knew I needed to feel safe and what better way to make me feel safe than to let me know Nate would be watching over me all night.

Nate pads towards me, brushing against me with the length of his body as he passes. *"Come on Frankie."* My eyes flick to Jesse in concern.

"Go. Nate will keep you safe," he states, setting my lingering worries to rest.

Knowing he was right, I turn and find Nate waiting

for me in the tree line. We run through the forest for hours, hunting scrub turkey's and rabbits, until finding a tree to curl up under and drifting off into a contented sleep wrapped in Nate's calming scent.

⁕

I slowly become aware of the beating of a drum. Upon opening my eyes a crack I realise the beating drum is Nate's heart as my head is resting on his bare chest. An arm resting over my side squeezes me gently as it hold me tightly against him.

"Morning," he whispers with a gruff voice full of sleep, before releasing his hold on me. Allowing me to sit up. The situation becomes ten times more awkward when I spot Big Mac curled around our feet, in his birthday suit. I lift my eyes to my knees not wanting to catch sight of parts of Big Mac I'd rather not see. I'm hyper aware of the fact that Big Mac isn't the only naked person here, I don't raise my hands to try and cover myself knowing that it's too late to hide anything that my hands could cover. Nate's hand drops into my line of sight and I realise in my moment of panic, Nate must have stood up as He's now leaning over me offering me a hand to help me up. "Come on let's get you some clothes. I remember how strange it is the first few times you wake up in the middle of the forest naked." Holding my hand in his he leads me on a short walk through the forest until we reach a shed. He opens the door and I step in the shed to see my neatly folded pile clothes sat on top of a cabinet. "I'll wait here while you get dressed," he states as he turns his back to the door allowing me the privacy of the shed to get dressed in.

I dress as quickly as I can and after tapping Nate on the shoulder, he moves a side and allows me to exit the shed feeling much more comfortable being fully clothed.

"I changed in a hurry coming after you so my clothes didn't survive. Luckily I have a spare set in the ute, although I'm sure I'd be able to find some in the house too. Jesse has heaps of spares lying around for any who might need them," he states as he walks in the direction of the house at a leisurely pace.

Feeling curious, I reach through the pack bonds to see if he feels self conscious about being naked. I can't believe he wouldn't, not even a little bit. No doubt feeling me tugging at his rope he lets to a chuckle. The charming sound sends a shiver down my spine. "Sorry," I apologise. "I wondered if you feel weird about being naked?" I admit sheepishly.

"You get used to it eventually," he says without breaking his stride or even looking back at me. "Both being naked and seeing naked people. It's part of werewolf life. It just becomes normal, believe it or not."

Nope. I just can't imagine ever feeling that way... ever.

I've been following Nate from the shed trying my hardest not to look at his nakedness but the perfectly round arse before me is making it pretty impossible. It keeps drawing my eye. We walk around the house and come to a stop by the front doors.

"I'll run and get my clothes out the car," Nate informs me as he dashes around the cars to his ute. He pulls the back door open and reaches in to the back seat. Making me remember my bag with spare clothes.

"Nate, could you grab my bag out the front, please?" I call across the drive.

"Sure thing," he calls back before heading around the car to the passenger side.

Once Nate gets back to me, we head upstairs and he leads me into the third bedroom on the right closing the door. He walks away from the closed door before spinning on his heel and glaring at it. I open my mouth to ask what is wrong when he suddenly strides over to a heavy dresser against the wall and pulls it in front of the door so it's effectively blocking us in.

Looking at his handy work his shoulders relax and he turns to face me. "You can grab a shower first," he suggests nodding in the direction of the bathroom to my left as he walks towards the window, passing my bag to me and throwing his clothes on the bed as he passes.

Thinking of Nate, naked in the bedroom has me hurrying my shower. After throwing on some clean underwear, I pull my clean tank top over my head and tug up a pair of shorts before stepping back into the bedroom blindly, rubbing my hair dry with the towel.

Feeling Nate's eyes on me, I drop my hand down and glance across at him. Our eyes connect and he looks away with a slight blush on his cheeks, not before I see an admiring look on his face. Making me feel much more attractive than I'm sure I deserve. My hair sticking up in all directions and having no make up on my face. Dropping my eyes to my feet to hide my grin, I walk across the room and I hear Nate moving, probably towards the bathroom. His feet come into view on the carpet and just as we are about to pass each other, my body steps into his path of its own accord. "Fuck!" I hop up and down on one foot, the other smarting due to Nate having stood on it.

Nate crouches down and rubs my foot. "I'm sorry, but you did jump in front of me." He stands to his full height of six-foot-five, and I stay there blocking his route. An internal debate battling in my head - to kiss him or not to kiss him.

I want to, my wolf doesn't. Winning the battle I place my hand on his bare chest, running up and reaching around the back of his neck as the room fills with our scents. Stretching up on my tip toes I can't take my eyes off his lips. He bends slightly meeting me halfway. Our lips connect, causing my heart to race. My wolfs energy racing over my skin to get to his skin. I can feel his wolfs energy doing the same to me, tracing every inch of my body. With his hands on my hips he pulls me closer to his body, making me hyper aware of my thin summer clothes being the only barrier between us.

The rattle of the door handle causes me to break away, gasping for air.

Nate clears his throat before trying to talk. "Who is it?" He doesn't take his hungry eyes off of me.

"Its me buddy. Is there something in front of the door?" Kelly's voice calls through the door as he gives it another rattle.

Continuing to hold me in place by my hips, he glances over at the obstacle before the door. "Yeah, Frankie's in here. I didn't want to shower, with her alone in the bedroom so I put the dresser in front of door." He gives my hips a gentle squeeze as he looks back at me. "That way, no one could get to her."

"It works." Kelly's laugh sounding muffled behind the door. I can just picture him shaking his head, like he does. "Are you gonna move it so I can get in? There are queues in all the other rooms."

Nate doesn't make a move to remove the obstruction form the door. "I haven't been in the shower yet. I was just getting in."

The door handle rattles once again. "That's alright, just let me in at least I'll be next."

With a sigh Nate releases his hold on my hips and walks over to the door. He drags the dresser back to where it belongs against the wall and opens the door, allowing

Kelly into the room. He Turns without a greeting and close himself into the bathroom.

Kelly enters the room, quickly closing the door behind him. "Whoa." Kelly waves hand in front of his face and rushes over to the window, cracking it open. "What have you been doing in here?" I glance at him and open my mouth to explain, only to close it again. I can't tell him I was making out with his naked best mate. "Actually, don't answer that I don't wanna know," he adds quickly.

My stomach churns nervously as I stand where Nate had left me, wondering whether I should wait for him to finish in the shower or just go downstairs. Surely I'd be safe in Jesse's house without someone shadowing me. I watch as Kelly wanders around the room showing off his ripped naked body. The sight's nothing new, I often find him walking around the farmhouse naked, he's extremely comfortable in his own skin.

Catching my eye he sits on the bed, patting the spot next to him. "How are you feeling after last night? I heard about what Colin, Bernard and the others did."

Shaking my head, I hand my damp towel to Kelly as I take a seat next to him. "I can't sit next to you while your naked."

Standing he wraps the towel around his waist before sitting down once again. "I'm sorry. I totally forgot I was naked."

I pick at a broken nail on my right hand as I answer

his earlier question. "To be honest, I don't think I've fully processed last night yet." I gasp as a sudden flash of my teeth sinking into Colin's flesh runs through my mind. "Oh my god. Is Colin okay after what I did to him?"

"It's nothing he didn't deserve." Nate's voice sounds muffled through the closed bathroom door.

Kelly stills my hands with his. "He's healed now. He's just got a bit of a bruised ego. Don't you dare feel bad for it."

I give him a grateful smile. As much as I know he deserved what he got I still feel a pang of guilt over what I did in return. "Will I be punished for what I did to him?" I ask.

Nate bursts out the bathroom with such force the door comes off it's hinges in his hands. He stares at it with wide eyes. Seeing the water dripping from his hair and over his tense muscles has me licking my lips and thinking of the kiss we'd shared only minutes ago. Leaning the door against the wall he takes a few long stride and just in front of me. A towel wrapped around his waist, he kneels down before me ensuring our eyes are level. "You did nothing wrong. You were defending yourself. Nobody gets punished for that."

"He's right." Kelly confirms, standing up. "I'm getting a shower and it looks like you're going to get a good view." He laughs, pointing at the doorless jamb.

Nate and I leave Kelly to enjoy his shower without an

audience and hope to find some food. I'm stopped in my tracks as I catch Carters scent coming from an ajar door. Placing my hand on the knob I ready myself to push it open wider, so I can confront him about not helping me when I'd been screaming his name.

Nate's heavy hand on my shoulder makes me pause. I turn to see a sad look cross his face. "He's not alone," Nate mouths silently, whilst tapping his nose.

I keep forgetting to use my nose to it's full capabilities. I breathe in Carter's scent picking up on a mild lavender hint it has attached to it. *Clarissa.* She must be with him. Their scents being mixed together, means they must be kissing like Nate and I had not long ago at the least. Knowing those two they would have been much more intimate. Frozen on the spot part of me wants to go in, not caring what I may interrupt. Clarissa was in league with Colin last night, I could kill two birds with one stone confronting the pair of them.

Nate tugs on my shoulder firmly, pulling me away. "Let Jesse deal with them," he silently mouths, seemingly having read my mind.

The door opens with a creak. "Did you have a good view?" The sound of Clarissa's smug voice has me regretting waiting around. "I thought I could smell you. You're the only one covered in almost every males scent. Lets see, there's Carter's, Nate's, Jesse's," she sniffs elaborately between each name, "Big Mac's, Colin's,

Bernard's and Paul's too. Wow, you have been a busy girl."

"*Bitch!*" I snarl as my fist flies out on its own accord, socking her in the temple and knocking her off her feet. I look at my aching fist feeling proud and somewhat astonished. Having never been in a fight before I had no Idea I was capable of that.

Carter exits the bedroom's ensuite in a rush and crouches next to Clarissa, a towel wrapped around his damp waist. "Frankie, what the fuck was that for?"

I turn away to leave. "Ask your girlfriend. She knows exactly what it was for."

"You deserved everything they did to you. Now you are a slut you've been acting like," she spits out venomously. Making me think she can't have heard the plan had failed.

I smirk at her over my shoulder, excitement running through me knowing she'll be disappointed when she hears what I have to say. "I guess you haven't seen your fellow gang rape organizer's since last night?"

"Gang rape?" Carter repeats hesitantly. He stands, stepping away from Clarissa and moving towards me perhaps catching on to my suggestion. "Frankie what's going on? Are you okay?"

"She's fine. No thanks to you," Nate answers, grabbing my hand and leading me down the stairs. As my foot hits the bottom step, I flinch at the sound of a fist going through wood at some force. "There goes another door," Nate states calmly.

"Another door?" Jesse's voice close behind me causes me to jump and my wolf to stir inside me.

Nate's hand tightens around mine and I can only guess he hadn't sensed Jesse either. "Yeah, I kinda pulled the bathroom door off its hinges in the room we changed in. Sorry, Boss."

"Don't worry about it, two's pretty good. We lost five last full moon." I spin to face Jesse, somewhat confused at his words. "The day after a full moon we wake up one of two things, angry or horny. It doesn't seem to matter which mood we're in, the doors always end up casualties," he adds, picking up on my confusion.

Opening my mouth to speak, I suddenly close it without uttering a word. My face blushing at the thought of what I'd almost blurted out. Jesse smirks and I know he'd guessed what I was thinking. He leans in towards me, the stubble o his jaw faintly scratches against my cheek as he whispers in my ear. "For me, it was the latter." The words are barely audible, but I hear every word as though he'd shouted it from the roof tops.

Stunned, I watch him walk away without another word.

Chapter Twenty Seven

Frankie

Hours later I walk back into the farmhouse with Kelly and Nate on my heels. Nate still taking Jesse's order of "Don't let her out of your sight" to heart, even though Jesse has since rescinded the order...*twice*. We find Gareth on the sofa eating pizza, his bedding neatly folded on the arm chair. Kelly heads straight into the kitchen, no doubt to look for something yummy to cook for us. He's always trying to feed us.

Gareth jumps up pulling me into one of his bear hugs. "Hey guys. Did you have a nice night?" he asks around a mouthful of pizza.

"It was okay, things got a little wild." I say to his shoulder as I squeeze Gareth a little tighter feeling the safety of his big burly body. Nate's scent flares behind me and I can hazard a guess that he's either not happy about mine and Gareth's hug, or the memories of the wild I was referring to from last night. Or more likely both.

"It smells like rain. Is it raining outside?" Gareth asks having caught Nate's scent. He releases me and peers towards the window.

"I think there might be a storm coming," I say hoping to give Gareth enough confirmation for him not to want to check things out for himself. I turn my attention to Nate. "Nate, will you help me get the horses in the stables before the storm comes?"

"I'll help you," Gareth offers. "I used to be a dab hand with the horses back in the day."

"No, have your pizza before it goes cold. I'll help Frankie," Nate throws over his shoulder as he walks out the front door.

Giving Gareth an apologetic smile I quickly follow Nate. He'll know there are no horses to deal with, as he's seen the guys who run the farm dealing with them plenty of times over the last couple of weeks. Plus there is no storm coming. Nate is the only storm that's coming.

Nate's rant starts before the door even clicks to. "You're not very good at making things up are you? He only needs to step out the door and he'll know there isn't storm, the sky is so bloody clear a star gazer would be in their element."

I step towards him menacingly, my anger easily matching his. "You're blaming me?" I state, my voice high pitched in disbelief. "It's your fault. You're the one that got tetchy and filled the room with your scent. If you had a regular scent like pine or sandalwood I could have blamed it on incense. The smell of rain didn't give me many options."

Standing toe to toe, squaring off for a fight. I gasp in surprise as he takes my lips with his. I hadn't even seen him move. My arms wrap around his neck of their own accord and I tuck my legs around his waist as he lifts me off the floor, all the while not breaking the kiss. The smell of rain invading my nostrils and turning me on. Regret fills me. I should never have complained about his scent. Feeling the need to apologise I lean back and break the kiss. "I'm sorry, I shouldn't have said the things about your scent. I love your scent."

Giving my lips one last look he glances up at my eyes and I see a mix of emotions flit across his face. "You were right, what else could you have said to Gareth?" He sighs and his shoulders slump in defeat. "I shouldn't have been a tetchy jerk. The shit that was pulled last night, on top of Rick's kidnap attempt has me on edge. I don't want you getting hurt, Frankie." His eyes bore into mine. "I don't like the sound of Danny. I told Jesse and he just brushed it off saying *'Frankie's a werewolf now, she can handle a human'.*" His impersonation of Jesse was so good I throw my head back with laughter. "It's not funny." The irritation is clear in his voice as he places me gently on my feet.

"No, it's not, but your impersonation of Jesse was." I can't help but giggle at the thought. "It was spot on. I dare you to do it in front of him." A broad smile crosses his face and I'm relieved to realise that he can't be that irritated at my giggling fit. "I know your worried about Danny, but Kelly is going to be sleeping in my room so he's not going to be able to hurt me. To be honest, Danny has a temper but I don't think he'll ever take it out on me. I'm more worried about him taking it out on you lot."

He rolls his eyes. "We're werewolves, we can handle a measly human." I glare at him with raised eyebrows and we both laugh at his contradiction.

Taking me by the hand, Nate leads me on a walk around the boundary making the most of a beautiful night.

"Jesse is your best choice as mate you know that don't you?" Nate asks ruining the moment in a split second. "That's why your wolf likes him and not me. He's the only one that can truly protect you." The sadness in his voice is palpable but it's the honesty that cuts through me causing a tight pain in my chest.

He knows my wolf doesn't want him.

Of course he does. He's seen how she reacts with Jesse. He'll have felt that she had no interest in him when we kissed. "You saved me from being gang raped last night not Jesse. Anyway, Jesse's my Alpha. He'll protect me regardless of who I choose." I take a calming breath before asking the one question that's been running through my head for days. "His last order from my father was to protect me, how much of what he does is of his own freewill?"

"I only knew to come after you because Jesse felt you and sent me. It was Jesse that protected you." Nate gives my hand a squeeze. "Your fathers order would have become void the moment he died, so everything Jesse does and feels is of his own freewill. "

Realising I'm not winning this argument I try a new tactic. "I was told wolf and human don't have to agree on a mate, that sometimes the wolf will let the human choose and the choice will grow on her eventually, she'll learn to love him."

He nods in agreement. "But it can also happen vice versa."

I glance across at him and watch as he stares out into the distance taking in our surroundings with every step we take. "I want you to know I made a deal with Jesse. After tomorrow's party, if I still haven't found anyone of interest, he'll accept my choice of him," I blurt the words out feeling the need to give him the honesty he deserves.

He flicks his eyes across to mine, guilt written on his face. "I know, Carter over heard you."

"Oh." That's news to me. My eyes fill with tears before they trail down my face. I feel like I'm stuck between a rock and hard place. I need Joey, he'd know what I should do. Who I should choose. Nate pulls me into his chest, wrapping his arms around me and holding me close. Feeling the safety his arms offer causes my tears to fall more freely. "How am I...supposed to choose? You are...both such good men," I say between wracking breaths. "I'm torn in two. Half of me wanting you and the other half wanting Jesse."

Nate's hand strokes my back as he holds me even tighter against his chest. "We'll both be happy as long as you're happy. Regardless of who you choose." The sincerity in his voice rings loud and clear allowing me to relax slightly. My choice won't kill either of them. "Come on we better get back. You know what Kelly's like, he'll have a hissy fit if the food gets cold before we get back," he states releasing me and once again taking my hand to lead me back.

Walking back into the house we find Kelly pacing the lounge and Gareth was trying to watch the TV around him, without much luck.

"What the hell have you been doing? The food will be ruined. I might as well just throw it in the bin." He glares at the pair of us before storming into the kitchen.

I chase after him not wanting him to follow through on his threat. Managing to grab ahold of him before he reaches the plates piled with burger and fries, I veer him out the back door and came to a stop on the porch.

Taking a deep breath he turns to face me. I relax slightly as I feel his energy, a little calmer against my skin. "I'm sorry. I think the moon is still affecting me."

"You and Nate both," I say, unable to hold the grumpiness out of my voice. "I'd just finished mission control with him, to get back and have to do the same with you." I sigh. Maybe I'm more affected from the moon than I realised too.

"But I don't require you sticking your tongue down my throat to make me feel better," he retorts as he reaches out and gives my shoulder a playful shove. The frown on my face must show my confusion clearly because he clarifies his point. "I can smell him all over you. Even on your breath."

"Please don't tell me you are jealous," I beg, only half joking. I don't think I can handle worrying about another guy in this scenario.

"I guess I am," he states, eyes wide in surprise. His answer clearly shocking himself.

I reach out and pull him into hug, which he accepts without question. "You're not jealous. You miss Gabby and this whole crap focus on me choosing a mate must be torture for you. I'm so sorry."

He cries in my arms for a minute before stepping back out of my embrace. "Thank you," he breathes the words barely a whisper, before turning and heading back into the house.

Nate's drying his plate as we walk in, evidently having already eaten. The microwave beeps and he takes my plate of food out, before placing it on the table. "Here, Frankie, eat." My stomach grumbles as I inhale the delicious smell and I don't have to be told twice. I take a seat and pick up my burger.

Kelly shakes his head. "I did not see where you got that from." He walks through to the lounge, all the while muttering about nuking good food.

I watch Nate hang tea towel in its place, out of the corner of my eye as I enjoy my meal. He gives me a kiss on the top of the head as he passes. "I'm going to head home now. See you tomorrow at Big Mac's?".

"You can stay… if you want?" I suggest. " It's not like we haven't shared a bed before."

Flashing me grateful smile he shakes his head and opens the back door. "Thanks for the offer but Kate will be wondering where I am by now. I was only meant to be dropping you off and making sure everything was good here."

By the time I finish my meal, clean up the kitchen and make my way into the living room, Gareth's got his head back on the sofa and snoring quite merrily. I turn off the TV and place a blanket over Gareth before turning off the light and heading upstairs. Like usual I skip the steps that creak but Kelly's voice calls out having heard me any way. "Is that you Frankie?"

I open his bedroom door a crack and poke my head in, seeing Kelly sat on the edge of his bed with a solemn look. "Yeah, I'm just heading to bed. Are you okay?"

"Some days are harder than others. Get yourself to bed, I'll be okay." The smile on his face isn't very convincing but I can't force him to talk.

A menacing growl and the slam of a door pulls me from my dream of Carter punching holes in doors. I dart out of bed alert and ready for an intruder, only to find my room empty of intruders. I'm just curling back up under the covers when I hear Kelly snapping at someone. "Who the hell are you? Better yet do you know what the fucking time is?"

"It's none of your business. Where's Frankie?" I'd recognize that voice anywhere... Danny. Deciding it would only end badly if I leave them to deal with each other. I run down the stairs two at a time, grateful for the T-shirt and shorts I'd slept in. Skidding to a halt in the entrance hall behind Kelly who is blocking the doorway, I can't see around him but I can tell from his posture that he must be toe to toe with Danny. "Just get her," snarls Danny his voice full of venom.

I can feel Kelly's energy pulsating with rage against my skin. "She's sleeping! Go away and come back at a decent hour," he lies, knowing full well I'm right behind him. He even Ben's energy was pulsating with rage.

"No one is sleeping, with you two shouting out here." I squeeze my way between Kelly and the doorframe. Danny smiles at me, probably thinking I'm on his side, as he steps back to give me room on the porch. I stroke Kelly's arm as I step in front of him, hoping my touch will calm him before I turn my attention on Danny. "It's two in the morning, couldn't you have waited until a reasonable hour?"

"I'm sorry but I couldn't wait another minute to see you." He pouts and I roll my eyes. "Now get over here and give me a hug."

A rumbled growl coming from deep within Kelly's chest causing me to turn and look at him. I flash him a reassuring smile before stepping into Danny's outstretched arms. The hug between us doesn't last long. I feel Kelly's eyes boring holes into my back and know Danny would be able to feel them too. I catch sight of the suitcase on the porch and raise an eyebrow.

Danny's face lights up with a cheeky smirk. "Room for a little one?"

"We're packed to the rafters as it is, Danny." I sigh, knowing I had no choice. He won't take no for answer, unless Danny has had a personality transplant in the time he's been interstate. "I'm sure we can squeeze you in somewhere."

Kelly grunts behind me and I catch sight of him heading into the lounge, I follow him, with Danny and his suitcase a few steps behind me. Gareth is snoring on the sofa, obviously in such a deep sleep the noise on the porch having not woken him up. Danny's sharp intake of breath tells me he's seen Gareth. I speak before Danny can go off on one of his tangents. "Gareth's on the sofa, as you can see."

Kelly disappears upstairs, hopefully to get some spare sheets and organise our sleeping arrangements. "Do you need a drink, or something to eat before I show you where you'll be sleeping," I ask heading towards the kitchen.

"No thanks, I'm good." I turn back to see Danny shaking his head.

I lead him upstairs, stopping on the landing outside Kelly's open door. I glance in the bedroom and see a neat folded pile of sheets on the stripped bed, but no sign of Kelly. I wave Danny into the room. "It looks like Kelly's left clean bedding on his bed for you." I point to a door across the hall. "That's the bathroom." Not that you could miss, with the flower plaque that states 'Bathroom' in big letters hanging on a nail on the door.

"Is that your room?" Danny asks, nodding to the only other door in the hall.

"Yes. Kelly's going to be crashing in my room while your here. Night Dan." I dart into my room and close the door behind me, not giving Danny the chance to argue about our sleeping arrangements.

I spot a bundle on the floor against the wall as I walk over to my bed. Feeling Kelly's energy radiating from that direction, I guess he must be in a makeshift bed. I lay in bed for at least ten minutes listening to Kelly huff, puff and fidget. Unable to take another minute of listening to his tossing and turning, I pull the covers back and shuffle my back against the wall. "Come and get in Ben, that floor can't be comfy, and neither of us are going to get back to sleep with you fidgeting like you are."

"I'm sorry, it's not the floor. I haven't slept without fidgeting since Gabby died." His voice sounds muffled from the covers.

Of course...he's missing his mate, he should be having pack comfort. If ever there was a moment for a facepalm this was it. "Please Kelly get in. Let me give you some comfort. You've done so much for me these last few weeks, let me do this for you."

Kelly stays still and silent for moment, before getting up with a grunt and sliding into the bed next to me. I feel his skin against my own and deduce that he is only wearing some boxers. I pull off my t-shirt leaving me in just a crop top and shorts, knowing more skin is better when it comes to comforting a pack member.

Kelly is laid on his back, staring at the ceiling. Obviously not willing to take what I'm offering. Turning over I face the wall, grabbing his left arm on the way. Giving him no choice, I pull him over me so he's spooning my back. Within seconds I feel him relax into the mattress and let out a deep rumbling snore.

***

Once again, raised voices pulls me from my slumber and I wonder if I'll ever manage to sleep tonight? I listen trying to make out any words but all I can hear is the deep baritone of two undistinguishable male voices. The sound of footsteps come up the stairs, before I can move Kelly's arm from over me.

The door bursts open and I smell Jesse before I hear his voice. "Something's wrong with Kelly."

I can hear Danny stomping up the stairs behind Jesse, muttering to himself. Something about "storming in uninvited."

Jesse isn't paying any attention to Danny or his muttering, his focus is all on Kelly laid beside me. Kelly who is deep asleep and feeling content through the pack bonds.

I slide out from under Kelly's arm and climb over him as quickly and quietly as I can so not to wake him. Although, I'm pretty certain that even an earthquake wouldn't wake him upright now, not that we ever get any of those here in Western Australia.

Grabbing my t-shirt off the floor, I push Jesse out of the room as I pull it over my head. "Down stairs," I order, pointing the way. They both follow my instructions without argument.

In the kitchen I boil the kettle and pull out three cups, knowing I need coffee before I can deal with any agro between Danny and Jesse.

Danny starts before I even have the instant coffee out of the cupboard. "This moron just stormed in here like he owned the place, and everyone in it." The snarl on his face and his fisted hands by his sides remind me of the Danny I used to know.

"This moron knocked. You told me to piss off." Jesse snaps, before turning his attention to me, his voice turning gentle, "I'm sorry Frankie, but Kelly felt comatose. He's done nothing but pace since Gabby died, until he vanished through the bonds couple of hours ago. It had me worried."

Contemplating over the fact that I'd at least had a couple of hours sleep and wondering if I'll get a chance to go back to bed before having to start the day, I turn to Danny. "Can you give us a minute, Dan?"

Dan throws a filthy look at Jesse before stepping into the lounge and closing the door behind him. Human ears wouldn't have been able to hear the grumbled, "fucking moron", under his breath. Our werewolf ears had no problem hearing them.

An amused smile crosses Jesse's face. "That guy has some serious issues." he states, settling himself against the cupboards behind him. "I'm guessing you sleeping with Kelly is the reason for his dramatic change?"

I shrug. Not really knowing the answer myself. "Neither of us were sleeping with him tossing and turning on the floor." I say, before explaining myself more. "He's still grieving over Gabby. Joey's death has added another hole in the pack bonds, which hasn't really helped him." I pause to take a breath, swallowing down the lump in my throat that the mere mention of Joey always seems to evoke. "The three of us spent a lot of time together these last few weeks. I just thought sleeping next to me might comfort him. Like it had for you after you were shot. I don't know why no one else had tried to do that for him. He was asleep in seconds."

Jesse rubs a hand over his face. He looks as tired and worn down as I feel. "We all did. We tried every combination possible. Male. Female. Both... We even had a puppy pile of five of us, myself included. Nothing made a bit of difference. He just stared at the ceiling all night." After a moments thought he asks a question that's barely audible, "how come it worked with you?"

I answer, even though I'm sure his question was to himself. "Maybe it's to do with my blood and it's strength within the pack. Like how I didn't need to be brought into the pack because of my father creating the pack with his blood. Rossi blood." I shrug my shoulders. *I don't have the foggiest clue why it worked, but need to try and come up with an answer.*

Watching him think my words over, I can almost see the cogs turning in his head. "Maybe. But there is another possibility. Your mother was always able to calm anyone down. Even the most rabid pack members. Leave Maria in a room with them for five minutes and they would be as calm as stone when you returned. She was an Omega. Maybe you are too." His words sound like he's working through his thoughts aloud, not looking for confirmation.

I put two spoons of instant into my cup and look to Jesse. "Coffee?"

He shakes his head and looks to the closed lounge room door. "Is he going to behave? Nate was concerned for your safety earlier and after meeting him myself, I'm starting to get concerned too."

I finish making my coffee an give him what I hope is a reassuring smile. "I can handle Danny. The only thing I'm concerned about is how he's going to act with you guys. He seems to find *all* guys a threat. I think I'm going to have to give Big Mac's a miss. He'll be picking fights left, right and centre if I go."

He gives me a kiss on the top of my head before walking out the back door. "Don't worry about us, nothing can get out of hand at Big Mac's. No one wants to be banned," he throws over his shoulder before disappearing into the early morning light.

Chapter Twenty Eight

Frankie

By the time one in the afternoon comes around I've come to the conclusion that if we wait for Kelly to wake up and feed us, we'll have died of starvation. I'm throwing together some miserable looking sandwiches as he walks into the kitchen, full of the joys of Spring. Prancing over to me, he slides his hands around my waist while smacking a kiss on my cheek. "I don't know what you did to me, but that was the best sleep I've had in months...I feel whole again." The sheer joy on his face, evidence of the truth of his words.

Feeling down the pack bonds, I can tell he's so much

closer to whole than the empty shell he was yesterday. "I'm glad I could help."

After casting a mournful look at my sandwiches, Kelly pushes me out the kitchen. "Catch up with your friends. I'll sort this mess you've made out and bring you all something edible." I thank him with a kiss on the cheek before joining Gareth and Danny in the lounge.

As I pull my clothes out of the wardrobe, I find myself thinking about how miraculous it is that the day has passed without anymore fights, before kicking myself, I've probably jinxed us all now. With Kelly in the shower it's the first time I've had two minutes to myself all day. As I slip my little black dress over my head there's a knock on the door and I hear it click open before I can say 'come in'. I straighten the hem and glance up, not surprised in the slightest to find Danny standing in front of me. I knew he'd manage to corner me sooner or later. Kelly had been good at keeping himself between us most of the day. The hours Kelly had been comatose, Danny had been catching up on his sleep too, thanks to his red eye flight. If Gareth is correct about his motives, now is as good a time as any to set him straight. I heard his sharp intake of breath and smelt his arousal. *I guess Gareth is right about his intentions after all.*

He takes a sharp intake of breath before speaking and I catch a sharp scent of arousal. "You look beautiful, Frankie." Any woman would be flattered with his attention, after all, he's a good looking guy. Unfortunately I've seen the ugly side of him one two many times. He's wearing tight faded jeans and a Rip Curl T-shirt. He's as well built as any of the pack guys, but his body is hard earned and nothing to do with werewolf genetics. Danny has been boxing since he could walk, his dad was a boxer and his hero. When we were fourteen, a bunch of us went to watch him. Danny was so excited, it was the first proper fight that his dad let him watch in person. Unfortunately it was the first and last fight of his dads he saw. He died during the fight, due to a punch that landed badly. Belinda, Danny's Mum, tried to stop him fighting after that but Danny wanted to make his dad proud by following in his footsteps, fighting. When the cops brought Danny home for street fighting, his mum decided the boxing clubs were much safer than the streets.

I smile. "You look pretty good yourself, Danny."

I rakes his eyes up and down my body. "I want you back, Frankie. We didn't give us a chance before." As I give him a sad smile, a frown forms on his face clearly confused. *Did he really think I'd jump at the chance to get back with him?*

I sigh. Mad at myself for jinxing us. "*We* didn't give us a chance? Danny, you ran back to Melissa without giving us a chance. Not we. *You!*"

He takes a step towards me and reaches out to pull me into his embrace. "I'm here now."

I knew this would happen, once Danny gets an idea in his head there is no changing it. No matter what you say or do. I step back shaking my head, vigorously. "No... it's too late." *Five years too late.*

The door bursts open and I send up a prayer, as a naked Kelly walks in without a care in the world. Used to seeing him naked I don't bat an eyelid. Going by Danny's wide surprised eyes and slack jaw, he isn't quite sure what to think.

Kelly let's out a wolf whistle. "Frank, you look hot!" Ignoring Danny, he strides over to me and kisses me on the cheek as he leans around me to grab his clothes off the wicker chair. "You okay?" he whispers as his lips brush passed my ear. I nod in reply as he steps back.

"You... You're..." Danny stutters as he stares wide eyed at Kelly's manhood. leaving his mouth open catching flies.

"Hung like a horse?" Kelly finishes for him. "I know," he adds with a shrug.

Getting a handle on himself, Danny quickly tears his eyes away to make eye contact with me. "Are you two...?"

I don't blame him for jumping to that conclusion, seeing a guy walk naked into a girl's bedroom, would give you that impression. I could say yes and he'd probably leave tomorrow. And I know Kelly would go along with me, no matter what I said. But I don't want to have to pretend to be with Kelly all night. I've made a deal with

Jesse. I want to follow through with it. I'm sick of feeling conflicted about all these men. It's time me and my wolf make a decision and choose one. If I was a normal wolf I wouldn't even have to choose a mate. I could be a free agent for as long as I wanted, just like Kate and all the other girls in the pack. My wolfborn status, and the ability to freely have children makes it too dangerous for me to be unmated. Although, being mated will make things safer regarding the men in my pack, unfortunately it might not make a difference to the wolves outside our pack. regardless of that I need to make my decision, and make it tonight. I shake my head. "No, we're not."

Kelly tucks himself into his jeans and zips up his fly whilst glancing out the window. "Nate's here," he states for Danny's benefit, knowing I'd heard the pick up, and felt Nate through the bonds, just as he had. As you become closer in proximity to a pack member the bond, like a rope, flexes and you feel them get closer.

I pick up my clutch off the bed. "Let's go party," I say, walking past Danny — who still seems to be deciding whether there's anything going on between me and Kelly.

My heart skips a beat as I open the door to the kitchen to find Nate dressed in a pair of black fitted jeans — by fitted I mean they must've been sprayed on. He's wearing a knitted sweatshirt, like the one he had on the first night I saw him. It leaves him looking mouthwatering as it molds to all those muscles. We Stand in silent appreciation of each other. Our scents telling us exactly what we thought of each other. The room becoming thick with arousal.

I feel Gareth step up behind me as Kate walks in behind Nate wearing a red version of my little black dress. It looks amazing with her long blonde wavy hair hanging over her shoulders and her bright blue eyes sparkling in the light.

"You look amazing Kate," I say, walking around Nate and pulling her into a hug. Only feeling slightly guilty for ignoring Nate as I did so, knowing that if I did paid any attention to Nate, neither of us would be able to control ourselves enough to seem normal in front of the two humans who were now in the room — Danny and Kelly having entered behind Gareth. It's not a big kitchen, and with two male werewolves, two large human males, Kate and myself: it's starting to feel minuscule.

Kate pulls back and flashes me a grin. "We're gonna knock 'em dead."

"I've definitely died and gone to heaven," Gareth states in an unusually deep voice causing me to glance back at him to see his lust filled eyes focused on Kate. She replies with a flirtatious laugh, causing Nate to storm out of the house with a growl.

"Now you've done it." I whisper with chuckle in her ear. Nate isn't keen on Gareth or Danny as it is. Gareth coming onto his baby sister isn't going to win him over.

Kate told me she's actually the oldest, by twelve minutes, but Nate is the protective type — as all werewolves are. I'm pretty sure, even if Kate was twelve years older he'd still treat her like his baby sister.

Looking at Nate's Colorado, it's obvious that there aren't enough seats. "We won't all fit." Dan says pointing it out.

"Sure we will, I'll sit on Handsome's knee," Kate says giving Gareth a wink and taking a step close to him.

I watch as a blush spreads across Gareth's face and he clears his throat. "Sure...that's... cool with me."

Nate's objecting growl makes the hair on the back of my neck stand on end. "Kate, you can ride shotgun, I'll sit on Kelly's knee." I insist, hoping to calm Nate down before he has to drive. He'd probably run us off the road if Kate sat on Gareth's knee for the trip.

As we walk into Big Mac's bar, *The Wolves Den,* I'm surprised to find it isn't as big as I'd expected it to be. It's a long narrow room, five metres wide at most. The shiny wooden bar runs the fill length of the room along the right hand side. Most of the stools placed along the bar are taken by customers. In the dark of the room I can just make out a stage at the back of the room with a small dance floor before it. The rest of the room has high tables scattered around, a handful of stools accompanying each one.

I'm not sure how busy a small bar like this would get

but it's packed tonight, people dancing wherever they stand. I can feel through the bonds that most of the pack here but some of the customers feel like regular humans, with no werewolf energy coming from them. I sense a strange vibe coming from the three barmaids I can see, making me think they may be some other form of supernatural beings.

We head to the front edge of the bar where there's a small free space and Big Mac strides over to serve us. "Hi guys, what are you after?" Nate and Kelly both order a large whiskey, Gareth and Danny ask for a bottle of larger, and Kate and I both order a Captain Morgans and Coke. "Coming right up," he says as he starts pulling together our drinks.

Beyonce's *Run the World (girls)* comes on and Kate starts singing and dancing away next to me. The way she's already grinding against Gareth tells me she is far from shy. My eyes flick from Kate to the door, a second before it opens and Jesse walks in. I just knew he was there and going to walk in the door, which is strange since I hadn't even noticed he wasn't here in the first place. Jesse is sex on legs everytime I see him. But the tailored black suit he's wearing now with an emerald green shirt and loose black tie just screams sexy. His body is full of muscle, which would catch any females eye ,but it's his energy that gets my attention. Not the power he radiates from being an Alpha but the connection of energy we have between us.

My inner wolf is drawn to him like a magnet.

His eyes find mine in an instant, as if he feels the magnetic pull too. Although I doubt that's it, he really had no choice but to make eye contact with me, since I'm standing directly in front of the door. I'd be hard to miss staring at him with my tongue hanging out of my mouth.

Danny taps me on the shoulder, pulling me out of my drool over Jesse moment. "You're not listening to a word I'm saying are you?"

I tear my eyes away from Jesse and turn to Danny with an apologetic look. There's no point denying it, I couldn't even hazard a guess to what he'd been saying. "I'm sorry, what was you saying?"

"I was telling you... I've not given up on us. I'm going to win you back." The truth in his words hit me. He means it.

Jesse's come to a stop behind me. I can feel his energy playing along my skin. I hear Kelly offering to buy him a drink. Jesse's voice as he replies sends goosebumps over my skin, and realise I need to put Danny straight because no matter what Danny does, he's not the man for me.

Someone hands me my drink and I take a large mouthful before opening my breaking the news. "Danny, I care about you. We were close friends at one time," He opens his mouth to speak but I held my hand up in a stop gesture. "Let me finish. Please..." he nods and I carry on.

"We haven't spoken for five years. A hell of a lot has changed in that time. I'm not the same girl you knew back then. Please don't waste your time on me," I plead before walking away and heading to the toilets before he can argue. No amount of arguing was going to change my mind. Danny blew his chance years ago.

Kate grabs me with a hand on my forearm, before I get two steps away and drags me towards the dance floor. "This is going to be hilarious," she states.

The DJ's voice flows through the speakers before I can question Kate. "Ladies and Gentlemen, we've got a special performance for you. One night only, Carter and Tim perform LMFAO's *Sexy and I Know It*." Kate had positioned us in the front row giving us a perfect view of the stage. The DJ sweeps his arm towards the far side of the stage where there's a curtain that must conceal a changing room. The music rings out and they stride out from behind the curtain. Thankfully, fully clothed. Hearing the song I'd imagined the worst. Within thirty seconds, I'm kicking myself for even having the thought as they both pull at their clothes effectively tearing them off to reveal metallic gold budgie smugglers.

I turn to Kate mortified. "We're gonna be scarred for life."

Kate pats me on the back in mock sympathy. During my mortification the crowd had erupted into laughter at their performance. They both have great bodies but they also know it, just like the song says. I'm sure I can't be the only person that finds it a turn off when someone loves themselves that much? The song finally ends and the bar fills with applause and wolf whistles.

I brush past Gareth and Danny as I head to the bar, and hear Danny grumbling under his breath. "Love themselves much?"

I squeeze into a space at the bar. After letting Danny down gently and seeing my ex wiggling *it* on stage, I'm feeling the need for a good strong drink.

"Hey Beautiful Lady, what can I get you?" Big Mac asks leaning across the counter so I could hear him over the noise. He's wearing the same MC vest, a black tee and jeans, I'm guessing he's not a man for colours. Being a big guy, as his name suggests, he's not really made to fit behind a bar. The girls serving must have to go under his legs if they need to get past him because there's barely an inch between the bar and his big burly body.

"Morgans on ice, you better make it large."

He scoops the ice into a glass and pours over the amber liquid. "Things can't be that bad, surely?"

I look at him, eyebrows raised in disbelief. "I don't have a job. I got stabbed, almost died and then changed into a werewolf, turning the world as I knew it upside down. My best friend was murdered by someone who was trying to kidnap me. Tracey smashed a bottle over my head trying to kill me. Four pack members tried to rape me." Giving me a pitying look he pours an extra shot of Rum over the ice. "Oh, and lets not forget the Ex who I haven't seen in almost five years, turning up on my door step expecting me to jump into bed with him. My life is just rosy."

He slides the glass to me and I hand him the cash before downing the glass and sliding it back towards him. He refills it without a word, waving away the cash I offer him. "On the house, Love."

I flash him a grateful smile. "Thanks, Big Mac."

"I might be able to help you on the job front. Unfortunately there's not much I can do about your other problems though." He reaches his hand over, placing it on top of mine on the bar. His wolf comforts mine at the small touch, it's as if someone's stroking the fur on the top of her head. "We all miss Joey," he adds his voice breaking on the name.

"Thanks. I forget you all knew him too," I admit before changing the subject, so the tears I can feel building won't have chance to fall. "What's the job?"

"How do you fancy a bit of part-time bar work? I can only offer you a couple of nights a week to start, but people are always coming and going I'm sure I'll be able to offer you more in a few weeks."

"Really? I could kiss you." As the words leave my mouth I pull myself up on the bar, just enough to reach his lips with a thank you peck. "Thank you," I say, letting myself drop back down.

Big Mac clears his throat before speaking. "Not a problem, Frankie."

Feeling eyes boring into me I turn to find Jesse standing where I'd left him with Nate and Kelly earlier. His eyebrow raised in question. I shake my head, no, knowing exactly what he's asking with that brow. *Big Mac?* His eyes shift over my shoulder just as a hand lands on it. The anger that crosses his face causes me to turn to see who he could be so angry with. I find myself face to face with Carter, thankfully clothed.

"Hi," he says, sounding unusually timid, his hands in his jeans pockets and his shoulders hunched. "I'm sorry about Saturday." He shakes his head in what looks like disbelief. "I swear I had no idea, you have to believe me."

Knowing it was true, I can't blame him for being played by Clarissa but I know my wolf will never want him. Not after he put sex before obeying an order of protection, that's a weakness she wants nothing to do with.

"Hey," I say with a genuine smile. "It happened. No amount of apologising can change that." It sounds blunt even to my own ears but it's the truth. "I think Jesse is angry. Has he punished you for disobeying his order yet?" I add, quickly feeling a little guilty about my bluntness.

He mock laughs. "*Ha!* You think? I can feel his energy whipping me from here. No punishment yet but I'm not foolish enough to think he'll forget. Jesse never forgets." Resignation shows with his half hearted shrug and I stroke his forearm to comfort him. He pulls his arm from under mine. "I disobeyed my Alpha and I deserve whatever punishment he may have in mind." He gives me a quick peck on the cheek before striding across the room to face Jesse's wrath.

I watch him go as the DJ's voice comes over the speaker. "Time to slow things down a bit for those of you with a lovely lady. If you don't have one, go and find one to drag on the dance floor for Adele's *'Someone like you'*."

Nate, who's standing next to Jesse catches my eye and flashes me a smile before walking over to me. He doesn't take his eyes off me as he works his way across the room, looking at me like I'm the only person that exists. Stopping before me he offers his hand, palm up. "Would you like to be my lovely lady for this song?"

"I'd be honoured." I answer, placing my hand in his. He leads me to an open spot on the dance floor before pulling me close. I rest my head against his chest and allow him to glide us gracefully around the dance floor.

I feel his lips brush a gentle kiss on my hairline before his breath blows against my cheek as he whispers in my ear. "I know you're going to pick Jesse." I pull back enough to be able to look up into his face, to see if he's serious. His defeated look tells me that he is. I open my mouth to deny it, but with a shake of his head and tugs me back into his arms so that I'm resting my head against his chest once again, and no longer able to see his face. "I've known all along, Frankie," he breathes the words into my ear. "You've got a connection with him, nobody else can compete with. Hell, he's been your best friend since you were seven years old. You've always loved him, just like he's always loved you."

He guides us to a lone stool at a high table, in the quiet corner near the front window of the bar. Sitting me on the stool and standing before me, he makes us the same height. "Do you know he has never shown any interest in anyone as long as I've known him? That was...until *you* released *your* wolf." He looks at me with sad eyes. "You'll be happy with Jesse and he'll take good care of you. I'm happy knowing that."

Listening to him spell it out like that I'm finally able to connect the dots. Causing my wolf to prance inside of me. Happy, that I'm on the same wavelength as her. Deep down she's known all along that Jesse's it for us. With tears in my eyes I reach up and cup Nate's face. "What about you?"

Nate brushes an escaped tear off my cheek. "My mate is out there somewhere and I'll find her... Someday." Placing a gentle kiss on my forehead he turns and walks away, towards Kelly.

I don't stop him leaving, because as much as I'm attracted to him, I know we could never be mates. My wolf just doesn't see him like that. Nothing would stop us dating and becoming lovers, but we would be hurting each other in the long run by keeping one another away from finding a mate. A wolf never quite feels complete, without their mate.

I watch him order a drink and join in Jesse and Kelly's conversation. If anyone can find their mate, the gorgeousness that is Nate, can. Whoever it may be, she will be one lucky gal.

My eyes linger on Jesse. I know he is the one. Jumping off my stool I decide it's time to show Him what I think of our stupid deal by giving him *the* kiss of his life. I'd barely taken two steps before Tim steps into my path.

"I think you owe me, a thank you," Tim says. A salacious grin crosses his face and he speaks again. "In fact, I think I deserve a thank you kiss, at least." He's right, I do owe him a thank you, but there's no way he'll be getting a kiss.

Leaning forward, I give him a platonic hug, making sure to turn my face away so he can't get his mouth anywhere near mine. I stiffen as I feel his lips brush against the pulse in my neck. He pulls me close with his hands on my lower back. Close enough to feel his erection between us, as his hands slide down my back and onto my arse. Shocked out of my stupor, I bring my knee up to crush into what lies at the base of his erection. Once my knee makes contact I push at his chest with all my might, effectively shoving him away from me. Stumbling backwards, I manage too stay upright as I put more distance between us.

I glare at him bent over double, cupping his groin in his hands.

"Don't. Ever. Touch. Me. Again!" I spit each word with as much command as I can muster. I walk around him giving him a wide birth, not daring to take my eyes off him and I collided straight in to a rock hard chest.

It's so well built that I rebound off it instantly and brace myself expecting to hit the deck, until strong hands grip my biceps and hold me steady on my feet. I look up at my saviour with a smile and open my mouth to say thank you for not letting me land on the floor. The words die on my lips as I catch sight of The anger on Danny's face. He doesn't even acknowledge me, his focus is on Tim.

"That fucking pervert," he shouts, pushing me aside to get to Tim.

Using my werewolf strength I grab his forearm and hold him in place. "Leave it Danny."

"I saw what he tried to do you, Frankie," he says not taking his eyes off Tim, who's still trying to get his breath back. A knee in the groin is good self defence, even against a werewolf. *I'll have to remember that, you never know when it might come in handy.*

I turn his face to with my free hand on his cheek, forcing his eyes away from Tim. "Then you'll have seen what I did to him in return."

"Have you got a problem? Are you jealous it wasn't *your* arse I was feeling?" Tim snarls having obviously gotten his breath back, and seemingly edging for a fight with Danny. My panic rises, hearing him closer behind me than he should be, causing me to spin around to face him. The last thing I want is an angry wolf at my back. I don't know Tim well enough to know how far he'll take this, but I've seen too many of Danny's fights to know it won't end good once it starts. I take a deep breath, swallowing down my fear before I make this situation worse.

"Is there a problem here? Tim? Frankie?"

Hearing Jesse's commanding tone allows me to sigh in relief. "No, it's sorted now isn't it guys?" They both grunt in agreement, causing me to think whatever this is, it isn't over. Not for a long shot. Jesse's appearance has bought us a reprise and I'll take it, Tim would never start anything with Jesse around. And if Tim behaves, I'll be able to handle Danny. I glance at him and realise the only way I can really calm him down is to get him out of here. Which means my plans for Jesse have to be postponed, no matter how much I want on talk to him. *Who am I kidding?* I don't want to talk to him. I want to kiss him senseless. I want to wrap myself around him, with nothing between us. Unfortunately I'll have to wait a little longer to give him no doubt about who I've chosen as my mate.

Gareth approaches Danny placing a gentle hand on his shoulder. "Hey Dan, You alright?" He knows how to read Danny's body language, as well as I do. Danny might look calm on the outside but he has tells, like the fingers twitching to make a fist at his side.

I answer before Danny has a chance to open his mouth. "I'm not really feeling up to partying. Do you two mind leaving early? We're staying at the apartment tonight and I need to show you where it is."

Dan and Gareth both nod in reply. "Yeah, sure thing, Frankie," Gareth says.

I glance at Jesse wistfully, not really wanting to leave him without letting him know my decision.

"We'll wait for you outside Frankie," Gareth states, no doubt having seen something on my face, as he grabs Danny by the arm and tugs him towards the door. *I love that guy!*

Forgetting about Tim, I step up to Jesse so were inches apart. My wolf sensing him, stretches inside me reading her energy towards him. Jesse strokes the back of his knuckles down my cheek, and with my wolf so close to the surface it feels as though he's running his hands through her fur. I grab his hand, holding it in place against my cheek, not wanting him to end the contact.

"Are you going to be ok with him?" Jesse nods his head in the direction Gareth and Danny had just left, not taking his eyes off mine. "Danny seems like a hot head. Are you and Gareth going to be able to handle him?" The concern in his voice causes my stomach to somersault, making me feel like a loved up teenager.

It brings a smile to my face. "I knocked him back, earlier. He's jealous of the other guys, I can't exactly explain pack touch to him."

He drops his hand from my cheek. "If you need me, you'll call." The command behind his words comes through loud and clear.

Deciding to set things between us straight before I leave, I gave him what I hope is a wicked smile and step up as close as I can before our bodies touch. I hold his eyes with mine to make sure I have his attention. The heat I see in them tells me that I do. Licking my lips I drop my eyes to rake over his lips. "I'll be round bright and early in the morning to collect on our deal."

His hand brushes through my hair and snakes around my nape possessively. "It's gone midnight. So technically you could collect now," he says through a growl.

I let my hands roam up his chest and around his neck, allowing a finger to stroke over his pulse as I contemplate his offer. "What I have planned will take a lot longer than the minute I've got, until Danny gets restless and all hell breaks lose."

His lips are suddenly on mine. I hadn't even seen him move. His tongue licking my lips, at my teeth. A ferocious kiss, a mass of tongue, lips and teeth. He pulls away leaving my lips feeling bruised and swollen from the fierceness. "Go... Quick. Before I change my mind and don't let you leave." He steps back releasing my body from his grasp.

The sudden distance makes me feel cold and lonely. "Jes—" I start, not liking this distance.

"*Go!*" The growled command cuts off my words.

I take note of the tension in his body and see the wolf in his eyes. Tony's joined us. His desire running over my skin and the scent of it filling my nostrils. My eye sight becomes stronger as my wolf comes forward, and I know its her eyes he'll see on my face.

The room falls quiet as other pack members turn in our direction, clearly feeling whatever is going on between the two of us. I realise my time is up, I need to leave. I start for the door, only making it a few steps before stopping and turning to look at Jesse once again. I don't want to leave with the pack smelling his desire and thinking I've turned him down. I can already see Tracey heading in his direction, no doubt ready to offer him comfort. She is not going to comforting him.

No woman is going to comfort him. My wolf growls at the thought. She wants to show everyone that he's ours and none of them can touch him. *Ever.* I want to agree with her, but she wants to take him here and now in full view of pack, making them all witnesses to our mating. Unable to agree with that I debate with her internally in the split second while I'm looking at Jesse. Deep down, we both know we can walk out the door right now and he would set *anyone* that offers themselves to him, straight. Still, we both can't ignore the need to do something.

I allow my body fill with desire, hoping its enough that everyone can sense it. "Tomorrow, Jesse... Tomorrow I'm going to have you, how I've wanted you from the very start and I can't promise I won't bite."

Jesse stares at me, staying frozen to the spot. The desperate look in his eyes and the tension I can see pulsing through his body, tells me how hard he's fighting to not come after me. A deep rumbling emanates from deep within his throat and I know I've pushed him too far. If I don't get out now my wolf might just get her wish of having him with an audience.

Turning, I leave the bar at a steady pace, forcing myself not to run. Running would cause his wolf to chase me. To hunt me. As I make it outside with no one following me I send up a silent prayer to whomever may be watching over me. Lately I've been thinking of Grams, but with Joey passing so recently and the pack connection between us, I can't help but feel that maybe it's him watching over me now.

"Frank, what's happened? You look..." Gareth starts, seeming to struggle to describe how I do look.

Danny steps forward, arms out, as though to catch me if I fall. "Uneasy," he suggests.

Gareth nods. "Yeah. Uneasy is close enough."

My heart's pounding in my chest but I swallow it down and start down the pavement that leads to my apartment, calling to them over my shoulder. "Nothing. I'm fine." My answer's too sharp and quick, we all know I'm lying.

<hr>

I unlock the door to my apartment, expecting to find the place a mess since the last time I was in here had been when I left Carter in bed to go to the cemetery. I haven't really had time to think about coming back to this place, not with everything that's happened since that day. It feels like a lifetime ago. Hell, it is a lifetime ago - I'm no longer the person I was back then. Being stabbed to death and turning into a werewolf will do that to you.

The door's barely open an inch before I'm hit with what feels like a sledgehammer to the chest. In reality it's Joey's scent. He must have been here sometime before he died. As I open the door wider I understand why. The room is immaculate, Joey had cleaned up after my night with Carter. Swallowing the lump in my throat I focus on trying to keep the padlock on my tear ducts. I force my feet to keep moving, by entering the room and leaving the door open for Gareth and Danny to follow me. I hear the door close behind us as my eyes fall on the note propped up against the coffee canister. I recognise the neat print that was Joey's, just as the padlock containing my tears unlocks. Grabbing the note, I hold it against my chest.

The need to be alone hits me and I glance around, being in an studio apartment with two guys makes finding that time a challenge. I head for the only place I can close myself away. The bathroom. "I'll be back in a minute. Make yourself at home" I say over my shoulder as I lock myself in the private space.

I sit with my back against the bathtub, hugging the note as if it's Joey himself, and I'm able to keep him safe from Rick causing his death. I initially tried to read the note, but seeing the words, *'Hey Frank'*, caused all the other words to blend together in a blurry blob, thanks to the tears that just don't seem to have an off switch.

A gentle knock on the door pulls me out of my trance, and the sudden ache in my arse as I shift on the floor leaves me wondering how much time has passed.

"Frank. It's me, can I come in?" Danny's voice whispers through the door.

Taking a deep breath I wipe at my tears and check my appearance in the mirror. I don't want to have to explain anything to Danny. I fold the note and slip it into my bra, before opening the door.

Chapter Twenty Nine

Nate

Watching Frankie leave the bar, I can't help but be glad that she has the sense not to run. Jesse's fighting his wolf's urge to chase the prey he desires as it is. If she was to run, someone would end up dead. It would either be Kelly and I, trying to stop Jesse from taking her right there in the bar, or it would be Frankie's Ex, Danny. After watching how he reacted to Tim and his grubbing hands, I'm certain that there's no way that Danny would just stand by and watch Jesse take Frankie in front of everyone. Having felt Danny's aggression when he was ready to launch at Tim, I can't leave her in his company for long. He may only be human but I'm sure he'd be able to do plenty of damage before she'd be willing to take him down. The need to protect Frankie is too strong, after two minutes of counting the seconds pass I take a step forward the dominant wolf in me, deciding we can't wait any longer before following them.

A hand taps my shoulder and I feel Jesse's energy running along my skin. "Nate, would you mind..." Jesse gestures towards the exit.

"I was just about to go anyway. I know you said he's human and Frankie could handle him, but I get an uneasy feeling about him," I admit, bowing my head in submission. I shouldn't be going against my Alpha's previous wishes.

Jesse ruffle his hair playfully. "I feel it too. I'd go myself, but I can't... not after that."

I meet my Alpha's eyes with a grin, knowing exactly why he can't follow them. "I'll stay out of sight. Unless he starts trouble."

Without waiting any longer, I follow Frankie's scent, Knowing she's had a big enough head start. Joey had shown me Frankie's apartment not long before he'd died, so as the first big drops of rain hit the floor I don't worry about losing her scent.

Standing outside Frankie's apartment door, I listen to her tell Gareth and Danny to make themselves at home. Her sorrow is screaming through the pack bonds. I know the cause is Joey, I can smell his scent too. My wolf is urging me to go inside, to comfort her. But I know that if I go in there now it would send Danny off the rails. The sound of a door closing and the guys talking to each other tells me she's most probably locked herself in the bathroom. I sit with my back against the wall next to the door and settle in for a long night. After about fifteen minutes, a repetitive snore fills the silence. One of the men must have fallen asleep.

A quiet hour passes before I hear a knock on wood and Danny speaking softly. I sit up straighter and focus all my attention on the room behind me, as a door opens and Frankie speaks. The need to hear what's happening in Frankie's apartment, forces me to allow my wolf to step forward and take over enough to increase my hearing. I stand and prepare myself to be ready to enter if I'm needed.

"I still love you, Frankie," Danny begs.

"Danny, we've had this conversation," Frankie says her voice sounds full of sadness.

"Frankie, give us a chance." Danny's pleading tone is gone and replaced with anger.

I hear footsteps, but can't tell if it's both of them or just one. "Danny, no. I haven't done anything to cause you to think there would be a chance. Lets just forget about this and go to sleep before we wake Gareth up. I'll take the floor."

"We won't wake Gareth, he'd sleep through an earthquake. If that's all that's stopping you..." There's a bang, like someone bumped into something following Danny's words..

Frankie makes a scared noise. "*Ah!* Danny, get your hands off me. We aren't doing this...EVER." Her voice turns from scared to angry by the end of the sentence. Tension runs through me as I listen and wait, knowing I can be in there in a split second if it sounds like she can't handle it herself.

"Danny!" I hear a fist contact flesh and hope it's Frankie throwing the punch.

"Bitch! You hit me. You've broken my nose." I almost laugh at how shocked Danny sounds. The slap of skin I hear followed by a female grunt of pain, sobers me instantly.

No one should lay a hand on Frankie. Unable to listen anymore, wolf and man both agree it's time for action. I barge the door with my shoulder and as expected it doesn't resist.

Chapter Thirty

Frankie

I look at Danny in shock as my cheek stings from his slap. The door bursts open and Nate's scent fills the room. His angry energy is tingling against my skin. Danny has me pinned to the wall, his hand up my skirt and his mouth on my neck, oblivious to the fact that someone had just broken down he door.

Nate tugs Danny off me. "Are you deaf? She said, *no,*" he yells in Danny's face.

Nate grunts and I instantly feel his pain through the pack bonds.

My mind scrambles trying to work out what's

happened. I see a knife sticking out of Nate's chest, right where his heart should be. I can't believe what I'm seeing. I scream. "*Nate!*"

Gareth appears out of nowhere and pulls at Danny, trying to get him off Nate. "Get off him, Danny." His voice jumps up an octave, and I can only assume he's seen the knife. "What the fuck have you done?"

Danny releases Nate and he drops to the floor, the hold Danny had on him being the only thing keeping him upright. Danny turns his attention on Gareth and saves him across the room. "You don't wanna fight me, Gareth. You won't win."

I drop to the floor next to Nate. My eyes roaming over him while I try to think of what I should do to help. The sound of a knife scraping out of the holder on my kitchen side catches my attention and I turn to see who has the knife. My eyes fall upon them as Danny lunges at Gareth and I watch in horror as the knife slides across Gareth's throat. He drops to the floor a hand clutched to the wound on his neck. This Danny isn't the Dan I once knew, he might kill someone in the ring by accident but he'd never kill someone cold blooded like this.

My wolf paces inside me. She wants out and she wants blood. Not Nate's or Gareth's, even though the room is filling with the scent of their blood. No. She wants Dan's. He doesn't deserve to live, not after we just watched him kill Nate and Gareth.

One second I'm me, crouching next to Nate, the next I'm shifting in mid air. I turn into a full wolf just as my teeth rip into Danny's throat. Shaking him as he's held in my jaw, rips him to shreds. I can't help but enjoy the feel of his warm blood pouring down my throat, and the meat of his flesh tearing between my teeth. The thought that this should be bothering me runs through my head for a second before the satisfaction of the kill takes its place. There's so much blood, it's pouring out of my mouth and pooling on Gareth, who is laid underneath the two of us. *Fresh meat.*

A howl from behind me pulls me out of my frenzy causing me to spin around, ready to attack and to protect my kill. "Please Frankie. You've killed him. We're all safe," Nate pleads between jagged breaths. *Nate!*

In an instant, I'm back to my human self and falling beside a barely breathing Nate. The knife still stuck in his chest. I reach for my pocket where my phone would be, if I had clothes on. Thinking about a phone makes me register ringing coming from Nate's jeans pocket. Seeing the bulge belonging to his phone, I reach my hand into his pocket, trying not to move him about too much. Managing to tug it out I answer, not bothering with a hello. "Nate has a knife stuck in his heart. He's losing a lot of blood and not healing." Panic rises inside me just saying the words. "Do I take it out or will he bleed more? It might be silver." I can hear the terror in my own voice. Nate's hand finds my free one squeezing it comfortingly. He's got a knife in his chest and he's trying to comfort me.

"How much is a lot? We don't usually die of blood loss, but silver slows the healing process or stops it altogether, that's why silver weapons can be deadly to us." Jesse's voice says through the phone. The growl behind his words tells me he's not as calm as he's trying to sound.

"I don't know, the room is full of blood." I glance around trying to work it out. "I can't tell how much is Nate's and how much is Dan's or Gareth's."

"Shit... What the fuck happened? If you took the knife out straight away, it would have had a better chance of healing, the longer silver stays in the worse he'll be. Why didn't you remove it straight away?" he snaps at me through the phone.

"I was fucking busy, eating Dan." I snap back halfheartedly, know he's right. I know the dangers of silver, I shouldn't have let it get to this.

Nate reaches up and grabs the knife in his weak hands. He lifts his hands but doesn't have the strength to move it at all.

"Take it out," Jesse says as I drop the phone to the floor, my hands already replacing Nate's on the hilt of the knife.

"I'm sorry," I say to Nate, pulling the knife free as quickly as I can. I grab the rags off the floor beside me, that look like they belonged to the dress I'd been wearing not long ago, and use them to compress the wound. Looking up at Nate's face, I find his eye's trained on mine. I will him to live. "Don't die on me, Nate. Please..." The tears streaming down my face. "You came to protect me. You idiot. Why did you have to do that?" I know yelling at him, and calling him names while he's dying isn't fair, but it I can't seem to stop myself. It stops me panicking.

He smiles with a wince. "I love you... didn't... want you...hurt."

Bending over him, I press my mouth against his in a passionate kiss. I feel him kiss me back for a fleeting moment before he goes limp beneath me. Knowing that he's died beneath my mouth, I pull him into my lap and hug him into my chest. I strokes his hair with my hand as I sob at the loss I feel. The loss of yet another pack member. And it was my fault, yet again.

Chapter Thirty One

Jesse

Feeling Nate cling on to life through the pack bonds, I know there's been trouble. Pulling out my phone I dial Nate's mobile. It rings out, going to voicemail after the allocated number of rings. "Dammit," I say to the phone as I instantly dial again. "Come on, pick up," I growl.

"Something's wrong with Nate." Kelly says right behind me.

I fumble with the phone dropping it to the floor, having not heard or felt him approach. I curse as it shatters. "*Fuck!*"

"Sorry." Kelly places his phone in my hand without

question and I dial once again.

Finally it's answered. "Nate has a knife stuck in his heart. He's losing a lot of blood and not healing." I'm momentarily shocked to hear Frankie's voice coming through the phone. The shake in her voice keeps my attention on her words. "Do I take it out or will he bleed more? It might be silver," she says, her terror coming clear down the line.

"How much is a lot? We don't usually die of blood loss, but silver slows the healing process or stops it altogether, that's why silver weapons can be deadly to us." I try to keep my voice calm, as not to panic her more. But try as I might, I can't keep the growl out of my voice.

"I don't know, the room is full of blood. I can't tell how much is Nate's and how much is Dan's or Gareth's." She speaks fast and it takes me a second to process the information she's given me. All eyes in the bar are on me, the pack having all felt Nate's pain through the bonds. I point to Big Mac and Carter, gesturing for them to join both myself and Kelly.

"Shit... What the fuck happened? If you took the knife out straight away, it would have had a better chance of healing, the longer silver stays in the worse he'll be. Why didn't you remove it straight away?" I snaps hating myself for it the second it comes out of my mouth. She doesn't deserve my anger. I leave the bar and head for Frankie's apartment, knowing without a word, the three men will follow.

"I was fucking busy, eating Dan." There's a growl behind her words but no conviction behind it. She thinks she deserves my anger.

I hear a clang and can only assume she's dropped the phone to the floor. "Take it out," I say, before disconnecting the call. I shove the phone in my pocket and taking the moment to hope we get there in time. In time for what? I didn't know, things feel bad through the bond. Nate is barely hanging on to life.

We run through the streets at full speed, praying that no one is looking out their windows at this late hour. I push the door to Frankie's apartment building open and my body stiffens as Nate's torn from the pack bonds in his death. A howl escapes from my throat without thought, I hear the rustle of clothes and the thud of flesh hitting concrete, as the three men behind me drop to their knees and release their own howls of loss.

Leading the way up the stairs, I take them three at a time and burst through the door leading into the hall. I keep the momentum going, aiming to break down Frankie's apartment door. Seeing the open door hanging on by one hinge, I manage to stop myself before flying through the open doorway. My bulk effectively blocking the door like a brick wall, causing the guys behind to collide into me. We'll all be hurting over the collision, once the adrenalin leaves us.

My eyes immediately search for Frankie, falling on her within seconds. She's rocking with Nate in her lap, sobbing with grief as she strokes his hair. My heart breaks into pieces at the sight. Frankie's pain coming through the bond, tells me she chose Nate. Regardless of what had happened between the two of us at Big Mac's earlier, she had chosen Nate as her mate. Nate may be dead, but Frankie won't find another mate. I know her well enough to know she'll never allow anyone to take his place in her heart, even if her wolf would allow it. An Alpha needs a mate and she'll never accept him now. Our chance together has died tonight.

Knowing there is nothing I can do to help Nate, I step towards Frankie in hopes to comfort her. Her deep threatening growl causes me to stop in my tracks.

Ever so slowly she lifts her head, glaring a warning at me through her wolf's ice blue eyes. The slow movement tells me how close her wolf is to the surface, even without seeing her eyes.

Holding up my hands in the air I try to show her I'm no threat. "Frankie it's me, your Alpha." I say in a hushed tone. "We're here to help. I'm going to send Big Mac in to help your friend Gareth, his heart is still beating.. Just."

"*Shit!*" Carter growls, on entering the room. His hunger obvious with the lick of his lips and his eyes trained on the blood that's calling to his wolf.

Placing Nate's body on the floor, Frankie crouches

before it in a protective stance. Clearly having picked up on Carter's hunger and therefore making him a threat.

"Carter, if you can't get a handle on your wolf, get out of here," I say without taking my eyes off Frankie. She looks ready to kill us all, or at least try to. "Go find Kate, she's going to need pack," I add, hoping to keep both Frankie, and Carter satisfied. Carter backs out of the room leaving the path clear for the other guys two enter.

Big Mac slowly walks over to Gareth giving Frankie a wide berth, her body turning to follow his every movement. He reaches down to staunch the wound and she turns her attention back the door, obviously satisfied with his actions.

I feel Kelly come to a stop behind me, his energy pulsating against my skin. "Oh, Nate," he cries, dropping to his knees on the floor. Frankie's eyes leave mine and fall upon Kelly, suddenly changing back to her own beautiful chocolate brown eyes. Making a feeling for Kelly, she brushes my forearm with her hand comfortingly as she passes. I turn and watch her crouch beside Kelly, taking her into his arms in a warm embrace. The last thing he needed was to lose his best friend - brother, so soon after losing his mate, Gabby. There have been to may deaths in our pack lately - Gabby, Joey and now Nate. Three deaths too many.

Leaving Kelly and Frankie safe in each others arms, I make my way over to Nate and crouch down beside him.

"Rest in peace, my friend," I whisper, reaching out and close the mismatched eyes of my Beta.

I straighten up after a moments prayer, deciding the best thing for me to do is to check on Big Mac and Gareth. Spotting a folded up piece of paper poking out from under a rag, that could have been the dress Frankie was wearing earlier, I pick it up and recognise Joey's familiar hand, from when he did some paperwork for my business. Seeing it addressed to Frankie, I use a piece of rag to wipe off the blood, before putting it in my shirts breast pocket.

"How's he doing, Mac?" I ask looking down on Big Mac and Gareth.

"Not good, Boss. He's still got a heartbeat - be it faint, but he's lost a lot of blood. I've surprised he's hung on this long. He's human and needs an ambulance before he bleeds out." Big Mac takes a second to tear his eyes away from his patient to give me a questioning look. *Do we call any one?*

Werewolves aren't out in the open. We like to clean up their own messes, if only to keep a lid on our secrets. If we call an ambulance, the police will need to be informed since there's a dead body. Frankie could end up in trouble, considering she's eaten any evidence of the actual murderer, not to mention the fact that she's walking away uninjured and covered in both the victims blood. It really doesn't look good for her. If we don't call Gareth will die, and Frankie, like Kelly has lost too many people in recent times. She can't lose Gareth too.

"Call an ambulance. Keep the wound staunched while we wait. I'll get rid of any Danny leftovers. Perhaps we can figure a story out - where we arrived just in time to see him flee?" I inform Big Mac as I rake through Frankie's cupboards looking for garbage bags.

There's hardly enough of Danny left for the chunks of flesh and bone to even fill a half the bag. Unfortunately I can't collect Danny's blood, since it's mingled in with Gareth's. My wolf's nose can smell the subtle difference between their scents but the police won't know the difference. Blood looks like blood As long as they don't do any lab tests, everything should be fine.

Tying the bag off, I glance around the room having one last check for any left over evidence of Danny. I catch sight of Frankie and Kelly, now sat comforting each other on the opened out sofa bed. Apart from the grief that's pouring off the both of them, they seem to be okay, at least enough to be left to comfort each other a little longer. I need to get this bag out of the apartment before the police arrive. With one last glance around the room I run, full werewolf speed, out of the apartment and down the stairs not coming to a stop until I'm behind a neighbouring apartment building. I lift the lid off a large dumpster and throw the bag inside. I take note of the building number so I can send another pack member to collect it when the police leave the area, not that they'll need the building number, their noses with lead them to it.

I step through the doorway of Frankie's apartment as the sound of sirens come to a stop outside the building. I push the broken door to, closing it as much at the one hinge will allow, before rushing over to the sofa. I kneel before Frankie. "Frankie, the police will be here any minute, we need to figure out what to tell them." I watch as she keeps mumbling incoherent words to Kelly, not even acknowledging that I'm kneeling before her. Taking in her shock I deduce that the police have no chance of getting anything out of her tonight. Standing up I gently pat her on the shoulder, the bare flesh under my fingers making me realise that she needs covering up before anyone enters the room. Removing my jacket, I place it over her shoulders. "Put this on sweetheart."

Her head snaps up to look at me, finally appearing out of that foggy shock. "Jesse. I ate him," she says, her voice full of disbelief. She moves away from Kelly to stand, and blindly places her arms into the sleeves of my jacket. As she fumbles with the buttons I take over, my calm hands fastening each button one by one.

Upon hearing the door to the stairs opening I know time is running out. I reach out and stroke her cheek with my knuckles. "Don't say that to the police. Just leave the talking to me. Okay?" I plead, hoping she's taking in my words. I catch sight of Frankie's head nodding as the first police officer pushes through the broken door.

Frankie sits down and pulls Kelly back into his arms. During mine and Frankie's interaction, he'd been sat with his head in his hands repeating the same three words. "No. Not Nate."

The medics enter, taking in the scene they immediately see where they are needed and head straight for Gareth without giving Nate a second glance. Catching the officer in charge's attention I pull him aside and explain what happened, or at least, what I want them to think happened. Seemingly satisfied with my detailed description of the suspect, he walks over to Big Mac with his notepad to get his details on the situation.

Chapter Thirty Two

Frankie

I ate Danny. Dan. My friend. Just the thought is making me feel nauseous.

On the night of the full moon, I ate my first rabbit, which was hard to get over once I'd turned to my human form and remember the moment it such clear detail. Somehow, I don't think I'll ever get over this. I ate my friend, bones and all. I keep telling myself, I'd watched him stab a friend in the heart and slit another's throat, but it isn't really helping... I still ate him. My wolf's content with how it turned out, happy for the meal she received and the punishment she had given.

I listen to Jesse tell his side of the story and watch as the paramedics take Gareth from the room on a stretcher. Once he's finished with Jesse the police officer moves over to Big Mac, Jesse hovers, watching over him and answering any extra questions the officer throws his way.

I look down at the sheet corner turned up on the sofa bed and try to straighten it under myself. Gareth had been snoring here only a short while ago. Kelly's repetitive whisper pulls my attention from the rumpled sheet and back to him, I continue patting his back, comfortingly. "No. Not Nate." He's been repeating the same three words since seeing Nate on the floor, he's obviously in shock. Losing three pack members, that he had a close relationship with, in such a short time is not going to be good for him. He was only just coming to terms with the loss of his mate, Gabby, and now his best friend has gone too.

My eyes flick to the door as I hear a kerfuffle outside. "It's okay, she's his twin sister." Jesse says to the officer by the door as he points to Nate's lifeless body on the floor, having recognised Kate before I did. Her overwhelming sorrow is pushing down on my making it hard to breathe.

"I'm sorry, Sir, but it's a crime scene we can't let anyone else in," the police officer apologises sounding genuine.

"I need to see him," she pleads with the officer, who was being pushed further and further in the room by her wolfs strength.

"Miss it's a crime scene, you can't go in," he says in his Irish agent getting stronger, as he tries to get her back firmly back into the hall.

"Sergeant, she's mighty strong."

"Are you finished with me for now, Sergeant?" Jesse asks not taking his eyes off Kate and the struggling police officer.

The sergeant looks over his shoulder at the door, and goes a short sharp nod of assent to Jesse, obviously realising his officer wasn't winning with Kate.

"Jesse, I need to see him. I can feel it... but I need to see him to believe it," Kate shouts over the officer's shoulder without slowing down her fight.

Jesse reaches the door and shoving the officer aside he pulls Kate into his arms. "It's true, Darling." My heart breaks as she sinks into his embrace without a fight, knowing Jesse wouldn't lie about something like that.

"I need to see," she whispers. I doubt the humans in the apartment would have heard her words, but I had no trouble with my wolf hearing and by the look of Big Mac's slumped shoulders and sad eyes, I wasn't the only one.

I turn my eyes back to Jesse, he's stroking his hand in large circles on Kate's back. "Maybe they'll let you see him before they take him away. Okay?" Jesse offer turning to look at the police officer he'd shoved out the way.

He nod's. "Yes, that shouldn't be a problem."

Kelly lifts his head out of his hands, pulling away from me and looks towards the door. "Kate?" he questions liking his eyes back to me for an answer.

I nod. "Kate's outside. She can't come in, it's a crime scene." We both glance across at Nate's body which now has a blanket covering it. It doesn't matter, I can still see the sight without the blanket in my mind. Looking at Kelly's frown, he probably can too. He stands, his knees cracking in protest and walks to the door.

The officer blocks his exit. "I'm sorry, Sir, but we need to get a statement from you before you leave."

Even though I can only see the back of Kelly, I can tell by the stiffness in his shoulders and the terrified look on the police officers face, that he's giving him a death stare. If the guy doesn't submit soon Kelly will lose his control. His emotions are already pushed to the limits, his wolf will be happy to take advantage.

"It's fine, Constable Jackson. Let him go. He came in with these two and won't be able to tell us anything more. We can take a formal statement in the next couple of days," the sergeant states, no doubt having picked up on the tension. Kelly's low growl was a telling sign.

"Y..yes, Sergeant." The constable's voice cracked as he spoke. He steps aside allowing Kelly to pass. His shoulders dropped in what looks like relief, probably being happy not to be the to toe with Kelly anymore.

Jesse allows Kelly to take Kate into his embrace,

before he walks back into the room with no complaints from Constable Jackson. He crouches in front of me and places a handoff my knee, giving it a gentle squeeze. "How are you feeling?"

I place my hand on top of his, needing to feel closer to him. "Okay... I think?"

"Do you feel up to telling the sergeant what Dan did before he ran out, and we came in?" he asks with a raised brow in question. Something in his determined stare gives me the feeling his real question isn't the one he asked out loud. I nod, remembering his comment earlier. I won't say anything about eating Dan.

Waving the sergeant over, Jesse takes a seat next to me on the sofa bed, placing his hand back on my knee. I take his hand in mine, the comfort of his touch holding me here in the present and giving me the strength to relive tonight's horrific events.

The sergeant stops beside the sofa bed, placing a chair from my dining table in front of us, before sitting on it with his notepad poised. "Miss Rossi, I'd like you to tell me exactly what happened tonight?"

I take a deep breath trying to think where to start. Jesse's hand gives mine a gentle squeeze reminding me I'm not alone in this. "I came out of the bathroom and Danny tried to... he wanted us to get back together as a couple. We dated about five years ago and haven't seen each other since. Don't know why he thought we could just get back together…” I pause, taking a moment to think how I managed to get off track. He doesn't need to know all this. He needs to know what happened tonight. “I told him, 'no', but he wouldn't listen. I told him we should go to sleep before we woke Gareth up—”

“Where was Gareth during this exchange?” he asks cutting me off.

“Here,” I say pointing to the bed beneath me. “He was asleep, pretty deeply going by his snoring. Danny thought I said no because we'd wake him. He came onto me stronger telling me Gareth would sleep through anything.” I pull at a strand of cotton on the hem of Jesse's jacket, nervously. Jesse puts his arm over my shoulder and tucks me into his side. “I punched him. When he realised I'd broken his nose he slapped me and that's when Nate came in.” I point to the broke front door.

“What happened then, did Danny let you go?” the sergeant asks. His pen scribbling away on his notepad. I momentarily wonder if his hands aching, mine would be if I'd been writing that much.

I shake my head. “No. He had me pinned to the wall. Nate pulled him off me and he was yelling at him… and… then I felt—“ Jesse's hand squeezes mine painfully cutting off my words. It only takes me a second to realise what I almost said. I can't tell the police about the pack bonds. I clear my throat, hoping to cover my mishap. “I heard Nate grunt in pain and saw the knife in his chest… I screamed and Gareth appeared pulling Danny off Nate. Nate dropped to the floor." I wipe at the tears running down my cheeks and turn to sob into Jesse's shoulder.

"You're doing really good, Miss Rossi. Do you think you could carry on with the story?" the sergeant asks. I breath in Jesse's scent and lift my head and offer the sergeant a small nod. I can do this. I need to do this. "Would you like a glass of water?"

I clear my throat, surprised to realise it does feel suddenly parched. "Yes, please."

The sergeant gets up, after filling a cup with tap water he comes back and hands it over to me.

I smile my thanks, taking the cup and sipping a mouthful. I place the cup on the floor beside my foot and take Jesse's hand in both of mine on my lap. "Okay... Nate fell to the floor and I dropped down beside him to help. I heard a knife being pulled from my knife block and as I turned to see who had it, I saw Danny slashed Gareth's throat before running out of the room."

"Okay, then what happened?" I frown at the sergeant, unsure what he means. Danny ran off, surely that's all he needs? "How did Jesse and the other guys know to come here?" he clarifies most probably catching on to my confusion.

"Oh... I reached for my phone so I could call Jesse, I didn't know what to do? Whether I should remove the knife or not? but I couldn't find it." I mutter, trying not to get myself confused. I don't want to say anything I shouldn't.

"I was a Medic in the army..." Jesse says, his tone so commanding that no one would question what he said, even if he'd said the sky was green.

The sergeant flicks through his notepad and frowns. "You say you didn't have your phone, where was it?"

I glance across the room and see it in a puddle of blood, not far from Nate. I think quickly and spin him my story. "I didn't say I didn't have it. I said I reached for it, to call Jesse... But I dropped it." I point to it in the puddle of blood. "Nate's phone rang in his pocket and Jesse was on the other end when I answered." I frown at Jesse unsure whether I've said something wrong. How would he know to ring, without telling the police he'd felt it through the bonds.

"I explained this earlier." Jesse's voice made it clear he doesn't like to repeat himself. "Nate had followed Frankie home because Danny seemed angry about something before they'd left. None of us know Danny very well but from things Frankie has told us about their past, she made it clear that he has an anger management problem. We were concerned for her safety. And rightly so as it turns out."

"Yes. Right." The sergeant doesn't seem to know how to get back on track and into Jesse's good graces. "So, Jesse called Nate to see how Danny had reacted to his arrival…" He lets his sentence trail off and gives me an expectant look.

"Oh. You want me to carry on." It's not a question but the sergeant does regardless. "I answered the phone and asked Jesse what to do… Nate tried to pull the knife out but didn't have the strength to move it much. I dropped the phone and pulled it out. Nate died in my arms…" The fall once again, but I won't let them stop me from finishing. "Jesse came in not long after."

Jesse gives my shoulder a squeeze and I take the comfort it offers.

After flicking through his notes once again, the sergeant looks up at me with his pen poised. "Ms Rossi, could you go through it one more time for me, please?" I look at him blankly, unable to comprehend what he's saying, knowing that I've told him everything.

"I'm sorry Sergeant, but you can see Ms Rossi is exhausted. I don't think she can give you anything more tonight." Jesse's tone sounding sure, making it clear he shouldn't be argued with.

The sergeant looks me over and closes his notebook. "I'm so sorry. Of course, we can go over this tomorrow. Perhaps Ms Rossi might remember more after a good night sleep."

"I hope not," I whisper, remembering what it felt like to have Dan's flesh tear between my teeth. The detective gives me a worried glance.

"She watched her friend, kill her boyfriend. I don't think she really wants to remember that any clearer than she already does," Jesse clarifies, halting whatever question the sergeant was going to ask.

Shaking his head, he opens his mouth to speak again. "Ms Rossi, you aren't going to be able to stay here for a few days. Do you have somewhere else you can stay, perhaps with a friend?"

"Erm..."

"She'll stay with me. You have my address." Both Jesse and I speak together.

Chapter Thirty Three

Frankie

Walking out into the fresh air I'm surprised how potent the blood in my apartment must have been. For a fleeting moment I even don't blame Carter for being so effected by the blood lust earlier, until I remember it was Nate's blood he was getting all hungry over. He shouldn't have been getting worked up over a pack mates blood. I shake the stupid thoughts from my head and look up to the vehicle Jesse is leading us to. Nate's Dual-cab Ute. Carter must have brought Kate here in Nate's ute. The sight of it makes me look for Nate, my breath hitches as I come to the realisation that I'll never see Nate again. Kelly stops in his tracks seeing the vehicle too. Kate slides her hand into his and leads him to the ute.

Big Mac stops on the pavement. "I'm going to walk back to the bar. Let the fresh air clear my head." He pulls Kate into a hug. "If you need *anything,* give me a call. Okay?"

She nods, stepping back and wiping away her tears. Kelly pulls her into his side and guides her into the front bench of the ute. She slides into the middle beside Carter who's behind the wheel. Leaving room for Kelly on her other side. Jesse opens the back door, gesturing for me to slide in. I watch as he slides into the seat next to me and places his hand on Kate's shoulder. She relaxes instantly, clearly feeling comfort from his touch.

Seeing one of Nate's knitted sweaters on the seat beside me, I pick it up, holding it to my nose and breathing in his scent. The solace it offers is too tempting to give it up. Placing it on the seat beside me, I try to lie down. I shuffle about trying to make the position comfy. Jesse pulls the sweater away from me, causing panic to race through me. I need that sweater, at least just for tonight.

"Here," he says placing the sweater on his lap, offering himself as a pillow. Tucking my legs up on the empty seat beside me I curl up with my head in Jesse's lap and fall into a heavy sleep.

Waking up on a bed full of people would normally

scare me to death, but the feel of Jessie's energy touching every inch of me was keeping me calm while I grasp where I am and why. I know without a doubt, the bare male chest that I'm currently using as a pillow belongs to Jesse, his scent and energy are a dead giveaway. From his deep, even breathing I deduce he's asleep. I slowly shift in the bed,and realise I'm wearing a baggy t-shirt and some shorts of some kind over my underwear. Someone must have dressed me, because I sure as hell don't remember putting these clothes on, plus, I'd never wear a bra to bed. They arrest the comfiest of things. I turn over trying not to disturb the sleeping bodies, wanting to see who it is I can feel against my back. It's Kate, spooning Kelly. Feeling a weight shift against my feet I look down the bed to see Carter sleeping lengthways across our feet, since I'm short he isn't actually only feet but he's using Kelly's ankles as a pillow.

Jesse shifts behind me cuddling into my back, his arm pulling my body towards him. I think back to last night, trying to remember how I ended up here, and in a puppy pile at that. It doesn't take long for the memories to flood back - Danny attacking Nate and Gareth, me tearing into Danny's neck, Nate dying. I'm suddenly wishing I could forget again. Considering I'm sharing a bed with four other people, I'm not weirded out like I'd expect. After all we're Pack, our wolves are comforting each other over the loss of our pack brother, Nate. It just feels right.

Jesse's breathing changes behind me and I know he must be awake. His body stiffens as he fills with tension. "Hey," he whispers against my ear, his voice gruff with sleep.

"Hi." Is all I manage to squeak out in reply. I'd been fine waking up on his chest, why do I have to panic now that he's awake. Letting go of me, he rolls on to his back. Most probably trying to give me distance. Not liking this new found distance between us, I turn over and snuggle close. He lifts his arm, offering me his chest. Taking his offer I place my head over his heart and drift off to its steady rhythm.

I wake out of a deep sleep that leaves me feeling like a lot of time may have passed. The fact that the bed feels much emptier makes me think I'm most probably right. Listening to the room I hear the steady breathing of a large male and a strong beating heart, a telling sign that someone else is with me. I can't feel their energy due to the fact that we aren't touching and the room is full of all our scents, so I can't tell who it may be. Feeling like I may be able to finally force my eyes open, I turn on the bed to face my bedmate. The door bursts open, I instinctively jump up and out of the bed.

Kelly, who was the other person in the bed, is now in a fighter's stance on the other side of the bed. "What is it?" he asks sleepily. The tension in his muscles tells me he'd have no trouble waking up if a fight was needed.

"Sorry, the door made me jump," I say as Jesse's face emerges from behind it.

"The police are here. Carter is giving them his statement first. I told them they aren't talking to you until you've eaten," Jesse says giving me a warm smile.

Hearing that one word *'eaten'* makes my stomach churn. The last thing I ate was Dan.I dive into what I hope is the bathroom. By some miracle my head is over the toilet just in time to empty my stomach of whatever may be left of Dan. Gentle hands pull my hair back out of my face until I'm finished. "I'm sorry," I say as I take the wet flannel Jesse is offering me, and use it to freshen up my face.

"There is nothing to be sorry for." Jesse gives me a stern look. "You did what had to be done." Jesse always has an uncanny way of knowing exactly what I'm thinking. I don't think he can read minds but it sure feels like it sometimes.

Standing up I glance in the mirror over the sink and it shocks me to see I'm still covered in blood. How could anyone sleep next to me like this. Raising my hand I touch a dry patch on my cheek and watch as it flakes of into the sink. I watch through the mirror as Jesse sets the shower going and pulls a towel off a shelf, before hanging it on a hook on the back of the door.

"I'll leave a shirt and some sweats on the bed for you. The police can wait. Come down when you're ready." He brushes my forearm with his palm in passing.

"Thanks, Jesse. You don't have a spare toothbrush, do you?" I ask, really wanting to get the taste of vomit out of my mouth.

He laugh, reaching into the cabinet under the sink. "An alpha's home is always full of spare things. There's always someone dropping by and crashing for a night or two." He places a new brush, still in the packet, on the counter before walking out and closing the door behind himself.

<hr>

It doesn't take me long in the shower. The longer I stood with the hot water being down on me, the more flashes of last night I saw running through my mind. I know I'll have to live through it all again with the police, deciding its best to get it over with I wrap a towel around myself and brush my teeth before opening the door to the bedroom. Stepping into the now empty room, I spot the sweats and t-shirt on the bed as Jesse promised. Sitting on top of the clothes sits some female undies and a plain white t-shirt bra, picking it up I search for the size tag, surprise surges through me to see that it's my size. I spend a moment wondering how he's know my size before dismissing it for a lucky guess. I pull the price tag off the underwear. Jesse obviously has more than just new toothbrushes handy. Tugging the clothes on I smile as I notice the t-shirt is the only thing that isn't a women's size or brand new. I can tell by the scent that it's Jesse's. The fact that he's wrapping me in his scent pleases me more than I'd like to admit. I've never been a girl wanting to be owned by a man but my wolf is more than happy. *He's protecting us with his scent.*

As I'm walking down the stairs the front door opens and Nate walks in. My heart jumps into my throat. I blink unable to believe my eyes. "Nate?" The whisper escapes my mouth before I have time to think. It can't be Nate, No matter how much I want it tone him. He died beneath my lips.

"Dave," he says, with a shake of his head. The sound of his voice clarifies this. It isn't Nate's voice. Even knowing this I can't tear my eyes away from him. I take in his features and realise his face looks slightly rounder than Nate's.

I drop my eyes to the floor, fighting the disappointment washing over me. "I'm sorry, it's just...you look like his double."

"Well I guess I am... was," he corrects himself with a frown. "We are... were identical twins. Kate was a bonus baby." My heart breaks listening to him struggle with referring to Nate in past tense.

"You're triplets?" I ask, my voice rising in surprise. Neither Kate or Nate had mentioned there was another one of them.

He looks me up and down. "I'm guessing you're

Maria and Rossi's daughter? You have such a strong resemblance to Maria. I can certainly see why Nate threw himself into danger for you."

My jaw almost hits the floor as my eyebrows rise high on my forehead. "You knew my parent's?" Nate had never mentioned my parent's. I'd assumed they'd died before his family had joined the pack.

"We grew up in the pack. We all knew your parents, they were the Alpha couple. He had a the biggest crush on your mother. Some would say he loved her. He only got a broken heart in return though." He takes a sharp intake of breath and nods towards the shirt I'm wearing. "I guess that runs in the family. Only there is no life after you broke his heart," he says with a snarl before walking towards the kitchen.

I drop to the stairs with the weight of his venomous words. Memories of Nate flashing through my mind. Why didn't he tell me, he loved my mother? Was it my mother he was talking to, when he said those last words, *'I love you'*, was it all a lie?

Chapter Thirty Four

Jesse

Telling the sergeant he'll have to wait a little longer for Frankie, one last time. I decide it's time I chase her down. I thought I'd be able to make him wait until Frankie had eaten but he's getting restless. He wants statements and he wants them now.

As I make my way through the kitchen Dave walks in from the hall, He looks so much like Nate that it takes me a second to realise that it's not him. They're identical, when they are together there's subtle differences a freckle here and a freckle there, or Nate's face was slighter longer than Dave's rounder one.

"Dave," I say pulling him into a quick embrace before releasing him again. Dave holds onto me a few seconds longer than I'd expected. He's has never been as touchy feely as Nate. "How are you doing?"

He releases me and leans against the kitchen worktop. "Honestly? I can't really believe it. It's..." He leaves his sentence hanging, clearly unable to put his feelings into words. "Where's Kate?"

"She's in the garden. There's a couple of wild one's looking out for her," I state referring to the wild wolves that belong to a pack that resides in the bush surrounding the pack house. They have been an extension to or pack since it began. With a nod he walks away, taking a deep breath as he goes to prepare himself to console his equally grieving twin sister.

Getting back to my task I find Frankie sitting on the stairs with her head in hands. Sitting beside her I place my hand on her back and rub circles on it, like I would her fur if she was in wolf form. I imagine the feel of her fur between my fingers. I've never actually done that to her wolf. Although she's done it to me many times, thinking about it now, I can feel her fingers running through my fur during the times I've visited her as the stray wolf, *Tony*, she'd called me. I miss those days. I miss sitting with her all carefree. Life is so much easer as a wolf. I'd find her sad, so I'd lick her cheek to make her giggle and I'd always feel her sadness drift away. Things are much more complicated as a human. The question that keeps running through my mind is a troubling thought. *Did she chose Nate in the end, regardless of what she'd said in the bar?* Her pain on the night felt like she had but part of me hopes I had it wrong. If she had chosen Nate, things are going to be so hard for her now, twice as hard since Dave is such a visual reminder of what she's lost. If she is still standing by those feelings she'd announced in the bar, I could move our relationship on and give her comfort for the loss of a pack mate. But if she had a change of heart, and Nate is the one, making those moves would just cause us both more stress and pain.

My wolf nudges at me, wanting to come out and play. Unfortunately it's not possible at the moment with the police in the house. There's no way I can just turn wolf. *Or could I?*

"Jesse, why didn't he tell me?" Frankie asks, her voice sounding muffled from behind her hands.

"Tell you what, Darling? Did you not know about Dave?" I ask, knowing that she will have just seen Dave walk by and the sight of him must be what has upset her.

"No, I didn't. But not that, about my mother. That he knew her. That he... loved her."

"Oh, Sweetheart. Nate grew up in the pack and yes he loved your mother, but you have to understand, she was the Alpha's Mate, every male pack member loved her."

Her head snaps up and looks at me with demanding

eye's. "Did you love her? Is that why you like me? Because I remind you of my mother? Is that why Nate said he loved me?" she asks, her voice a mixture of hurt and anger.

I brush a loose strand of hair out of her face and tuck it behind her ear, so I have a clear view of her. "No Frankie, I love you for you. Maria has nothing to do with it. I promise you that's true for both myself and Nate. Nate had a teenage crush on Maria, before that changed to the love of a pack mate. Just the same love we all have for each other." I kiss her temple. "He chose you as a mate, that has to show you he loves you," I add in a soft tone, not wanting her memories tainted with a question for the rest of her life. A werewolf can live a long life.

She frowns. "He didn't chose me," she states, leaning back slightly to look at me clearer. "He told me I was meant for someone else. To be honest I knew it all along too. When I asked him 'What about you?' He told me his mate is out there somewhere and he'll find her one day. Only now, he never will."

I reach out with my thumb and wipe away a lone tear as it runs down her cheek. "Her path has changed, she'll find another mate now," I say, guessing what has upsets her about that thought.

Chapter Thirty Five

Frankie

Listening to Jesse clear up all my stray thoughts, solidifies my feelings on our relationship. He's the one. My mate. He knows me well enough to know what I'm thinking without me having to spell it out. Nobody else would of known I was crying for Nate's unknown mate, but Jesse did.

With that knowledge I lean into him and place my lips on his in a gentle kiss. After a moments hesitation he kisses me back. Not fiercely or full of passion like in our previous kisses, but soft, gentle and full of love. As I pull back I see a flash of Tony in his eyes and I'm not surprised as he gives my cheek a long sloppy lap with his tongue, before pulling away laughing.

Hearing his laugh makes me feel euphoric causing me to play along. "Eww," I say wiping at my cheek over dramatically.

"Excuse me, Mr O'Keefe. Ms Rossi. We need to take your statements now." An young constable stutters nervously, as he stands in the pool room entrance.

The happy moment between us is gone and the weight on my shoulders is once again heavy. Jesse stands, looking down at me he offers me his hand. I may not need the help up but I take his hand regardless, feeling his energy crawl along my skin makes me feel safe and solid.

The constable leads us through the pool room, past the table and stops beside the bar and Jesse's closed office door. "Sergeant Sanchez is waiting for you in there, Ms Rossi," he says turning to me. "Mr O'Keefe will be right here giving me his statement," he adds, pointing to the stools at the bar. I don't know if he picked up on the panic rolling over me but I know Jesse did. He gives me hand a gentle squeeze, giving me the strength to push down the panic, let go of his hand and enter the room. I have to go over the events of one the worst days of my life one more time, and then I can move on.

It turns out Sergeant Sanchez is the same sergeant with the pot belly, from last night. I don't recall hearing his name last night, maybe he never told me it. Perhaps I was in too much shock to take note of it. "Good afternoon, Ms Rossi." His words make me look at the clock on the wall. *Two in the afternoon.* We must have slept for a long time in that puppy pile. "Please take a seat," he suggests pointing to the sofa against he wall as he sits behind Jesse's desk. "Let's get started. In your own words, could you please go over last nights events for me."

Taking a deep breath I tell him what he wants to hear. It doesn't take me long to get through the evenings events. Not the first time anyway. The third and fourth time seem to take me longer. I start to question myself, wondering whether I'm telling him the right things, trying to make sure I'm not slipping up and telling him something I shouldn't. Like the fact that I became a wolf, and ate his suspect.

Finally he states the wonderful words I've been waiting for since I finished the first time around. "Thank you, Ms Rossi. You're free to go... For now."

Dashing out of the room, I close the heavy door behind me and sigh in relief as I slump against the closest barstool. I'd expected him to ask me to go over it, '*Just one more time*'. I can't believe he hasn't.

At first glance it looks like the room is empty. My stomach grumbles and I decide the best place to go is the kitchen. Not only will I find food there, but I'll probably find Kelly since no matter whether he's stressed, happy or sad, he cooks. Most of the other pack members there too, being a werewolf seems to mean you have a bottomless pit for a stomach. Before I became a werewolf I used to wonder how Joey managed to eat such massive meals, without being obese, but now I totally understand it.

Something moves in the corner of my eyes causing me to stop in my tracks and look over to the window seat. My eyes fall on Kate, she smiles and pats the seat next to her in invitation for me to join her.

"Hi," she says, as I sit down beside her. "How are you?"

I can't believe my own ears. *She's asking about me?* She's the one who has lost her brother, a triplet brother, how can she think about how I'm feeling. "Oh, don't worry about me, Kate. I'm fine," I answer automatically.

She shakes her head and gives me a sad smile. "You're forgetting I can feel you through the pack bond's. You are not fine."

"I just had to live through last night five times. It turns out, it hurts more every time. You'd think it would get easier but seeing that light in his eyes fade, feeling his mouth go slack beneath mine, it..." I stop myself mid-sentence, realising it's her brother I'm talking about. "I'm sorry," I say shaking my head in disbelief at the things I had just told to her.

Kate takes my hand in hers. "No, it's ok. I'm glad you were with him, it means he didn't die alone. What were his last words?"

'I love you... didn't... want you...hurt.' His last words run through my mind and I know there and then, I can't tell her them. I could never tell her his last words wee for me and not her. "Tell Kate I love her."

"Don't lie to me," she demands, as a sad look crosses her face. "He told you he loved you didn't he?"

I nod as guilt from the lie surges through me. "Yes."

"Dave told me what he said to you. About your Mother... About you breaking Nate's heart for real." She squeezes my hand n hers. "He's wrong. He never saw Nate around you. I did. Nate loved you and it was nothing like the crush he had on your mother, it was love. That's how I know what his last words were. If he thought it was the end, he'll have wanted you to know." She stares in my eyes for a moment. It's as if she's deciding whether to add something or not. "Nate told me about his theory... About you and Jesse. Having seen you and Jesse together, I think he is right. That didn't stop him loving you, though. Nate chose to go and protect you, even though he knew the danger he'd be putting himself in. I don't blame you, Frankie, so please don't blame yourself."

I give her a grateful smile, trying to convey how thankful I am for her words. I can handle Dave blaming me. I don't really know him, but I wouldn't want Kate to feel that way.

"Ignore Dave. He doesn't know what he's talking about. Nate and Dave hadn't spoken for years, so he feels guilty about that. It's easier for him to blame you than face his own guilt," she says, before twisting and pulling me into a hug. She pulls away holding me at arms length. "He's always been the jerk of the three of us," she states making us both giggle.

Jesse's office door opens and Sergeant Sanchez walks out, his eyes widen in surprise as they fall on the pair of us sat in the oncoming dark. "Ms Rossi, I'm glad I caught you." My heart sinks at his words thinking he's thought of more questions to ask me. "I just had a call from the forensic team. They've got everything they need, so you're free to go back to your apartment," he says, before leaving the room, no doubt in search of the young constable he'd come with.

I don't ever want to go back to that apartment. The words run through my head and decide then and there, first thing in the morning I'll call a cleaning crew and tell the landlord I'd like to break the lease. I don't care how much he charges me. I suddenly feel a whole lot lighter with a decision about my future made. My stomach suddenly lets out a loud growl, causing both Kate and I to burst out laughing. Her stomach follows suit letting out it's own little growl.

"Is someone hungry in here?" Kelly asks from the archway. My eyes flick in his direction. "You'd better get yourselves in the kitchen before Carter finds your plates."

Not needing to be told twice, I dart straight into the

kitchen leaving Kate in my dust. Carter will not be eating my lunch. I come to a holt in an empty kitchen that smells of the most delicious food. I open the oven and find two plates piled high with roast beef, vegetables, and mashed potato, all drowned in gravy. I hear Kelly and Kate enter behind me and praise Kelly as I pull out our plates. "This looks and smells amazing."

"Of course it does. I cooked it," Kelly says, unabashed, blowing his own trumpet as always. It's not like anyone can argue with him, after all, he is a fabulous chef.

Kate and myself laugh. "If your head gets any bigger Kelly, you will be forever trapped in the kitchen," Kate states, as her laugh dies down.

"Shh, I wouldn't complain about that," I say. The kitchen is the best place for Kelly to be.

"Frankie, what would you do if I got stuck in here? I wouldn't be able to cook your every meal."

I look at him with wide eyes as I place the two plates on the breakfast bar. "You would. Jesse would have a lodger."

Kelly leaves the room, his laugh trailing away with him, as Kate and myself tuck into our meals at the breakfast bar. After cleaning our plates, we find everyone in lounge. Clarissa, Carter, Tracey, Mel, Dave, Kelly and Jesse are all lounging around on the sofa's. I head for an empty space I spot beside Jesse, as Kate squeezes between

Dave and Kelly. Jesse places his arm around my shoulders and pulls me close into his side as I sink into the sofa.

"How are you doing, Sweetheart?" he asks quietly in my ear as the others converse between themselves. Before I can answer he flashes me a knowing smile. "Don't be telling me you are fine because I know you're not. I want to know what's worrying you?"

Resting my head against his shoulder, I look out into the darkness, remembering the smell of the forest I know to be there. "Detective Sanchez told me they've finished at my apartment."

"And you want to go back there?" he asks giving my shoulders a comforting squeeze.

My heart jumps into my throat at the thought of going back. "No. I don't want to go back there... Ever. But that's not what's worrying me." I glance up at him and his reassuring smile spurs me on. "What if they find something that proves Danny never left? They'll put it all on me, even Nate and Gareth. I'll go to jail and both you and Big Mac will be in trouble for lying about seeing him leave."

He pulls me tighter to his body. "I bagged all his remains up. They're in the shed and they'll be getting cremated later. Nobody is going to jail. I promise you that."

"Thank you." I stretch up and place a gentle kiss on his lips. My wolf wants more, her energy flares towards him, before I manage to rein her in we have an audience. "You're a good Alpha, Jesse," I tell him, resting my head on his shoulder once more.

"If he's such a good Alpha, how come we've lost three pack members with in the as many months?" Dave says bitterly. Clarissa gasps in astonishment as everyone else in the room seems to hold their breath.

"Dave!" Kate admonishes him. "None of it is Jesse's fault."

I flick my eyes around the room to see that everyones eyes seem to glued to Dave. I can feel the tension in Jesse's body as I sit against his side, his arm a solid weight around my shoulders.

"Really? Another Alpha killed Joey, and Jesse still hasn't retaliated," Dave states as he glares at Jesse.

"Rick lost men at our hands that day, too," Jesse interjects gently. Too gently. The tension is body doesn't match the gentle tone of his words, making me suspect if Dave doesn't drop it, Jesse may just explode.

Dave laughs harshly. "Why was Rick in your territory again? Oh yeah, trying to kidnap Frankie because she's an Omega and isn't moon called. Looks like she's more trouble than she's worth, if you ask me. I say we should throw her to the wolves."

Jesse's anger as it whips each and everyone of us, before hitting Dave with the full force. Dave's energy flares back towards Jesse, causing a number of gasps from the pack members in the room. Jesse stops it with his own power, throwing it back at Dave before it could contents with him. Dave flinches at the pain of his own power. "Don't forget who is Alpha here. If you want to challenge me for the role, go about it the proper way but be prepared for a losing battle."

Dave glares at Jesse, causing Kate to touch his forearm in a warning. It pulls him out of his anger and he lowers his eyes in submission.

Jesse rises and leaves the room in silence, closing the kitchen door behind himself.

"Who want's a brew?" Kelly breaks the silence with an offer of tea and coffee. Everyone gratefully takes him up on his offer and conversation's commence as though the power play had never happened.

Kelly passes me and I stand, making him an offer. "I'll give you a hand." I'm not really bothered about helping Kelly, I know he can easily make half a dozen coffee's without help. But the offer gives me an excuse to leave the room and find Jesse without every knowing what I'm up to. I don't like the way he feels through the pack bonds. Guilt. Anger. Sadness.

"Thanks, Darlin'," Kelly says as I follow him out the room. "I heard him go upstairs. Take care of him. Alpha's are always looking after their people. An Alpha needs someone to look after them, once in a while," he whispers in my ear once the door closes behind us.

I turn and head for this stairs, calling over my shoulder. "I will." Knowing he'll be in his room, that's exactly where I head. I remember which room it is from the night Tracey cracked me over my head with a JD bottle. I have no idea what I'll do once I get there though.

The door is suddenly right in front of me, before I'm ready for it. Taking a deep breath to calm my nerves I give a sharp knock on the door. Receiving no answer I turn the door and peer into the empty room. It doesn't look any different how it looked a few nights ago. "Jesse?" I call into the room. Getting no reply I raise my voice. "Jesse, are you in here?"

The bathroom door opens and Jesse steps out with a towel around his waist and water dripping down his shoulders. As his eyes connect with mine in the doorway, the surprise written in their width tells me he can't have heard me over the shower. "Frankie? Is... everything okay?" he asks before looking down at himself, obviously realising he's only wearing a towel.

I feel my face blush as I follow his gaze, taking in the appetising sight before me. I quickly avert my eyes, they land on the bed which causes my face to blaze even more. "I'm sorry. I knocked and you didn't answer. I wanted to make sure you were okay? I can see you are so I'll leave you to it." I state, turning to leave.

Jesse's hand falls on my shoulder before I can take a step. "Stay... Please." His pleading makes him sound so vulnerable, causing me to turn. "I thought the shower would calm me down." Feeling through the pack bonds I can tall he's anything but calm. No doubt feeling me tugging on the bond between us, he opens himself up to me and me alone.

I stumble on the spot as I'm flooded with emotions. Love. Guilt. Shame. Anger. Sadness. Loneliness. Oh, this man who gives himself to a whole pack of werewolves is so, lonely. Tears well in my eye's as Kelly's words run through my mind, *'An Alpha needs someone to look after them, once in a while,'.* The amazing alpha before me is in need of someone. He's been alone for too long. Seeing the tears in my eyes he closes himself up enough so that I'm not overwhelmed by his feelings.

In this moment, I know the man standing before me will be my mate. Jesse's a strong, proud man. He'd never let a pack member that close. Not unless they meant more to him, like a Mate. I may not be able to help him with all those emotions, but I can ease some. His loneliness. I step towards him, closing my eyes as I leant in to kiss him. Only to find empty air where his mouth should be. Opening my eyes I find him standing on the far side of the room. Folding my arms across my chest, I raise my eyebrows in question.

"Frankie, I can't take advantage of you right now." He takes a step backwards as though to make his point clear. "You still have options but if you kiss me now—" he starts.

I don't give him time to finish.

Instead, I allow my wolf to surface. She's angry and sick of hearing him throw the 'options' card at us. "No, Jesse." I shake my head vehemently. "You say you're giving me options, but you aren't. You're pushing me away from the choice I've already made. I chose you from the start and I choose you now." I lift my hand in a stop gesture as he opens his mouth to speak and walk over stopping in front of him. "Jesse O'Keefe, you are still making excuses to get out of this. You really know how to give a girl a complexion," I say with a grin, trying to break the tension I can feel building in the room. I'm not letting him push me away any longer.

He places his mouth on mine and I relax into him, thankful that we're finally on the same page. His hands roam all over my body, before he lifts me in his arms and carries me to the bed, all without breaking the kiss. He rips my clothes off, as my hands run over his chest and arms, loving the feel of hairs sprinkled on his chest. My hands move lower and I smile into the kiss as I discover his towel is long gone. Finally our wolves energies are free to roam over the bodies they have been dying to touch from the start.

Our Mates.

Chapter Thirty Six

Frankie

Opening my eyes, I find myself alone in Jessie's bed. Glancing around, I see my torn clothes scattered around the room and deduce last night wasn't some wild dream. We'd spent most of the night learning each others bodies, it was more than fun finding out how to make Jesse growl in a whole new way. The bathroom door opens as I'm reminiscing and I sit up pulling the sheet tight over myself. My eyes flick to Jesse as he steps into the room, a small towel wrapped around his waist. I watch as one small trail of water runs down his chest, I lick my lips wanting to follow its trail with my tongue.

Jesse gives me a wide grin as our eyes meet. "Sleeping beauty finally awakes."

I giggle and can't stop myself from playing along with the theme he's set. "I didn't even have a prince here to wake me with a kiss." I stick out my lip in a faux pout.

"Oh, let me fix that for you," He strides towards me confidently and leans over me, placing his hand behind my neck as he brushes his lips against mine in a gentle, soft and exploratory kiss. His scent wraps around me like a blanket, the wonderful freshly cut grass mixed with something else I can't quite place, but makes it all him. He pulls away all too soon for my liking and I reach out to pull him back to me forgetting the sheet I'd been holding. He groans deep in his throat and in a split second decision he rips the towel from his waist and pushes me down onto the bed, to give our bodies what they are craving from each other. Fully aware of the others in the house and their wolf hearing, I try to stay as silent as possible but before long Jesse sends me shattering into a million pieces and the others are the last thing I'm thinking about as I let out a scream of pleasure.

I come back to earth as he collapses beside me on the bed, and as we lay in silence I feel the bed shaking. I crack open an eye to look at him. He's shaking with laughter. "*What!*" I demand, feeling slightly affronted. We just had what I thought was great sex and he's lying there laughing.

"If they didn't hear us last night... they did just now...

I'm surprised… they didn't barge in… thinking I was… murdering you," he manages to say between laughs.

I feel myself blush, and break eye contact. "I'm sorry. I tried to stay quiet, but…"

Rolling onto his side, Jesse faces me before reaching out his hand to turn my face towards him, forcing me to look directly at his eyes. "Don't be sorry for that, ever! You be as loud as you want, okay?"

I nod and give him a kiss, he sighs as we break apart. "I suppose we both better get dressed and show our faces downstairs. Kelly's here so there'll be a great breakfast spread on."

Knowing if one of us doesn't move now, neither of us will get downstairs for breakfast anytime soon. "Is Kelly the pack chef or something? He seems to do all the cooking here." I ask as I stand pulling the sheet off the bed with me.

Jesse settles into his side of the bed with his hands behind his head. "Yeah, I guess so. Keeping us fed seems to keep him happy. Cooking is Kelly's life really, he has a restaurant in Subiaco but he hasn't been back to work since Gabby died."

We've only been mates for a few hours but hearing him talk about Kelly losing Gabby, it causes fear to ripple though me for a moment before I chase it away. I lean over the bed and give Jesse another kiss, before wrapping the sheet around myself sarong style, not feeling comfortable enough to walk through the room naked, yet. "Okay, I better get showered and dressed because I can't exactly go down dressed like this." I point to my get up.

He grins warmly as his eyes roam my body. "You'll get no complaints about your fashion sense from me, not while you're wearing that at least. It'll be extremely easy to remove, just a little tug." He winks.

"Behave!" I warn him with a laugh, as I walk to the door, heading to the bedroom I should have slept in last night. Unable to wipe the smile off my face I blow him a kiss as I close his door.

Turning around I bump directly into Carter, his hand's gripping my arms are the only thing stopping me from falling. Once I'm steady on my feet again he releases his grip. "We need to talk," he says. No, I'm sorry for sneaking up on you, or anything.

Walking past him to my room, I reach for the door handle. "I need to get showered and dressed," I say bluntly. If he wants to be rude, then two can play that game.

"I'll wait," he says, leaning against the wall in preparation for the wait.

I sigh, as I start to feel sorry for him. "You'd better come in and sit on the bed. You may as well be comfortable while you wait." It's only when the words have left my mouth that I start to wonder whether its was a good idea to offer that. I can't imagine Jesse being happy with it. I certainly wouldn't if the boot was on the other foot. As I walk into the room I notice a backpack on the bed, one of my backpacks.

"Kelly brought some of your stuff from the farm. He brought your bike too," Carter states, having clearly sensed my confusion.

"Oh, right." Opening the bag I'm surprised to find the clothes I wear most often, along with the usual essentials like underwear, a hair brush and a little bag off makeup. "How did he know what clothes to bring?" I wonder aloud, more to myself than expecting Carter to know.

"He probably picked the clothes that had the most of your scent on them. Although he's been living with you for weeks now, he probably knows what you wear on a regular basis, by sight," he answers.

It's kind of creepy thinking of a guy sniffing my clothes, I much prefer the latter idea. Grabbing my jeans, my favourite emerald green tank top and my underwear, I go to the bathroom. Closing the door behind me I Feel immense relief at getting away from the anxiety radiating off Carter.

Being aware of Carter waiting for me in the other room means I can't spend time enjoying the amazing water pressure of Jesse's shower. The farm's shower system is in desperate need of an upgrade, I might have to ask Jesse who he used. Once I'm dressed I walk out the bathroom with my hair wrapped in a towel. My eyes meet

Carter's, who is sitting on the bed looking all stoic, facing the bathroom. I break eye contact by turning my head upside down and rub my hair dry, before heading over to the dresser to brush my hair. I meet Carter's eyes through the mirror having felt them on me the whole time. "You wanted to talk. So, talk," I state unable to warm my icy tone.

Carter runs his hands through his hair and takes a deep breath before speaking. "I'll forgive you for sleeping with Jesse."

Not believing my own ears, I spin around to look at him in the face. "*What?*" I yell, unable to stop the question flying out of my mouth.

"We're good together Frankie. I can forget you slept with Jesse. Please," he begs, leaning forward on the bed holding his hands in prayer.

Anger surges through me. "Carter we are *not* together. We won't be together again... Ever." I glare at him, as my hands form fists at my sides. "You lost the chance of us getting back together when you were too busy chasing after Clarissa in the woods, to stop me from getting raped." I shake my head as I remember the fear I felt that night. "I screamed your name in fear and the only person that turned up was Nate."

"Nate," he says with a vehement laugh, as he stands and walks towards me. "Oh yeah, it would've been him you slept with last night, if he wasn't dead. You shagged with him in the forest after all."

"How dare you?" Unable to hold my hands at my sides any longer, I slap him across the face. "I was not the one having sex in the woods, that was you! I slept and yes I was next to him, but no there was nothing sexual in it. Hell, Big Mac was there, ask him what happened." I pace a few steps away from him, to stop myself from lashing out again.

Carter rubs a hand over his cheek. "I notice you didn't deny the fact that if Nate was here, you would've woken up with him, this morning." His words cause me to regret stepping away from him and I silently hope his cheek stings like a bitch.

Grabbing my hairbrush, I throw it in the bag roughly. Taking my anger out on inanimate objects is nowhere near as satisfying as that slap was a moment ago. "I don't know how you can stoop so fucking low, bringing him into this? No. I wouldn't have been with him. My wolf and I had already picked Jesse I thought I had made that perfectly clear before I left the bar." Giving up on my bag, I turn to face him not caring if I take my anger out on him. He bloody well deserves it. "Nate had already told me he knew I was meant for Jesse. The only reason I am telling you that is because I don't want to hear you mention Nate like this, to anyone downstairs do you understand?" I put as much power to my words as I can, giving him a death stare to make it clear I'm serious.

"As if you could stop me," he mutters under his breath.

I walk up to him making us toe to toe and poke a finger in his chest. "You saw what was left of Daniel. Granted I might have a fight on my hands with you, since you'll have more chance and strength to fight back but so help me I'll try."

He opens his mouth to reply as a fist raps on the door. We break apart and I walk over to the door knowing it's Jesse, his scent entering the room through the gap under the door. He'd been in the next room, so he'll have heard everything. The way our voices were raised he wont be the only one. I pull open the door grateful for the interruption.

Jesse's eyes go straight to Carter, who is still standing at the other side of the room where I'd left him. I turn my head to see Carter staring at me with wide eyes, he's clearly shocked at my reaction. "Are you coming down for food before we go visit your buddy, Gareth?"

I whip my head back around at his words. Guilt surges through me, I've been so focused on Nate's death, I hadn't really thought about Gareth and his recovery. Reaching out I take his hand, entwining our fingers with a smile. "Yes," I say before looking back at Carter. "We're finished here," I add for his benefit.

About halfway down the stairs the smell of food hits my nose and my stomach growls in appreciation enticing a laugh from Jessie. "You have done a lot of exercise since that roast last night." I can't help but laugh too. "Are you okay?" he asks stopping on the stairs and turning to face me.

I look at him blankly, unsure about what he's referring to. He nods towards the way we'd just come, making it clear he's meaning what just happened between myself and Carter. "You heard everything." I state, not really needing a reply but he nods regardless.

"I nearly went downstairs, but when I heard you tell him to go inside and wait while you showered, I just couldn't make myself leave. I'm sorry I didn't mean to listen in on the conversation but you weren't exactly whispering. I'm pretty sure the guys in the kitchen might have even heard bits." He looks down at the floor breaking eye contact, showing me exactly how sorry he is. Being Alpha, he would never be the first to break eye contact with anyone, unless he believes he's in the wrong. To be honest I don't think Alpha's even admit to being in the wrong, it goes against their nature.

I tilt his chin with my finger, so our eyes connect once again. "I'm glad you heard everything you did. You're my mate, there is nothing I want to keep from you so if it concerns me, it concerns you."

Jesse cups my face in his hands and kisses me on the forehead. "Mate." I lean in to plant a kiss on his lips as a phone rings downstairs, I open my eyes to find him already taking the rest of the steps two at a time. "I better get that," he calls back up the stairs.

Following my nose the rest of the way to the kitchen, my stomach growls loudly with each step I take. I find Kelly facing an army of pans on the stovetop. As I get closer I can see what's in each of the pans, sizzling sausages, poaching eggs, beans, tinned tomatoes, bacon and mushrooms sharing the last pan. "It smells divine, Kelly," I praise, practically choking on my saliva.

"I'm just about to dish up then I'll start on your pancakes," he says, pointing to a bowl full of pancake mix without taking his eyes off the food before him.

I give him a quick peck on the cheek. "You're a star, Kelly."

"Hey, don't distract him. He might burn it all," shouts Clarissa. I turn to find her peering though the open french doors which lead to a courtyard positioned in the middle of the house, windows on all sides.

"Well I don't want that. I'll leave the chef without distractions," I say, throwing a wink at Kelly before making my way through the french doors.

Stepping outside, I notice everyone is sitting around a large wooden table. Quickly choosing an empty seat I lower myself into it, my arse barely touches the seat before the subject I'd been dreading approaches it's ugly head. *Well one of the two subjects I'd been dreading.*

"Come on then give us the juicy details," demands Nicky as she plans over the table seemingly on tenterhooks.

Remembering Jesse's earlier comment about my screaming, and putting it together with Nicky's comment makes my face blaze.

"Here," says Kelly, placing a plate full of food in front of Nicky. "Get this down your neck and leave the poor lass alone. She isn't going to tell *you* a thing." He winks at me before placing another equally full plate in front of Tracey who's sitting next to Nicky, with a sour look on her face.

The centre of the table is loaded up with a pot of coffee, a pot of tea, and a jug of juice, along with clean glasses and cups. I help myself to a coffee and take a long savouring sip, hoping the caffeine fix will calm my nerves down.

Clarissa, sitting on Tracey's other side sits back in her seat and looks at me, eyeing me up and down for what feels like hours. "You've got a good pair of lungs on you, girl," she states, causing the table to erupt in laughter. *Fantastic!* I'd only just gotten rid of the burning cheeks caused by Nicky and now I can feel them burning twice as bad.

Kelly walks back in, a plate in both hands and one resting on the crook of his arm. He places one on the table in front of Kate and another in front of Clarissa. Kelly places the plate from the crook of his arm at an empty place on the table. After pouring himself a cup of tea he sits down and digs into his breakfast. Carter follows him in his own plate in hand, making a beeline for the seat beside Clarissa, placing his plate of pancakes in front of me and pulling a squeezy bottle of golden syrup out of his front jean pocket as he passes.

I look up at him dumbfound. "Th...Thanks," I manage to stutter. Glancing around I can see I'm not the only one shocked by his actions, everyone else is staring at him in silence too.

Cutting a cross into my stack of pancakes, I squeeze a lovely sticky dose of golden syrup onto the top one and watch as it pours through the cross, covering them all. I close my eyes as I take my first bite enjoying the taste way too much. Kelly makes the best pancakes I've ever tasted. He cooks them in the same pan he cooks the bacon in, and that makes them so delicious. Swallowing the first mouthful, I open my eyes to find everyone's eyes on me, even Jesse who had taken the seat next to me without me even noticing.

"Did you just orgasm on a bite of pancake?" Big Mac asks, having also managed to take a seat at the table without me noticing. Some werewolf I am. Give me plate of pancakes and my instincts are shot.

Feeling my face burning it's way to that lovely beetroot colour again, I feel the need to say something to make them understand and take away my embarrassment. "He cooks them in bacon fat," I state as if that's a perfectly clear answer to such a question.

The table erupts into laughter. Hating being the butt of everyone's joke I ignore them, making sure to eat the rest of my pancakes with my eyes open and definitely no appreciative noises. After a few more giggles, conversation picks up once again. I listen to everyone as I sip on my coffee, Jesse and Kelly seem to be discussing something pertaining to the pack in quietly muttered words. Struggling to follow their conversation I let my ears wonder to Kate, Clarissa and Carter who are discussing the latest movie releases I almost choke on a sip of coffee as I hear Clarissa getting excited about the latest Marvel movie. "Civil War, have you seen it? Bucky Barnes, I love that man." Clarissa is the last person I would expect to be into the comic movies.

Kate giggles. "He is rather nice, with that long hair and those muscles."

"I'm not growing my hair, I don't care how much women dig it," Carter states, as he drinks some orange juice.

Clarissa ruffles his hair. "I like your spikes more than Bucky's hair." She gives him a quick peck on the cheek before turning back to Kate and their conversation.

Tracey's laughter catches my attention and I turn to see her and Nicky both laughing at something Big Mac had said. I suddenly realise that even though these people are all so different and even seem to be from completely different walks of life, like Big Mac being the president of some bikie gang and Tracey being a barbie doll nurse, it doesn't matter because essentially they've known each other forever. They're family. I can't help but feel out of place. I may be part of their family now but it doesn't really feel like it. These people are essentially strangers to me, as I am to them. If Joey was here, I wouldn't feel this way. I'd known him for years and I know he'd help tether me to the pack. Not liking the loneliness surging through me I quickly collect the plates from around the tables and take them to the kitchen to start on cleaning up.

In no time I'm grabbing the last dirty pan and placing it in the sink before rubbing the grease off with a soapy scouring sponge. A large warm hand grabs my arse and I drop the pan and sponge into the sink, causing a wave of dirty water to pour out of the sink, over the side and down my front. I take a sharp deep breath with the shock of both the hand and my wet top and catch Jesse's scent.

"Sorry," Jesse says as he spins me around by the waist to face him. Gabbing a tea towel off the side he dabs at my wet clothes. "I thought you would've heard or smelled me."

I laugh as I bat his arms away, knowing my top is past saving by a tea towel. "I was in my little dream world."

His hands slip around my waist and he leans back to weigh me up. "Penny for your thoughts."

Looking into his lovely flame eye's I can see the love

and trust he has for me pouring out of them. As much as what I'd been thinking about would be slightly inappropriate to admit to my lover. I know he'll understand. "I was thinking about Nate," I admit. "Who he'd be talking to and what he'd be saying, if he was here?" I glance down at my feet, feeling stupid for thinking such things. Nate's dead and nothing can change that. Why should it matter what he'd be doing if he was here.

Jesse's lips brush my forehead in a gentle kiss. "He'd be here talking to you. He loved you whether you knew it or not. He'd probably be making the moves on you by now. As you much I love what you said last night about your wolf choosing me and what Nate had told you." His words cause me to get over my embarrassment and meet his eyes as I listen to him carry on. "Last night wouldn't have happened if Nate was still here." I open my mouth to argue but he doesn't give me a chance to get a word in. "Your wolf might have picked me all along, but I think you would still be undecided if Nate was here." Guilt surges through me as I wonder whether what he says may be true and I drop my eyes to the floor once again. After a second's contemplation I know he's wrong. My mind had been made up well before Nate had die and in time I'll make sure Jesse understands that. Jesse lifts my chin with his finger. "You have nothing to feel guilty about," he states clearly picking up on my guilt through the pack bonds. He gives me a gentle kiss on the lips before changing the subject. "Why didn't you use the dishwasher?"

My gaze roams around the kitchen, looking for a dishwasher but all I can see are identical cupboard doors. My gaze meets Jesse's to make sure he isn't having me on but his straight face tells me he's serious. He pulls open the cupboard door to the left of the sink and, low and behold, it's a dishwasher. I glance at the pile of pots and pans on the draining board and then to my wet top. "Damn!" Is all I can think to say.

Grabbing another towel out of the drawer to his right, Jesse starts to dry as I finish washing the last pan. Just as I place the pan on the draining board, Clarissa walks in and reaching out she takes the towel off Jesse. "I'll finish up here. You guys wanted to go to the hospital before visiting hours end, right?"

Jesse lifts his arm to look at the watch on his wrist. "Yeah, I didn't realise the time. We better hurry. Thanks," he says kissing her on the cheek, before grabbing my handed dragging me out of the room. I manage to throw the wet sponge in the sink, before I'm completely out of range. Clarissa's squee after the sound of splashing water helps push down the jealousy that I felt at the harmless kiss. Jesse pushes me up the steps and I throw him a confused look over my shoulder. The hospital is not upstairs shouldn't he be pushing me out of the front door? At my look he shakes his head and tugs on my wet top. "You might like the taste of bacon fat but you don't want to smell like it all day long."

Realising he's right, I take the steps two at a time and run into the room with my bag. Making quick work of getting into some bacon fat free clothes I'm soon running down the stairs again. I find Jesse waiting for me at the open front door, catching sight of me in my leathers he looks as me through narrowed eyes. Picking up on his confusion I wave my bike keys in front of him. "We'll get there quicker than we would in car. Kelly won't mind if you borrow this," I say while throwing him Kelly's spare helmet. I walk past him and out the front door as he hesitates slightly staring at the helmet in his hands before following me. Straddling the bike, I pull my helmet over my head and start her up. The bike wobbles as Jesse gets on behind me and I have to adjust my hold on the bike to compensate for the extra weight. It's been a while since I've driven with someone else. Jesse's hands slide around my waist and I take that as permission to go, speeding off down the private lane leading to the main road into town.

***

Stopping just outside the door the nurse had told us was Gareth's room, I turn to Jesse with concern at the fact he hadn't uttered a word since leaving his house. Taking in his pale face and shaking hands I worry he may be ill. "Are you Okay?"

Jesse gives me a stern look. "I'm driving back in Tim's car."

I feel my eyes widen. "What? Why?" I ask, trying to think back to our journey and what may have made him feel so against going back the same way.

"Why?" he repeats my word, sounding dumbfound. "Why?" He laughs, shaking his head before stepping up close to me and stroking my cheek with the knuckles of his right hand. "Because, Sweetheart, I thought I was going to die out there. If not from being crushed between the bus and truck you squeezed us in between, then from the heart attack it caused me to have."

Thinking back to the moment in question, I guess to someone not used to being on a bike may get a little worried during that move. "Oh! It was perfectly safe. Honestly, you was in no danger," I say hoping to reassure him and maybe talk him into rethinking his plans for the return journey. I quite liked his body pressed against my back and his hands around my waist.

"Well, that being said I'll still be going back in Tim's car, thanks. Anyway, you better get in there quick before the nurse comes and kicks us out," He says stepping away from me. "I'll grab us some crappy coffee only hospitals seem to provide," he adds before kissing my forehead and leaving for the vending machine.

Taking a deep breath I prepare myself for what I may see, remembering the last time I saw Gareth he was at deaths door. Walking into the room I'm surprised by how well Gareth looks and I wonder why I'd been so worried.

The only thing that gives Gareth's injury away is the bandage around his neck. Gareth has a hand full of cards the deck placed on the bed by his side. Tim's sitting in the visitor's chair next to the bed with his own hand of cards. Seeing me enter they both place the cards down and Tim stands and steps back to lean against the wall, giving me access to the chair he'd vacated. I squeeze past Tim, through the little space he'd left me and immediately throw my arms around Gareth, forgetting about his injury.

"Hey Darling, it's nice to see you too but can you maybe squeeze my neck a bit more gently? It's still a little sore."

I pull back quickly and apologise profusely, patting him down gently and treating him with the tenderness you would a baby. I feel Tim take a step closer to my back a second before his hands slide down my rear.

Jesse's scent instantly fills the room and a deep growl of warning come from the doorway.

Tim's hands freeze on my arse before they completely disappear as he jumps across the room and as far away from me as he can get in this tiny space. "S...s...sorry Boss. I had no idea," he stutters looking down at his feet, fear radiating from him.

"Use your nose next time," Jesse orders with a growl. "Wait outside I'll be out in a minute." Tim's out the door faster than my eyes can follow him. Jesse places the coffee's on the table at the end of Gareth's bed, before looking me up and down. Seemingly satisfied with whatever he sees he nods before leaving the room.

"Wow that was...tense," Gareth says causing me to tear my eyes away from the door where Jesse had just left and look at him.

As I wake him up, taking in his blush that no man that was so close to deaths door just the other day should have, I realise my actions have caused him to have his life completely changed. Forever. We most certainly have a new pack member.

"Gareth, you look well...too well. Has Tim explained what might have happened?" I ask as guilt surges through me. I've caused all of this.

"What...I might start howling at the next new moon?" Gareth asks clearly finding the concept amusing.

"It's a full moon, not a new moon." He laugh's at my correction. "I'm serious. It's not something to joke about. It's life changing."

"She's right." I jump at the sound of Jesse's voice coming from the doorway. "I've spoken to one of our nurses, Tracey. She's going to get you discharged to a private nursing centre before someone starts questioning your speedy recovery. You'll stay at mine for the time being, so if you do end up releasing the wolf there will always be a strong wolf close by to keep you in control. I'll get Tracey to stay too, so she can change your bandages and such."

Gareth looks from Jesse to me, clearly wondering if he should agree. I nod my agreement and give Gareth a reassuring smile before Gareth accepts. "Okay. Thanks."

Chapter Thirty Seven

Frankie

Tracey works her magic and in no time we're leaving the hospital together and walking through the carpark. Jesse stops beside a silver Holden Commodore and as Tim pulls a key fob out of his pocket and unlocks the doors, I know Jesse is sticking to his guns. He won't be returning to the house on the back of my bike. The big wuss. I can't help but feel somewhat annoyed, it wasn't as if I was driving like a maniac an the way here. "Tim, give me a minute I need to get Jesse's helmet off my bike," I say as I walk past the car and towards my bike parked in the motorcycle spaces, two rows over. I take the spare helmet off my bike and head back over to Tim's car. The three of them are sat in the car with the engine running, most probably making the most of the air-con, cars get mighty hot in WA's summer. Opening the back door on the car I throw the helmet onto the empty seat and close the door without saying a word. I hear a door open and a hand gently grips my arms stopping me in the tracks.

"Hey, don't be mad." Jesse spins me around and kisses me until my knees feel weak before releasing me and getting back in the car.

I watch the car pull out and drive away before I come back to my senses. I can't believe I just let him win me over with a kiss. Climbing on my bike I pull on my helmet and mentally kick myself for being so bloody weak and giving in that easy. As I make my way back to Jesse's house, I consider going back to the farm but it doesn't take me long to realise how stupid that idea is. Kelly is at Jesse's and if I was to go back to the farm, I'd have to feed myself. That is something I can not face. Not to mention the fact that Jesse wouldn't be at my farm and I'd like to have a repeat of last night's event's in Jesse's bed.

We spend most of the afternoon in the backyard playing cricket before retiring to the lounge with some of Kelly's homemade pizza. I'm sitting on the end of one of the L shaped sofa's with Jesse's arm around my shoulders. Kelly is in the seat on Jesse's other side. Kate, Gareth and

Tim are spread out on the L shaped couch opposite us. Kate and Gareth seem to be getting closer to each other every time I glance at them, a shuffle here and a shuffle there. They probably don't realise we all see it. The phone lets out it's shrilling ring, breaking the happy chatter. It may be turned down to its quietist tone but it still makes a werewolf's ears ring.

Tim grabs the phone off the sideboard behind his head. "O'Keefe residence, he answers cheerily.

"The cops are on their way to arrest Frankie," the voice says down the phone. We can all hear it with our wolf hearing, even Gareth who seems to be taking to the idea of becoming furry once a month pretty well. Hearing my name I sit forward on the edge of the seat.

"What the fuck for, Alan?" Jesse asks, not bothering to raise his voice as Alan's wolf hearing will have no trouble picking up Jesse's voice. He mirrors my movement, shuffling to the edge of the seat. His back ramrod straight with the tension I can feel coming from him.

"The murder of Nathaniel Michaels and the attempted murder of Gareth Murphy. A witness came forward giving Daniel Black a solid alibi for the time of the murder." All eyes seem to bounce around the room from one person to the other, disbelief written on all our faces. We all know Danny was there. Who the hell would give him an alibi? It's not as if he could be asking this person to do it. He's dead.

"Who?" Kelly asks the question we are all probably thinking as e sits straighter in his own seat.

"I don't know. I'm not on the case but I'm digging. I'll get a name. Just get Frankie out before they get there." He pauses as though something has caught his attention wherever he is. "They're leaving now," he whispers into the phone before hanging up.

I can't seem to take my eyes off the phone, even as time puts it back in the cradle. Shock surges through me. The police are coming to arrest me for murder. The wrong murder. I'm going to go to jail.

Jesse's face appears infant of me blocking my view of the phone. "Frankie, come on we have to go. Now!" He tries to tug me to my feet but I can't move. I feel cement to the sofa. "Frankie please," he begs.

"They think I killed Nate," I say as I stare into Jesse's worried gaze. "I didn't kill Nate." My eye's find Kate's, who is still sitting beside Gareth opposite us. "I didn't do it Kate."

She stands up and takes my hands in hers. "I know that babe." She tugs me to my feet. "Quickly, go with Jesse. Let him take you somewhere safe."

Allowing Jesse to take my hand out of Kate's, I follow her request and let him pull me out of the french doors that lead to his yard. He starts to jog tagging me along by his hold on my hand and I vaguely notice as he seems to be leading us into the forest that surrounds his house.

"Frankie. You need to run. Okay?" he asks his voice sounding full of concern. I nod even though I know he isn't looking in my direction. *Run, I can do that.* Doing as I'm told I pick up my pace.

We haven't run far before the wind blows away the shock and my head starts to clear enough for me to start asking questions. "Why would someone give Danny an alibi? Why would they lie about something like that?"

"I don't care why. I want to know *who*?" Jesse says with a growl in the back of his throat.

The sound of police siren's travels on the wind seemingly coming from back at the house. It sounds like they are chasing us but I know they would have no idea that we'd had a tip off so they won't be chasing us yet. Jesse stops at the edge of the tree line, turning to face me he places his hands on my shoulders and holds me still hidden in the trees. "Wait here. Tim's coming with a car. I'm just going to go wave him down." He kisses me on the forehead before turning and disappearing through the tree line to the road.

It's only a matter of minutes before his arm reaches through the trees, his hand grabbing hold of mine and pulling me out of the trees and into the open road. I recognise Tim's car parked a couple of metres up the road its engine running and the red tail lights lit up like a beacon. I glance up and down the road expecting to see police cars screaming towards us. I jog behind Jesse towards the car. He opens the back door and as he gestures for me to get in, I slide in. I'm surprised as he bends and slides in along side me. Once the door clicks shut Tim slams his foot on the accelerator and we speed off down the dark empty dirt road.

Tim drives us north past all the suburbs I'd expected him to turn into. I'm just starting wonder how far he's going to take us, as he pulls into one of the newer housing estates. One that only popped up about a year ago. It's only a thirty minute drive from one of the larger suburbs but people don't like driving that far to get to a decent shopping centre. The council have been promising the residents their own little town centre, but nothing like that has gone up yet, and I'm pretty sure it won't be happening for another couple of years. Tim pulls onto the drive of a modern looking house that looks like it could be painted a light grey, but I can't be certain of that in the dark. He stops the engine and both him and Jesse open their doors and exit the car. Following their lead I climb out of the car and follow them to the house. Opening the door Tim gestures for us to go in as he flicks on a light switch just inside the doorway. "Mi casa es tu casa," he says with a grin.

"Thanks Tim, I appreciate this," Jesse says stepping into the house. "Can I use your phone. I left mine at home, just incase they try putting a trace on it."

Tim nods. "Of course. It's in the kitchen." He points to one of the doors and Jesse disappears into the back of the house. Tim watches me as I step over the threshold and closes the door behind me, the click of a lock tells me we are securely locked in. "The living room is through there," he reaches around an archway and switches a light on, lighting up a perfectly normal looking living room. "Make yourself at home. Do you want a drink or something to eat?" Tim being the perfect host is not what I expected of the creepy Tim I've come to know and hate. The fact that he isn't being creepy is actually more creepier than when he is his normal creepy self.

"No, I'm ok thanks," I say, flashing him a thankful smile as I walk into the large living room. The large TV hung on one wall catches my eye first, before they fall on the three seater sofa opposite it. There's a two seater sofa sideways on to the TV, and a coffee table in the middle of the room. The carpet is a luxuriously thick charcoal grey, even with my shoes on I can feel its soft cushioning under my feet. Choosing the three seater sofa, I sit down and Tim chooses to sit at the other side leaving the seat between us empty. We can both hear Jesse taking on the phone in the kitchen, but the walls and doors between us make the words undecipherable leaving just the rumble of his voice. Leaning forward Tim grabs the TV remote off the coffee table and flicks through the on screen program, too quick for my eyes to keep up, and selects a channel. On the screen theres a shot of an arm with a tattoo it moves and spells the name *Charlie Hunnam* and I relax into the sofa grateful that he has good taste in shows. Its one of my favourite shows. *Son's of Anarchy*. We're well into our second episode as Jesse walks into the room.

Tim hits a button on the remote turning off the TV and focuses his attention on Jesse. "What's the go, Boss?"

Jesse lets out a deep sigh before filling us in. "The police have left the house but they've parked a patrol at the entrance to my private road. Kelly went back to your farm and there's a patrol watching there too," he says not taking his eyes off me. Making me wonder if he's waiting for some reaction from me. He leans against the back of the two seater sofa. "I spoke to Marco, Alpha of Verona Pack. He's willing to let us hide out there for as long as it takes to fin the witness and clear your name."

"You'll need passports organising. I'll get on with Nicky, she can sort that," Tim says as he goes to stand.

"Already done it." Tim settles back on the edge of the sofa. "She said she'll have them in a day or two. Are we alright staying here until then? As soon as we get those we can book the first flight to Italy."

That gets my attention. "Italy? as in the country, Italy?" I ask. Thinking there must be another Italy I don't know about.

"Yes. The country Italy." He laughs. "Marco is your Uncle, Antony's brother. I never thought to mention him before. Did your Nonna never mention him?"

"No." I say, stunned to learn that I have family I didn't even know existed.

Jesse shook his head and runs a hand through his hair. "It doesn't matter, you'll meet him in a couple of days. He said we can stay as long as we need, forever, if that's what it takes to keep you out of prison."

Forever. I can't stay in Italy forever and Jesse definitely can't. Surely Jesse knows that. I bite my lip, unsure of how to ask. "Jesse... What about the pack?"

"He's given us his invitation. His pack will be welcoming." I can't believe his words. A quick glance at Tim and seeing him staring at the blank TV trying not to speak tells me he knows Marco's Pack wasn't the one I was asking about.

I shake my head baffled with Jesse's idiocy. "No. I'm not talking about Marco's pack. What about our Pack. Your pack, Jesse."

He runs a hand over his face showing me how third he is, before tucking them both in his jeans pockets. "They'll be fine for a little while without me." His voice doesn't sound as certain as his words imply.

I know that the pack won't last long without him, it will fall apart. I can feel it though the bonds. He's at the centre of the pack. He's their lifeline. "What if it turns out that I can never return? What will happen to the pack then?" I ask, sincerely concern.

Jesse glances at Tim, whose blank stare hasn't left the TV. "Someone will take over. Someone else will become Alpha," Jesse whispers and we both watch Tim's shoulders slump in defeat at the thought of losing his Alpha.

Tim's sorrow overwhelms me through the pack bonds and I reach over the empty seat between us, taking his right hand in mine, from where it was resting loosely in his lap. Tearing his eyes away from the TV he looks at his hand in mine, like it's an alien. I stroke the back of his hand with my thumb in a circular motion, hoping to comfort him. "You can't leave the pack. They will be devastated if you leave them. They'll fall apart," I plead, knowing I can't let him leave with me. He'll never return to the pack without me.

"They'll be fine. There are plenty of people who could be Alpha. Dave, Big Mac, even Tim here," he says pointing to Tim. Suggesting those people tells me he hasn't really considered this far ahead because he knows better than I do that these people could never be Alpha.

I tell him as much. "I haven't known any of them as long as you but even I know none of them could be as good an Alpha as you are." Dropping Tim's hand, I count them off on my fingers. "Dave likes taking order's. That's why he's comfortable in the Army he doesn't like giving them. He could never be Alpha." I count off another finger. "Big Mac has his bar, That bar is his life, he wouldn't take the pack on because it would take him away from his bar." I grab Tim's hand once again in my own. "Can you feel how sad Tim is at the mention of you leaving? Do you really think he could take your place. No offence Tim," I say turning to look at him. The small smile he gives me in return tells me he isn't offended. "Our pack is strong, but it's strong because of you. *'For the strength of the Pack is the wolf, and the strength of the Wolf is the Pack.'* Jesse they need you."

"Did you just quote Rudyard Kipling?" Jesse say with a small laugh.

"Yes." I snap, wondering if he even listened the rest of what I said?

Jesse walks round the sofa. Sitting on the coffee table in front of Tim and myself he places a palm on each of our knees. "But you need me Frankie. You're my mate now."

I shake my head. "I'm not tearing you away from the Pack, they need you more. They deserve you more than I do."

The thin line of his lips tell me I'm not winning. "I need you," he whispers causing me to remember that loneliness he I felt within him just the other night and I know in that second that his words are nothing but the truth. He does.

"What if it was Tracey, or one of the other members who was running from prison? What would you do then?" I argue, knowing he wouldn't go with them not even to settle them in.

"I'd get them to another pack. Somewhere safe, where they could be protected. Or transferred permanently if need be," he admits, the slight slump in his shoulders tells me he knows what I'm saying.

I forge on anyway. "But you wouldn't go with them? You wouldn't leave the Pack for them?"

"No, Frankie. But it's not just someone else. It's you. My Mate." He growls deep in his throat and stands up before pacing back and forth in front of the TV. Having seen Jesse pace like this before I know he'll be pacing for a while. No one is going to win this argument anytime soon.

I turn my attention to Tim, who's watching Jesse pace. The look on his face makes me think he's trying to read Jesse's thoughts but that isn't possible. Jesse's face is too blank to be able to read anything from it. Jesse would make a good poker player. "Tim. It's getting late. Can you show me where I'll be sleeping, please."

Tim shake himself like a wolf would after sleeping or being still for a length of time. "Of course. Sorry." he says, standing up and leading me through the house. "There's a couple of spare bedroom's upstairs. Do you want to take a drink up with you?" he asks as we pass a door which must be the kitchen.

"No, thanks," I say with a shake of my head. I glance back in to the living room and catch sight of Jesse still pacing back and forth. I've argued my point with Jesse. If he doesn't take what I've said on board, no amount of my repeating myself will make a blind bit of difference. I know leaving him to pace is the right thing to do because I need to think of a Plan B and watching Jesse pace back and forth isn't going to help me do that.

Tim leads me up stairs to a plainly decorated room, which practically scream bachelors house. It's lacking the little decorations that only a woman seems to think of. "Here you go, Frankie," he says stopping in the doorway behind me.

"Thanks Tim. Sorry about invading your home like this." I turn and pull him into a hug. He squeezes me back and holds on a little longer than I'm comfortable with but as I feel his shock still clinging to him through the bonds, I relaxed into it realising how much he really needs the comfort of pack touch.

"We'll fall apart," he whispers so quietly in my ear, I can only just make out the words.

"He won't leave, I won't let him. I promise," I whisper back just as quietly.

He pulls away to search my face with his eyes, probably looking for the truth of my words. After a moment he nods, clearly satisfied with whatever he may see and releases me completely before leaving me alone in the room. I close the door to, leaving it ajar enough so that Jesse can catch my scent if he wants to come and find me when he's done his thinking. Having changed from my leathers into shorts earlier in the day, I now tug down my shorts and take off my bra from underneath the tank top I'm wearing, before placing them on the end of the bed knowing my feet won't reach that far down. I lie awake for what feels like a good hour, thinking about all that was said down stairs and falling on the same conclusion. Jesse will not let me leave without him. Yet, if I let him go with me to *'settle me in'*, he'll never leave me. We'll both be in Italy until my name is cleared. If I stayed here in Tim's house? The police would find me eventually. Going to Italy is a good idea, but I have to go on my own. I eventually fall asleep with thoughts of Italy going around my head.

I wake to the feel of someone slipping into the bed behind me. Jesse's energy roams over my skin before he spoons up behind me, sliding his arm over my side and hugging me to his chest. I grab his arm and hugged him back. "I love you," I say sleepily. My brain momentarily panics, thinking it's too soon to say something like that but my heart shuts the thought down. It's the truth and life is too short not to speak it.

He kisses my hair, my neck, my shoulder. "I... Love... You," he says between kisses.

His kisses have me moaning quietly and my body alert. His hand slides up my stomach and to my breast, the brush of his fingers over my nipples have me begging for more, leaning into his touch. He flips me over so quick, one second he's behind me, and the next he's on top of me with his mouth where his fingers just were. I arch my back enjoying the teasing of his tongue and teeth.

My hands run wildly over his biceps, shoulders and around his neck. My nails digging into his skin trying to find purchase as his hand moves between us. I moan into his mouth as I feel him steady himself at my entrance. Impatiently I slide my hands down his back, using them to pull him towards me and effectively slamming him home. Exactly where I need him. The guttural sound he lets out makes me want to do it again, just so he'll make that noise again.

He spends what feels like hours showing me exactly why we need to be together. How much we both need each other. His torturously slow steady love making almost has me agreeing to anything, just so I can fall off that precipice and shatter into a thousand pieces.

"Oh, Jesse," I moan, my mouth barely able to form words as I come back to my senses and he falls onto his back next to me, before pulling me up to rest on his chest.

I feel myself drifting into sleep, just as his voice rumbles through his chest under my ear, pulling me back from the edge of sleep. " I've only just got you. I can't let you leave without me now. I know what you were saying is right. I know the pack need me, but I need you. You're my Mate. I can't lose you."

I run my fingers through his chest hair, liking the feel of it under my fingertips. "You wouldn't be losing me, Jesse. I'd still be yours. We'd just have an ocean or two between us and that will only be until you clear my name. If anyone can do that you can."

He brushes a hand over my head, soothing down my hair. "What if I came and settled you in?" he asks.

As much as I like that idea, I know deep down that I can't allow that to happen and I tell him why. "You can't go, Jesse. You would never leave me there. You have to let me go on my own."

"You still need my protection from people who want to use you for breeding or use your Omega abilities," he argues.

I run with the only counter argument I have, no matter how much I trust the words. "Marco is my Uncle. He'll protect me."

"I don't know. Your father didn't speak to Marco and I don't know why. I went to him as a last resort. All the other Alpha's I asked felt too threatened to allow me into their territory. Marco wasn't and as odd as that is in itself, I was ignoring that because I'd be there with you. I won't trust him with you on your own." His hand rests on my bicep and squeezes me into him.

Realising there is no way we are going to come to an agreement about this. He won't let me go alone and I won't let him come with me. I decide the only option I really have is to hand myself into the police. "What if I hand myself into the police." I ask. "You can still look for the witness and I'll be safe in prison."

"No. What if we can't find or get to the witness? You'll be stuck in there for how ever long they give you. It could be years, Frankie."

"I have a long lifespan now. Years wouldn't be the same as it would have been if I hadn't released my wolf," I state not seeing a big problem with it. I know it wouldn't come to that because they would find the witness eventually.

Jesse turns on to his side to face me and I slip my head onto his arm. "Being locked up would be a huge problem. For a start your wolf wouldn't like it, she'd never be able to come out. You're also forgetting that you age differently now, the humans would notice that. A life sentence for a Were, is a death sentence." His drawn eyebrows and the biting of his lip shows me how worried he is about this.

My eyes widen in disbelief at the thought of Were's being assassinated for being jailed. "There would be a hit out on me?"

He rubs at his chest with his free hand. "To save us from exposure? Yes," he admits.

Surely there is a way out of the death sentence, I blurt out any reason I can think of that could mean I won't be killed. "But I don't have to change with the moon.

Wouldn't that give me some time? Time for you to find the witness." Hope surges through me. This is our only option it has to work.

He shrugs. "It's too small a chance. Once you're in the prison I lose control of the matter. I'm not willing to take the risk."

The options seem to be having worse outcomes. Too tired to think anymore, I know I need to reassess this in the morning with a fresh head. I kiss him on the lips, the nose and the forehead. "I need to go to sleep. We can figure it out in the morning."

Jesse smiles. "Sure, we'll have all the answers in the morning," he says not sounding convinced, before kissing me deeply, making me feel as though with all the talk of death he thinks it may be our last.

Turning over, I shuffle towards him so my back is pressed to his chest and he pulls me close ensuring there isn't any air between us. "I love you," I whisper, closing my eyes.

"I can't lose you," I hear him whisper just as I doze off into a deep slumber.

Chapter Thirty Eight

Frankie

Opening my eyes to a dark room I deduce that I can't have slept very long, the sun isn't even starting to show it's face through the gaps in the blinds. I stare at the ceiling listening to the deep rumbling of Jesse sleeping and think about the options before me. Going to Italy which will result in tearing the pack apart or going to prison which will most likely result in my assassination. Neither of these options appeals to me but I have to choose one of them. There's only one that even with the worst outcome, less people will be affected. And if by some miracle the worst doesn't happen, it will work out for everyone. The Pack.

Jesse. Me. That miracle relies on Jesse finding the witness, whomever it may be.

As the sun starts to shine through the gaps in the blinds my decision solidifies in my mind and a plan is formed. I just hope I can pull it off. The main issue with the plan is that it relies me getting up without waking Jesse. I slowly slide out of the bed, pausing midway out as he grumbles something incoherent, before rolling over. I stay stock still until his breath comes deep and regular indicating that he's fallen back into a deep slumber. I slip out the rest of the way and quietly pull on my clothes before stepping out of the room, gently closing the door behind me. Walking down the stairs I work out the best place to find a pen and paper would be the kitchen, so that's where I head. Glancing around the room I spot what I'm looking for on the side next to the phone in its cradle. Sitting down at the breakfast bar I write a note to Jesse.

Jesse,

I'm sorry. But I can't let you hurt the pack, it would kill you.

I Love You.

Always

Frankie xxx

I fold the note in half and write his name on the back

before placing it on the side before me, knowing he'll have a clear view of it as soon as he enters the room. Seeing Tim's car keys on a hook above the phone I tear off another piece of paper and scribble a quick note to Tim, telling him where he'll be able to find his car. I leave Tim's note open not caring who reads it laying the pen placed on top of it.

After quietly slipping out of Tim's house I get behind the wheel of his car and drive into Joondalup, Pulling up to the modern looking one story building, I park in the visitor's section of the car park. I lock the car up and place the keys on the drivers side front wheel before making my way over to the doors of the building. Taking a deep breath I push my way through the doors knowing I have no other choice. Walking up to the receptionist's desk, I watch as the lady finishes with a call before addressing me.

"Good morning. How can I help you?" she says flashing me a cheery smile.

I force the words out of my mouth before I can chicken out and leave. "Hi. My name is Rosa Rossi and I believe Sergeant Sanchez needs to speak to me."

The second my name leaves my lips she picks up the phone and presses the number three. I can easily hear it ringing on the other end with my wolf's hearing. *"Ring...Ring...Ring...*What is it, Claire?" Sergeant Sanchez snaps.

She eyes me up and down for a moment as if weighing up whether I'm going to make a run for it or not before looking at me, her head tilted to the side in curiosity as she speaks. "Rosa Rossi is at the desk, Sir."

To be continued...

Turn the page to see Joey's letter mentioned in Chapter Twenty-Two.

Hey Frank,

You know how useless I am at speaking about feelings, I am a guy after all. But I feel the need to tell you somehow, I can't stand to see the hurt and worry in your face every time you look at me. So here I am writing my you a letter.

Every time you look at me, I can see those question's bouncing around in that brain of yours.

IS OUR FRIENDSHIP ALL A LIE?

WAS HE ONLY MY FRIEND BECAUSE OF JESSE'S ORDER?

I need you to know it wasn't a lie. Yes, He ordered me to go to your Gram, ask for a job and befriend the girl called 'Rosa'.

But the thing is, I never met that girl. I met a beautiful, quiet girl called 'Frankie'. She is the girl that became my best friend.

That first time we met, I knew I'd found that last puzzle piece that was missing from the puzzle that was my soul. You were it Frank. You was that missing puzzle piece. So please don't ever doubt our friendship. If that doubt does get ahold of you and starts bouncing around your head like a pogo stick. Remember that puzzle piece.

I love you Frank.

Always your best bud,

Jo xx

Other Books By Aimie Jennison

Pride to Pack

Book 1 of the Mount Roxby Series

Rosabel McGuiness, orphaned Werewolf, has finally decided to leave the Werelion Pride she's been living with for the last eighteen years. She's been challenged to one duel too many. It's time to find a pack to call home.

Theodore Wilson, Alpha of the Mount Roxby Pack, has never cared about finding his Mate. He swore off women when his Wife, a human who knew nothing about what he was, cheated on him. But now a new wolf has walked into town, and stirred up feelings he never imagined he would feel.

Mount Roxby has a plethora of supernatural beings, unbeknownst to the humans that live there. After a series of mysterious disappearances, and fatal attacks on both Werewolves and Vampires alike, Rosabel decides something needs to be done. But can she persuade the Pack Alpha and Vampire King, to put old prejudices behind them long enough to work together, and solve these attacks? Or will one bite too many cause a war?

Forever Young and Beautiful

Book 2 of the Mount Roxby Series

Beautiful eighteen-year-old Ruby Wilson always wished she'd inherited the werewolf gene like her brothers. They were her father's favourite, leaving her to feel hated, or even worse, like she never even existed.

Once her father took her brothers to live with him in his pack when they reached the age of sixteen, Ruby was left all alone with her heartbroken mother, who turned to drugs and drink, to get through the day.

Realising she needs to get away and accepting her fate she finally starts to settle down and starts to enjoy living as a human among her brother's pack.

Life runs smoothly for a while - until the unthinkable happens.

And life for Ruby will never be the same again.

Coming Mid 2017

Reclaiming the One

Book 3 of the Mount Roxby Series

At nineteen, Cain Wilson met his true mate, Selena. But their short-lived romance was doomed from the start for one simple reason - she belonged to someone else.

At twenty, he killed his father and handed control of the pack to his more capable, older brother Theo.

At twenty-five unable to watch his mate with another, he left the pack and became a lone wolf.

Now at twenty-seven, family troubles have brought him back to Mount Roxby and unbeknown to him, his true mate. Will he be able to put the past behind him and reclaim the one? Or has time built an impenetrable wall around both their hearts?

About the Author

Aimie is a Yorkshire lass living in Western Australia. She is a mother to three boisterous boys, who drive her up the wall on a daily basis.

Aimie loves to people watch, it's her favourite way to come up with new characters and stories. So next time a stranger is staring at you in the street don't panic, they could be an author basing a character on you.

Aimie has always loved to read and write. Her favourite place to listen to her characters is at the beach.

Aimie would love to hear from you. Comments and questions are always welcome. You can reach her at aimiejennison@gmail.com or through her website http://www.aimiejennison.com. Thanks in advance for your correspondence.

You can also connect with Aimie online via
Facebook * Twitter * Goodreads

Acknowledgements

I want to thank *my family* for supporting me unconditionally, for sticking with me and understanding when my scatterbrained mind forgets everything. I can remember what happens to my characters but I can't remember when I'm meant to be taking someone to their swimming lesson. I love you all to pieces.

Sara Cartwright, thank you for the amazing cover again. It took us a few goes but we got there in the end. You're a trooper for doing it again and again, until I was happy.

Jane of Tiny Tiger Edits, thank you for making my words sound great with your editing.

Leigh Stone of Irish Ink Formatting and Graphics,

thank you for making my book look so pretty.

Reggie Deanching of R + M Photography, You are an amazing photographer. Thank you for taking the perfect photo for this story and allowing me to use it on my cover.

Alfie Gordillo, when I saw your photo by Reggie I saw my character and I knew I had to have it. Thanks for bringing my character to life.

Sam Destiny, I am so grateful that this book world has brought us together. You are the best support a girl could wish for. I can't wait for the day we finally meet in person. Thank you for being the world's best beta reader. Once again, I'm sorry I broke your heart.

Early in the year I had a challenging couple of months. I want to thank everyone who stood by me through that time. Anyone, that sent messages of support. Thank you, from the bottom of my heart, because it's you guys that kept me going in those dark days.

Thank YOU.

* 9 7 8 0 9 9 4 4 3 6 8 3 2 *